Born on the Isle of Wight, Christine Harrison now lives
in West Wales where she has been writing for the past ten
years. Her short stories have won prizes and commen-
dations in national competitions, and have been broadcast
on BBC radio. In 1990 she won the *Cosmopolitan* Short Story
Award – her winning story being later published as part of
an anthology, *The Best of Cosmopolitan Fiction*. *Airy Cages* is
her first novel.

# CHRISTINE HARRISON

# *Airy Cages*

PAN BOOKS

First published 1994 by Macmillan London

This edition published 1995 by Pan Books
an imprint of Macmillan General Books
Cavaye Place London SW10 9PG
and Basingstoke

Associated companies throughout the world

ISBN 0 330 34029 8

1 3 5 7 9 8 6 4 2

A CIP catalogue record for this book is available from
the British Library

Typeset by CentraCet Ltd, Cambridge
Printed and bound in Great Britain by
Cox & Wyman Ltd, Reading, Berkshire

The author wishes to acknowledge the support of
the Welsh Arts Council

My aspens dear, whose airy cages quelled,
Quelled or quenched in leaves the leaping sun,
  All felled, felled, are all felled.

GERARD MANLEY HOPKINS

# PART ONE

*London and Brighton*

# I

S HE saw him first. As she stepped off her train, she saw
him. He was going through his pockets looking for his
ticket, the other passengers streaming past off the Irish boat
train into Paddington Station. It was getting dark, a band
was playing 'See Amid the Winter's Snow', and she fell in
love at first sight with this travel-stained young man who
couldn't find his ticket.

It changed everything. Small things were suddenly
charged with importance, things like a poster advertising
Chekhov's *The Seagull*, the words underlining the great
white soaring bird, even a litter bin full of orange peel and
empty cartons, how beautiful litter could be, the shining bits
of tinfoil, the brilliant orange peel.

We throw away years of life. We walk in mist. Then
unexpectedly something shifts, subtly, hardly at all, and
everything is changed. It was like that.

She spoke to him. 'Have you looked in your top pocket?'
she asked him.

His smile was vulnerable, a bit flash. 'You're a
genius,' he said, fishing out a scruffy-looking ticket, nar-
rowing his eyes as if scrutinizing it. As if it must be a
forgery.

'Yes, I know.' She spoke softly, almost under her breath.

Her breathing seemed to come lighter and faster, making it more difficult to speak.

He helped her to the barrier with her case, then handed it back. How was she to keep him with her? She didn't know. She wanted simply to say to him, 'Stay with me. You have greeny sort of eyes and a certain look of rough grace about you and I have fallen in love with you.'

But he smiled again and rambled off towards where the Salvation Army band was playing. Most people rushed about in straight lines. He rambled as if at a village fair. She watched him for a minute as he stood with a little knot of people, mothers with their children mostly, listening to the carols. She reckoned he was a country boy.

Her intuition was working overtime.

So she wasn't surprised when he came into the cafeteria. That was why she had gone in – to wait for him to walk through the door.

'You again,' he said, and sat down.

'You're a very pretty woman.' It wasn't said in the usual flirtatious way, but with a sort of abstract joy. It was the last straw. Then, 'I'll get myself some coffee,' he said. 'Don't go away. Isn't the music a treat?'

His soft accent lingered in the air round her as she watched him go off to buy coffee – and come back with beer. He took a sip before he put the glass down. As he sat near to her she breathed in his breath, malty from the beer and a clean male smell.

She wanted to keep that scent near her. Don't go, she told him without words, silently, don't go. You have made everyone into shadows now.

When he sang, very quietly, a snatch from 'See Amid the Winter's Snow' she smiled; and then suddenly, softly he came out with his own descant to the melody.

'It's my favourite carol,' she said; if it wasn't before, it was now. A sliver of ice on a nerve whenever she was to hear it from that day to her dying day.

'Are you a singer?'

'A flautist, chiefly. But I do sing after a fashion. What's your name?'

'Maisie. Maisie Shergold.'

'Maisie.' He repeated it. She gave him her card, shameless, in case he suddenly went off to be lost in the London crowds. He put on gold-rimmed spectacles to read it. A country boy but educated well by priests, she guessed.

'My name is Michael. Michael Curran. Flautist and singer of true songs.' He put out his hand, rough and warm, she took it in hers. At last she had touched him.

'What sort of true songs?'

'Bit of folk, bit of blues, bits of pop, mixed with madrigal. My own slightly unusual mixture.'

'Your own unusual truth?'

'Everybody's truth.'

She raised her eyebrows and smiled. 'Tall order.'

'Do we have a sceptic in the railway station?' He looked at the card again. 'Doesn't say sceptic,' he said. 'Says art historian. Eastern Orthodox iconography.'

'Perhaps historians have to be sceptics. But romantic too. My own slightly unusual mixture.'

She hardly knew what she said, or what he was saying. What the words meant was less important than that these sounds and smiles between them were lightly bonding two strangers together; beyond the bonds of sight and smell and touch already established there were bonds of the intellect, not to be underestimated. Maisie was the last person to despise such bonds – but they came last. And still the intellect had not yet been yielded a place, still they hardly heard what the other said, only the timbre and mood of the words. But now it was time for words to be used in a different way; discovering, probing.

'Tell me about Maisie Shergold. She's more than a pretty face.'

'Yes.'

'She's clever.'

'Yes.'

'I thought that was it. Clever.' He smiled.

He got up.

Don't leave me, Michael Curran. I want to hear you sing and play the flute. I want to feel your warm rough touch again.

'I'm going to get another beer. What would you like?'

'Nothing.' Only for you to return. Never to leave me. While he fetched his drink, she got out her diary for something to do. It was nearly the end of the year, the little book thick with numbers, reminders, names, appointments. She wrote in faint writing, 'I met Michael Curran on Paddington Station. They were playing "See Amid the Winter's Snow".'

But as they left the cafeteria the band were packing away their instruments.

'Taxi or underground?' he asked. Whichever takes the longest. Pluto took Proserpina to the Underworld. It was lucky she was ever seen again.

'Underground,' she said. 'It's quicker at this time of day.'

'Time matters not to me,' he said. 'Where are we going, anyway?'

'Somewhere where we can have a meal, a glass of reasonable wine. A wash. The Andromeda. It's a sort of club for sort of ladies.'

'Oh, good,' he said. 'Do they let in men?'

'Sometimes. But sometimes they are captured and kept there. Especially musicians.'

'Oh, good,' he said.


Brushing her hair and cleaning her skin with damp cotton-wool in the washroom, she filled the deep basin, with its old brass fittings, with water and plunged her hands in up to the wrists.

'I am nearly forty years old,' she told herself, 'and old enough to know better than this.' But she knew it was not a question of anything like that. For she knew suddenly but obscurely that his image had been with her before she had ever met him.

She looked at her hands under the water.

It was as if she had loved him before she had seen him. As if there had been a template of who she would love in her mind's eye, her heart, her secret mind. Always? She did not know that – or when that particular face, and mien, and bright smile, and way of turning the head, and walk, and light, easy way of standing about, but particularly that face – that especial face – had imprinted themselves on her. It was not an accident that she had met Michael on Paddington Station; her life had led up to that point – she had been looking for him, searching for him without knowing that she was. And when she saw him, she knew him from the first glimpse, the first second – she knew him at once.

She dried her hands, and flicked her dark hair about. Large brown eyes looked back at her from the mirror, faint circles under them, as in a water-colour painting.

When she went into the dining-room, she found him, waiting for her, in a still, quiet way, standing by the bar with a whisky. 'Shall we eat?' she said.

They had their meal tucked in the privacy of a dining-booth. These had been used in the past by men about town to entertain ladies from the theatre, but were now mostly used by women who wanted to entertain business clients in a certain casual privacy.

'What are you up in town for, anyway?' she asked. 'A concert?'

'Practice session,' he said. 'We're all meeting up later at the Fiddler's Cat, Shepherd's Bush way.'

7

'Oh.' She rested her chin on her hand, elbow on the table.

'Yes, come if you like. This is very good beef.' He ate in a simple way that she liked.

'They do good plain cooking here. Shall I come?' she said.

'Yes, come. You might be bored. But come.'

Maisie helped herself to a small spoonful of cauliflower. 'All right, I'll come.' She had forgotten that she had been looking forward to going home, resting after an irritating meeting about a museum purchase. All that had happened a long time ago. To someone else.


It was in an upstairs room over the Fiddler's Cat. Michael leaped ahead up the tattily carpeted stairs and then up another bare-boarded flight. But she could see straight away, as he opened the door and took a gulp of the thick, solid atmosphere, what this was all about for him – it was a drug to him. A curtain of smoke. Someone playing the same trapped phrase over and over again on the bass guitar, with insistent melancholy.

He changed as the drug pumped through him. His eyes even changed colour, she could have sworn. He drifted off in that sure, aimless way that was his own and was at the heart of something important about him, a contradiction, and left her to her own devices.

'What the hell am I doing here?' she asked a thin bearded man sitting on the floor against the wall carefully rolling a cigarette paper.

'Wasting your time. You ought to be out there making money.'

'Do I look the type?'

'You look like my English teacher at my old school.'

'I see.'

'I was in love with her. She was the only teacher who was any good.'

Michael had kind of taken charge of the room. 'The sound I'm after is – well – sort of sensual madrigal – a contradiction in terms, you might say. Virgin and the whore. Well, let's kick it around, anyway.' He grinned. He sang a phrase. He had no voice as voices go, but it made the skin prickle. An erotic reticence.

'Try it out. Yes, that high pure sound. Yes. We're nearly there.' He grinned again.

'Sensual madrigal.' The bearded man laughed a high-pitched laugh.

'There's something else,' said Michael. 'Underneath, a kind of throb. Got it? That's the sound. A blood-throb. And a sort of nervous tension. Fear, perhaps.'

'You're an intellectual, Michael,' said the bearded man, glum now.

Michael was sorting out the rhythm section, the drummer using a brush, listening to the others, listening to what Michael was saying, listening to the sound of his brush, ear cocked.

She watched him as he sang a phrase or two, one hand cupped over his ear. He seemed to have forgotten about her. Abandoned her. They couldn't get the pause right before the last phrase came in. 'It's right when it's easy,' said Michael; and next time it was right and they went on a bit until they faltered again. 'It's easy when it's right,' said Michael; and they tried again and it was easy and right.

'This could go on all night,' the bearded man said to Maisie.

Again she wondered what she was doing there. Wondered what she was doing loving Michael Curran, watching him as he sang, swaying very slightly behind a curtain of curling smoke, his figure neither tall nor short, elegant and sturdy. But what was she doing, how did she get into this?

9

It was as if she had been pulled down a path she had always known was there somewhere inside her. And already the whole thing was confusing her life.

She had to be in Brighton the next day, she had an appointment with an old man, a White Russian émigré, one of a handful of exiles dedicated, it seemed anachronistically, to the restoration of the Russian monarchy. He had something to tell her, to do with an ikon. It sounded interesting. She did not want to miss that Brighton train. She smiled, remembering his letters, so vivid even in their formality and courtesy.

Taking her smile for an invitation, the bearded man put an arm round her. Impatiently she stood up. She'd get a taxi and go. She felt angry then. What was stopping her going up to Michael, taking his hand, saying, 'Come back with me. I've fallen in love with you'? She was too tired now to go through any subtle foreplay, any waiting. Tired and angry. Surely she had lost him.

She went to look for a telephone. The bare landing looked infinitely melancholy.

He put his hand over hers on the telephone.

'Don't disappear into the night, will you, Maisie? I want to come with you now.' There was something in his voice that hesitated.

'Why don't you?' she asked.

'It's the others. I can't let them down.'

I would, she thought, I'd let everyone down.

'We only get together once in a while and then we have to make the most of it. You can see that, can't you? I can't let them down.'

'Of course you can't let them down,' she said. 'You can't possibly.'

'Oh, hell, I'm coming with you. Hang on a minute.' He was back in a couple of minutes. They clattered down the stairs.

'Did you get a taxi?' he asked her.

'Yes. How do you escape out of this place? It's all bolted and barred.' They would have to stay all night, after all.

'Easy,' he said, and led her out of an unlocked side door into the quiet, bitter cold of the street, with the taxi throbbing.

'Off Kensington Church Street,' she told the taxi driver. She looked up into the sky, rich with stars, then bent her head inside the cab.

She had that feeling again. Of being inexorably drawn towards something. A haven. An abyss. How was she to know?

'I live in an enormous room on the second floor,' she told him, as they drew up outside wrought-iron gates flung open on to a path shining in the moonlight like a strip of water. She found her key with a sure blind movement.

'Rose lives in the rest of the house – Rose is my daughter. At least she lives in two rooms and has filled the rest of the house with her junk – antiques and so forth – she has a fledgling antique business in Knightsbridge. It's a shop about as big as a sentry box, so everything ends up here.'

Michael closed the door behind them and stopped the flow of her words. He covered her lips first with his fingers and then with his mouth, as if tasting something for the first time. She felt herself go straight into his arms. It was what she had been waiting for all evening, ever since she saw him standing there fumbling for his ticket. She sniffed delicately at his special smell, and he acquainted himself with hers.

He followed her upstairs.

Inside her room, he dropped their bags on the floor and put his arms round her again. Gently she released herself and went to draw the heavy curtains.

'Whisky?' she asked. 'Or a sort of Chablis? I'm not a great drinking woman.'

'Whisky's fine,' he said, taking off his coat and then flopping on her bed. 'It's a great room,' he said, looking up at the beautiful moulding round the high ceiling. A fine carpet worn in the centre. Lots of books. Great armful of white chrysanthemums in a glass jar dumped on the table cluttered with papers, typewriter, word processor, reference books. A graceful wicker chair (rescued by Maisie from the endless stream of second-hand furniture that passed through the house) by one of the windows. The four-poster on which Michael sprawled and which could be concealed with heavy lace curtains. A small kitchen and a bathroom. Maisie's living quarters.

'What do you actually do?' he asked, taking the whisky and drinking it down in one go. 'What does an art historian do?'

'I'm a freelance consultant. My special interest is in religious artifacts, most particularly of the Eastern Orthodox Church, eleventh to fifteenth centuries.' It sounded a mouthful.

'You're clever.'

'You asked me before. Yes.'

'Don't know any clever women. Not really clever. Only pretending to be.'

'I'm not pretending. Do you avoid them?'

'No. It's just they don't cross my path.'

'Rare beasts?'

'Come here, Maisie. Rare beast.' She sat on the bed and he caressed her wrists, her forehead.

'What sort of thing do you have to do?' he went on, as he stroked her.

'A typical day?' Words counterpointed touch.

'Well, what are you doing at the moment?' He nodded towards the sheaves of paper on the table. His hands tried to span her waist. His words came as from some ethereal region somehow hovering above her.

'I've been working on the authenticity of a relic. Authentic in a historic sense, that is. Actually, it's the reliquary I am interested in. The relic itself is just a nasty bit of bone or something. The reliquary which houses it is the wonder – to me, that is.'

His little finger caressed the soft inner skin of her wrist.

'You have to travel a bit, then?'

'Yes. Russia, mostly. Orthodox countries, or ex-Orthodox. But mostly Russia, and what used to be Russia.'

'Didn't they do away with all that religious stuff in the Revolution?'

'Treasures like that. Art objects. They usually find a home before the invading hordes batter down the doors. Then they surface again in more propitious times – like these.'

She was finding it a bit hard to string her words together, aware too much of his slight touch and that their bodies were having a different conversation.

'I read somewhere', he said, 'that the Russians dug up all their saints during the Revolution and put them on show to prove their corruptibility. Nasty.'

'It's true,' she said. She stood up. 'I'm going to have a shower.' She hesitated.

She had lived so long without sex, so very long, that it was a stranger to her, like this man – who had brought it suddenly back into her life. It was like starting all over from the very beginning.

He was looking at her curiously, intently.

'Don't worry,' he said.

'Help yourself to a drink.'

'Please don't worry,' he said again.

'I'm not worried.' She bent to sniff the chrysanthemums. A wintry smell. Time seemed to stop for a moment, like a snapshot. Maisie knew it was one of those flashed moments that would stay with her for life – the vibrant presence of the man, a young stranger; the fresh, slightly bitter smell of the flowers, their crisp, curling petals, ice-green in the centre.

She had a bath, instead of a shower. She wanted to

reflect. You can't reflect in a shower. She wanted to remember how he had peered short-sightedly at his crumpled ticket. She wanted to hear again in her head how he sang the descant to a carol. She thought over his words. 'When it's right it's easy.'

As she got out of the bath she smiled at her reflection in the gold-rimmed ornate mirror. Thin shoulders, the hollows beneath them; long thin thighs, her hand reaching out for the snowy white towel. Her skin not white against it, but creamy. Her brown hair. Her mirror image looked like a sepia photograph in its gilded frame. She rubbed her body lotion over her thighs. She smelled her hand: it smelled smokily expensive.

As she put on the kimono she had brought back from a trip to Eastern Russia, she heard him playing the flute. It was the song they had been practising, but he was adding embroideries of his own; it sounded like Mozart now.

Perhaps it was the moment before the opening of Pandora's box, when the mind was made up but all the consequences of action had not yet begun to tumble and flow. She opened the door and went back into the big room.

'You look like a flower,' said Michael, putting the flute down on the bed. 'You look flower-like.'

'What sort of flower?'

'A bunch of flowers,' he said, and they smiled at each other and he held out his hand.

# 2

MAISIE walked along the sea front at Brighton and rejoiced in the glistening winter waves. She had left Michael that morning sleepily drinking the coffee she had brought him.

The square she was looking for now was just off the front. She found it, elegant, empty in the cold air, only a large dog nosing around.

She rang the bell labelled Denisov, and waited for a long time. Eventually the door was opened by a frail old lady who showed Maisie upstairs and into a rather splendid room. She was left to wait and look round at the high ceiling with its chandelier, rose-wood book-cases inlaid with ivory cherubs, richly coloured Persian carpet, an ikon of Our Lady of Vladimir gleaming darkly in the corner, for what stretched into nearly half an hour.

Maisie thought about how she had kissed the corner of Michael's mouth where a little saliva had dried in his sleep. How she had put a key into his hand and said, 'Don't lose it.'

Now the old woman was bringing tea in a samovar, and a little plate of lemon slices.

'Thank you,' said Maisie. She sipped her tea. Three different clocks ticked. A seagull screeched against the window. She did not mind the wait. She sat on the high-backed upright chair, the taste of lemon on her lips, and thought about Michael Curran.

She closed her eyes. She saw Michael at Paddington Station watching the band, his look of light-hearted intensity; the way he had stood there, forgetful of having met her, listening. She could never forget him like that, he was with her everywhere. He was part of her as she was not part of him, she thought. Though she was not sure.

'It is very good of you to come.' The old man who came in looked cobwebbed with age. 'Dr Shergold, thank you for answering my letters. Thank you for coming to see me.' He took her by the shoulders, with slightly trembling hands, and kissed her cheeks; it felt like moth's wings touching her.

'I was so interested in what you had to say,' said Maisie. The old man spoke in careful English with a faint, perhaps French accent. Certainly his English sounded unlike that of Russians she knew. His voice was breathless and muffled as if someone was trying to smother him with a cushion. And what on earth was he talking about?

'During the frightful turmoil of the Revolution,' he went on, 'it was thought the ikon was looted, lost track of for ever. But it has been in safe keeping all the time.' He paused, to allow this to sink in and to get his breath. He sat down and poured himself some tea, but did not drink it. 'When it is restored to its rightful place a Tsar will occupy once more the throne of Russia – God's representative on earth.'

'How interesting,' Maisie said again. She sipped the dregs of her cold tea to fill the gap of silence which followed this speech. Last night her love had raged like a fever, like a sickness. She had even whispered, 'I love you Michael,' as he had unlocked her. After all the long dry time, love had engulfed her, overwhelmed her. Like a predator, she had thought sadly, I will eat him up. Yet she had covered these feelings. Do not cling, do not grasp, do not want. She wanted this man. She had covered her feelings. Cover them, cover them, she had told herself.

'Yes,' the old man was saying, 'we have been working towards this end all our lives.' He trembled a little, as if the effort of that life's long work had at last suddenly caught up with him. He seemed to go into a sort of trance.

'It is very good of you to come,' he said at last. 'Good of you to make the journey.'

'Oh, not at all,' said Maisie. 'I am actually glad of a chance to come to Brighton. My mother lives here.'

'Your mother. That is very pleasant,' he said, 'she will like to see you.'

'Yes.'

'Of course.'

Seagulls screamed faintly across another silence.

'You would wish to see the ikon?' Denisov spoke more strongly.

'I would need to do so. Yes.' Maisie smiled.

'I believe you are an expert in such things?'

'Yes, I am,' she said.

'Yes, yes.' The old man got up and went over to the window. Maisie had to strain to catch his words.

'The holy ikon is at this moment in the vaults of the Westminster Bank here in Brighton. Not a suitable place for it, but until it finds a Russian shrine, it must stay there safely. I will arrange for you to examine it.'

Maisie told Denisov she would call again, she would telephone first for an appointment, and hoped to see the ikon.

'That would be very kind,' he said. 'Yes, I will have the ikon here for you to see. I look forward to seeing it again myself, touching it.' His voice became more and more muffled, as if someone was slowly stopping his mouth with snow. 'We wish to know everything about it that is possible to find from any source,' he urged faintly. 'Its origins, its

17

travels, we need an expert, Dr Shergold.' His voice was a whisper. He was obviously very tired, his bluish lips could hardly move now, as if frozen. Maisie stood up.

What made her kiss him she did not know. Perhaps because his days were so obviously numbered. He received her kiss naturally, without surprise, and rang the bell for the old woman to see his guest downstairs and out into the now entirely empty square.

Maisie was glad to be out in the fresh cold air. As she walked along the sea front, the sea, against a darkening sky, looked deeper, more mysterious, and the realization began to flood Maisie that she would not be going back to London that night. It was as if something outside herself had decided this.

Her mother lived in a road only ten minutes' walk away. At that moment, though, no one knew where she, Maisie Shergold, was. Not her mother, who had no idea she was coming. Not Michael, who would expect her by now to be on the train home. Not Rose, whose thoughts, anyway, would be on preparations for one of her so-called soirées.

Then she suddenly wanted so much to catch the next train back to London. What was stopping her, like a hand on her shoulder? It wasn't only because she wanted to see her mother that she had decided to stay overnight in Brighton. Was she testing Michael in some way? Testing herself, perhaps? Her ability not to be with him. To function alone. She did not want to examine what she was doing too closely. Her motives or her courage might fail. She entrusted herself to the hand she felt on her shoulder.

She ran up the steps of the large double-fronted four-storey house, where a Christmas tree glittered from one of the upper-floor windows, and rang the bell labelled in neat black lettering, E. Sharpe.

Evelyn Sharpe opened the door and clutched her head in a characteristic gesture. 'Come in,' she said.

'Would you put me up for the night, Ma?'

'Certainly not,' said Mrs Sharpe, laughing. Maisie laughed too.

Mrs Sharpe lived in the ground-floor flat, and her sitting-room window overlooked the little garden, at this time of year colourless except for a flourishing red-berried shrub, which leaped like quick-fire about the little garden over dead leaves and stones. The bright berries were now being slowly drained of colour by night's fall.

'I was just thinking about starting dinner. Now I can cook for two. Lovely. Come into the kitchen and tell me everything, all the news, you never write. I wish you'd write, people always used to write letters. Now they never do. Why are you in Brighton? Apart, that is, from coming to see your mother.' She gave Maisie an apron. 'Omelette and salad. Raspberries from the freezer and cream. All right?'

'Anyway, you never write to me.' Maisie sliced the cucumber thinly.

When it was ready they carried everything through to the living-room at one end of which there was a dining area with a highly polished table. Mrs Sharpe drew the heavy tasselled maroon curtains, threw a white cloth over the table and lit the gas fire.

'This big room is so hard to heat,' she said, 'I live in this quilted jacket.' It was one Maisie had brought back from one of her journeys abroad.

'You look nice in it,' said Maisie, looking at her mother and thinking really she was looking much older, smaller and thinner, and the bones were beginning to show, especially at wrist and jaw. 'That shade of pink suits you,' she said.

'Yes, it's funny, as one gets older it seems that baby colours suit one again. I used always to wear black. Couldn't wear it now, I'd look like a death's head.'

Maisie smiled. 'You're pretty good for seventy-odd, Ma, don't complain.'

They sat down to eat. 'How's Rose?' asked her mother, 'She rang me last week. Says her business is doing well. Any boyfriends in view?'

'She's seeing someone – scarcely a boy – one Bernard Glantz. A doctor – psychiatrist, that is. Haven't actually met him. He'll be at her soirée thing, no doubt – she'll be busy getting ready for it now – only time she ever clears up. He's somewhat older – Glantz.'

'She'd better be careful. I expect it's just a silly phase. All girls go through it. Always falling in love. I did. You did. It's nice to have done with all that, isn't it?'

'Yes,' said Maisie. 'It's nice to have it all over.'

'How's Leo?' Mrs Sharpe had always had a soft spot for Maisie's ex-husband.

'Fine. He's going to be a father again.'

'Oh, my dear.' Mrs Sharpe put down her fork. 'Oh, my dear. You must be so upset.'

'No. No, I'm not. Really.'

Mrs Sharpe looked at her curiously and Maisie said, helping herself to raspberries. 'You've always had a weakness for Leo. I think you're in love with him yourself – never mind being over all that.'

'Yes, I am a bit,' admitted Mrs Sharpe. 'He's so easy to get on with. So sociable and knowledgeable about things that interest me; like history, for example, or politics; as well as the antique business, of course. He's interesting. And he never puts one into an age group. With Leo you are just yourself – whether you are a child or an old lady.'

'Bit of a saint, really.'

'You can be sarcastic. I think it's rather a good thing to be sociable and knowledgeable and all of those things.'

'He was a bit too sociable, Ma.'

'You didn't fight for him, Maisie, too proud for this wicked world.'

'It wasn't pride. It was fear, really. I couldn't go into battle like that, like you would have done. I just had to watch from a hill nearby as it were, and see how things turned out.'

'I always thought he'd come back.'

'I didn't, once he'd gone. I don't want him back, Ma. Irene can have him now. He is Irene's husband.'

Mrs Sharpe looked at her, her old eyes only slightly yellow in the whites, the iris tawny-coloured.

'You're looking well,' she observed.

'I must telephone.'

'Of course – help yourself.' And Mrs Sharpe began clearing the table, taking a tray of things to the kitchen.

'Leave that, Ma.' Maisie said as she dialled. Mrs Sharpe took no notice. But the phone rang and rang. Michael had probably gone over to the Fiddler's for a beer and a chat with his friends in the band, he would be back soon, expecting her on the evening train.

Mrs Sharpe came back into the room, putting on her coat. 'I've got to go out, dear, I hope you don't mind. It's my bridge night.'

'Oh, Ma! I picked a silly night to come, didn't I? I'd forgotten about your bridge night.'

'It doesn't matter. I'll see you later on and you'll be here for breakfast. I can't not go.'

'I'll be fine,' said Maisie. 'I might go to bed quite soon, I'm really tired.'

'I'm not surprised. You're always here, there and every-where. There we are,' she said, hearing a car door slam.

When her mother had gone Maisie dialled her flat number again. There was still no answer. She went through to the kitchen and made some coffee, feeling disorientated at being alone in her mother's flat. It made her think too much about what it might be like to be her mother – over seventy years old and living alone in a draughty flat.

She took her coffee into the living-room. Even with central heating and a gas fire the room was chilly. She looked inside the Christmas cards on the mantelpiece, to see who had sent them. One from Rose, a minimalist type of card, typical of Rose, thought Maisie. A rich, festive one from Leo, threaded with a nice bright red ribbon. Hers was a representation of Our Lady of Walsingham, and one from someone called Imre, an un-Christmassy Bonnard, full of Mediterranean light.

Who was Imre?

She'd go to bed soon, she thought, and began looking on the bookshelf for something to read in bed, Evelyn Waugh – practically everything he'd written. Raymond Chandler, another of her mother's favourites. An old copy of *Alice Through the Looking Glass* that Maisie had grown up with. She picked out the Waugh *Diaries* and, as an afterthought, the *Alice*. She turned off the gas fire and went into the spare room and made herself up a bed with sheets from the airing cupboard.

Then she telephoned again. She let the phone ring for five minutes. She was beginning to feel a sense of restless uneasiness. Why hadn't she gone back today? What a fool she was! What was all that about testing herself, or was it testing him? What a fool she'd been! She couldn't get a train now, could she?

Throwing the books on the bed, Maisie went back to the phone and rang the station. There was another train. She could leave a note for her mother.

Then she felt the same hand on her shoulder she had felt walking by the sea.

She would have a bath. Go to bed. Let things take their course. Perhaps everything was predestined from the start. With love affairs, she thought, that was probably true. All that was to happen was laid down from the beginning of time. And if she interfered with the fates, looked over her shoulder, turned back, she would lose him. Like Orpheus and Eurydice. She put the phone down.

In the bathroom she turned the taps full on and watched the jets of water quickly fill the bath.

After her bath, she wrapped herself in her mother's thick blue towelling dressing-gown and went to telephone again. When there was no answer she started to dial Rose's number and changed her mind. She really was very tired. Things must take their course.

In bed, she opened the old copy of *Alice* and read favourite bits of it. Then she closed the book and went to sleep.

She dreamed about the Tsar. In her dream he was called the Red Tsar. And her mother was the White Queen.

In the morning, she woke up early and got up at once. She went quietly into the kitchen and made a cup of tea. Later she took a cup to her mother.

'Don't get up, Ma. Would you like breakfast in bed?'

'No, I'd rather get up. I hate eating in bed.'

'Did you enjoy your bridge?'

'They're such a lot of old fogeys,' said Mrs Sharpe, sipping her tea.

'I'd better be off, Ma. I want to get back.'

'But what about your breakfast?'

'I'll just have a bit of bread and jam.'

'I've got bacon, mushrooms, everything.'

'And I'll see you soon. I'll give you a ring. I have to go, Ma. Take care of yourself. Give me a ring if you need me. If you don't need me, even. I may see you next week – I've got to come down on business. 'Bye now.' Maisie kissed her mother's soft, dry cheek.

'Is anything the matter, dear?'

'No, of course not. Everything's fine. I must get back, though. I'll telephone.'

And she was gone.

Mrs Sharpe sighed and leaned back on the pillows, closing her eyes. She really missed seeing her ex-son-in-law. She had enjoyed it when Leo and Maisie had been together, when they had come down to Brighton, full of their busy lives, and Rose had been a little girl, thrilled to go out to a tea-shop with her grandmother. Nothing stays the same, she thought, not for five minutes. She went back to sleep and slept unusually soundly until nine o'clock.

By which time Maisie's train was pulling into Victoria. Railways stations were different for Maisie since her meeting with Michael. They had taken on an almost paradisical aura, it was not too much to say that. A railway station, the platforms, the people, the mysterious trains themselves, the cafeteria and kiosks, the whole being of the place, its sounds and sights and smells, were like walking in the Garden of Eden, the pillars rose up like trees to support the airy fretted ceiling. An unearthly voice came over the tannoy. Happiness rose up in her, a new fresh feeling, a flow of sweet energy – she had forgotten she could feel these things.

She decided on the spur of the moment that before she went home she would stop off at the Andromeda and have a shower, make herself beautiful.

The place was practically empty. She had a shower, a coffee, a chat with someone she vaguely knew.

Outside she bought anemones from a thin young man. She bought six bunches.

Now it was time, it was really now. She would soon be with Michael. Her heart soared; with a smile, clutching the flowers, she hailed a taxi. She nearly said Michael Curran as her destination. Laughing at herself, she sat in the back of the taxi, thinking to herself, hugging the thought to herself, in ten minutes or so, in five minutes I shall be with him. She felt so well and happy, so very well and full of vigour and kindliness to everyone in the world. She could do anything. Achieve anything. Only all she wanted was Michael.

She loved the way he walked; loosely from the shoulders. She loved his voice, soft and precise. She loved his love of music. The way he needed to use his glasses to read. The way he folded them and put them back in their case, and tucked the case in an inside pocket. His strong hands with clever-looking fingers. His eyes which lit his face. His quirky humour.

And even before she had opened the door of her room she knew he wasn't there.

# 3

WHEN Maisie had telephoned from Brighton, Michael had not been far out of earshot; the telephone rang in the room above him. He was downstairs at Rose's soirée.

When Maisie had not returned, he felt deflated, because he had geared himself to seeing her at a certain time. He had spent the day quietly exploring the area, walking in the park, sitting in its Orangery, watching the birds in the wintry flower-beds, watching other solitary figures wrapped against the bright cold weather, withdrawn into themselves, thinking their own thoughts as he thought his, and now, coming back to the flat, he was bored.

He wished he'd gone over to the Fiddler's for the lunch-time practice session. He'd been neglecting his music and was thirsting to get back to it.

So when he met Rose on the stairs, and heard the Stones' music coming from her room, he stopped and chatted.

'I'm Rose,' she'd said. 'Mummy left a note about you. You're Michael Curran.' And she invited him to look in on her soirée.

Maisie never came to these occasional evenings, Rose explained, because her father would bring Irene and it was a bit awkward. It was just that the two women tended to avoid each other. So Michael had said he'd come in for an hour or so as Maisie was late.

'Red or white, or vodka with cider, a vile and almost lethal drink?' asked Rose. 'This is Bernard, Bernard Glantz. But don't listen to his tosh,' she added, as Glantz came up behind her.

'You let fate take over,' Glantz was saying, 'you relinquish control. A manipulative relationship is not true love.' His ugly face looked serious and anxious.

Rose laughed, she was a bit drunk. 'True love,' she said scornfully.

Michael took a glass of wine from her. 'So young and so untender,' he said, looking grave.

'Some people are capable of it,' Glantz went on, 'some are not, being hedged about by their own neuroses and not free to love. That is what my work is about – freeing people to love.'

Rose glared at him. 'Is that what you do, Bernard?' she said rudely.

'I try to, but I seldom succeed in full.'

'Whoever succeeds in full?' said Leo Shergold. Rose introduced Michael to her father and to the thin, dark young woman with an attractive cast in one eye.

'What are we talking about?' she asked.

'Love,' said Rose. 'At least, that's what Bernard is talking about.'

'That's what Bernard usually talks about,' said Leo.

'Are men really interested in love? I mean, do they know about it?' Irene asked. The cast in her eye seemed accentuated as she spoke.

'What on earth do you mean, my darling?' Leo took a sip from a glass of white wine, then passed it to her. She drank for a little while, delicately, like a wild creature at a secret pool.

'It's all to do with women's different conception of time.

27

A woman's idea of time is cyclical,' she said. 'Women feed back into the creative cycle – clever little things, aren't we?'

'Perhaps the tide is going out for men,' Leo said in an unworried voice.

Michael was not listening now, he was wondering if Maisie was back. He excused himself, quickly draining his glass, and went upstairs to see if she had returned. If was late now, she must have stayed in Brighton for the night, she had said something about her mother being there. But he felt let down.

There was a certain quality about Maisie, something ungraspable; something vague, floating, about her, she wasn't real, corporeal in some sense. Even in bed she had been like that. It fascinated him, but fed his loneliness.

He made a cup of coffee and took down a book from the neatly filed travel section on Maisie's shelf. Kinglake's *Eothen*. He drank his coffee, reading bits at random, half-waiting for the telephone to ring. It didn't. After nearly an hour, he began to feel at a loose end again and went downstairs to rejoin Rose's little gathering.

There were about thirty people there by this time, and the room was full of voices, nearly drowning the chaste Indian music on tape. He drifted to a group near the window, Rose was among them; they were talking about art and politics. How people went grinding on over the same things, chewing on them like bones they couldn't bury or leave alone, he thought.

'Take Solzhenitsyn,' someone said. 'His books are really political tracts, not novels. A work of art can never have any lesser aim than to be art. With Solzhenitsyn the aim is political.'

'What utter nonsense,' said Rose. 'We read *Paradise Lost* at school. Would anyone dare to say that wasn't art? Yet all Milton's work was political.'

'It depends what you mean by politics,' said an old man with wintry blue eyes and a foreign accent. 'You could say that everything, even this glass I am holding, or that marble-topped table, is in its way political. A piece of spare Amish furniture makes a political statement, so does an elaborate eighteenth-century desk.'

'Politics is part of life,' agreed Rose. 'We breathe it in. It is carried in our bloodstream.'

Michael regarded her. 'What particular politics are in your bloodstream, Rose?' he said, reflecting that, at the moment, there was probably too much vodka in it.

'She is a puritan,' said Glantz. 'That says everything.'

'On the contrary,' said Rose, 'I bend with the wind. I float.'

Michael laughed, and the old man looked at him severely.

'If we have sense,' he said, 'we keep our politics secret to ourselves, keep it in the bloodstream only. You have never learned about that in this country – perhaps you will.'

'What is your country?' Michael asked. Habitually he kept his own Irishness out of things, it caused less trouble. He felt Irish only in Ireland. It was different with this old man, who wore his country on his sleeve.

'I am a Russian,' he said proudly, as if to say, 'I am highly born.'

There was a pause in the chatter amongst the little group, not an awkward pause, but one in which something of significance was being absorbed. Something that actually mattered to someone had been said.

'I have never seen my own country,' the old man went on. 'My parents were made exiles and I was born in Paris.'

'Mr Menshikov lives in London now,' said Rose. 'He has come to discuss business, he has some wonderful pre-Revolutionary pieces.'

'Business not politics,' said Michael, smiling and accepting a glass of wine and a plate of food – supermarket delicacies arranged artistically on a Victorian flowered dinner-plate.

'Art not business,' grinned Menshikov.

'We're back to politics, then,' said Rose.

'Exactly,' said the old man. 'And power. Power is the root of everything.'

Oh, well, thought Michael, it passed the evening. He would rather have been with musician friends.

The old man was talking about money for the organization. He spoke of this organization in a low voice, as if talking about God.

Where was Maisie? wondered Michael. He supposed she was all right. A woman of the world, used to looking after herself. He was surprised how very much he missed her and wanted her. If anything had got into his bloodstream, it was her; and how quickly it had happened, like a fix, a strong drug. What would have happened if he had known where his rail ticket was that afternoon on Paddington Station? By now he would be immersed in practice and recording sessions and soon be thinking of going back to Ireland – and Kate. Instead of waiting for Maisie, listening to an old guy who lived in a sort of time-warp and seemed to be trying to raise funds for a secret society by selling his furniture. But the old man's voice was clear in his head as he went upstairs to Maisie's room, which had quickly become a sort of home to him now. 'Power is the root of everything.' Was it? Was it?

But if you were in love you relinquished power over your loved one, as Bernard Glantz had said. Maisie had some kind of power over him. And why did he mind that?

She hadn't come home. He felt somehow diminished, enslaved now by his wish to hear the telephone ring, hear her voice. She had not come home. Was she showing she wasn't enslaved by him? Showing who held the balance of power?

Of course she'd just missed her train, or been persuaded by her mother to stay . . . or mugged on the last train home. Or she'd met another stranger on another station. This last prospect was the worst to contemplate. Worse than thinking of her bruised by a mugger's blows, blood trickling from her nose. Why was it worse to think of another man caressing her than being hurt by another man? With Kate it wasn't like that. With her it was the other way round.

Impatient with his wandering, feckless thoughts, Michael took out his flute and began playing a piece by Corelli. Music was the thing. It was the only thing you could rely on.

He finished up the beer in the fridge, ate some cold ravioli, went to bed and slept well.

Next day he went over to Shepherd's Bush and found them in the Fiddler's Cat having a lunchtime session. He apologized for his absence, and got straight down to work.

Maisie was still at the back of his mind, but the music was what was in control of him. They worked, and laughed, worked and drank and smoked, and worked. It was his niche, his home, his heavenly home, his hiding place.

About nine o'clock that evening he telephoned Maisie from the telephone on the bare landing.

'I've got to go to Kiev,' she was saying, 'for a conference on the twenty-fifth.' Her voice sounded vague, far away, as if in Kiev already.

'But that's Christmas Day,' he said.

'Yes, well, everything doesn't stop for Christmas Day there and it's twelve days later in the Orthodox Church. Anyway, will you come?'

'Yes, I'll come, Maisie.'

And they were back where they started.

# 4

THEY caught a mid-morning train down to Brighton. Brighton Station was bustling with life, festive with holly and bunches of mistletoe; chrysanthemums, white and bronze, stood in buckets of water.

'Everyone's doing their Christmas shopping,' Maisie said, taking Michael's arm. 'Let's do ours.'

'Food first,' said Michael.

They found a red gingham table-clothed little café and had scrambled eggs and good coffee. Then they wandered about the Lanes, arm-in-arm. Maisie bought a scarf with roses on it for Rose, and perfume, 'Elle-Même', for her mother.

Michael bought a cameo brooch and a little gold brooch set with pearls in the shape of a violin, both Victorian, to send to Ireland.

'What does your mother look like?' Maisie asked.

'Like a witch,' said Michael, 'a fierce, intelligent old witch with a bleak sense of humour.'

They found a post office and Michael wrapped the gifts there and then and got them off to Ireland. Maisie watched as he absorbedly wrote messages on two cards. Then, folding away his gold spectacles with a deft movement, he said,

'What now, my love? What time is the appointment with your Russian aristo?'

'Not for another couple of hours. I'll take Ma's present round. She'd like to meet you.'

'Is she like a witch too?'

'I don't think so, not my idea of a witch, anyway. She's my mother. I'm probably too close to see her or describe her objectively, I suppose she's like me, only older.' She felt his arm tighten about her.

'Are you sure she won't mind a strange man turning up? I could wait for you.'

'She loves men. I want you to come.'

'And I want to come.'

'Really, you wouldn't rather go for a drink?'

'It's tempting.'

'Go on, then.'

'I'm coming.' He squeezed her arm and kissed her quickly as they walked. 'No drinks. I wish to meet your mother cold sober.'

Which was why he laughed when Mrs Sharpe filled up his glass with whisky.

They sat by the window looking out at the winter sunshine caressing the little front garden, and drank whisky and ate smoked salmon. Maisie gave her mother her gift, not to be opened until Christmas Day.

'I always open my presents after Midnight Mass,' said Mrs Sharpe. 'Suppose I didn't last out the night, I'd never know what I'd got. Coffee, anyone?'

'Oh, yes, a quick cup of coffee, then we really must go. I'll make it, Ma.'

And Maisie left Michael and her mother weighing each other up and chatting about the person they had in common.

'She's a clever girl,' her mother said, as Maisie brought in the tray of coffee. 'She speaks Russian and she makes a nice cup of coffee.'

33

'Yes, I know.' Michael smiled at Maisie. She had once thought that wide, bright smile was a bit flash. What she had thought was flashiness was a sort of bitterness in the smile. She couldn't quite define it, understand it; the bitterness was part of the smile, part of its warmth and gaiety. It turned Maisie's guts to water.

As they drank their coffee and chatted, Maisie could feel the slight disapproval her mother felt for Michael, not really for him, but for the relationship, the situation. She had not accepted the break-up of Maisie's marriage. As far as she, Evelyn Sharpe, was concerned, her daughter was still married to Leo Shergold. But she was friendly enough, hospitable, of course.

'More coffee?' she was saying.

'We must get off,' said Maisie.

'She's always dashing about,' said Michael. 'A restless lady.'

'Send me a card from Kiev.'

'I'll probably telephone.' Maisie picked up her briefcase and pulled on her gloves; she was dressed quite formally for her meeting with Denisov.

And when she got there she was glad that she was. For when Maisie and Michael were shown up to the large room overlooking the square, it was obvious that something extraordinary was happening.

Often it is the sense of smell that reacts initially, picks things up, and it was the smell that Maisie noticed first. The room was blurred with the pungent fumes of incense. It is, like chloroform, a smell that touches the mind and clings to the memory. Denisov was there, sitting in a high-backed chair, looking very frail, perhaps ill. Michael was startled to see beside him the old man with the wintry-blue eyes, Menshikov, who had been at Rose's soirée. Standing opposite was a robed priest of the Russian Orthodox Church who was swinging a censer back and forth in front of a small ikon, which Maisie recognized as the Ikon of the Mother of God of the Black Steppes. With a queer stirring of excitement, she knew that this was not a copy, but the legendary original.

The atmosphere in the room was intense. With an involuntary movement, Michael crossed himself. It was something like the numinous sense of wonder that comes immediately after the birth of a child. A quietness. A sense of fullness, as if something had at last been accomplished; something that had been long waited for, long expected.

Maisie moved forward to acknowledge the old man's greeting and his apologies for not getting up. The priest was chanting in Russian, his deep-bellied voice resonated from the walls of the room as if from a sounding board.

Then suddenly all that stopped and the old servant brought in the samovar and some little sweet biscuits, and everyone including the servant sat down and started chatting. They were seated in a circle round the ikon as if the tea and almond biscuits were part of the ceremony, a sort of love feast, the samovar humming away.

Michael sat opposite Maisie, the ikon with its frame of beaten gold gleaming darkly, softly between them. They sat as if round a fire, warming themselves, eating their biscuits and sipping tea.

They all chatted quietly, regarding each other, companions of this strange circle, with friendly, even loving eyes. Time seemed an irrelevance, suspended as it sometimes is in the night-watches, when a circle of friends may sit around a fire in the open, under the stars in some desert country. Only it was early afternoon in Brighton and there were no stars over their heads. Only the moulded ceiling with acanthus leaves and cherubim holding the chandelier above their heads.

After they had finished eating and drinking, Denisov invited Maisie to examine the ikon. The priest made his farewells and left. Maisie opened her briefcase and took out reference books, a notebook and a small camera, and started making careful notes and taking photographs.

The ikon was quite small. It might have been first used for private devotional purposes. It had a certain intimate quality about it. Maisie was instantly struck by its delicate harmony. The Virgin looked at the Child, and He at her. He clung lightly to His mother, sitting on His mother's hand, leaning against her arm, quite upright and lively. The colouring was ochre, olive-green, gold-brown, black and umber. A gold glow behind the figures indicated the heavenly light from their nimbi. Both the Virgin and Child had a nimbus or halo, the mother's of a warmer, solid glow, the Child's more transparent, new, with a new-moon quality.

The thing that held the viewer was the loving intentness of the gaze in the mother's eyes, a serene, calm but wakeful gaze, as if an invisible thread hung in the look between them.

The Virgin's robe had a Byzantine appearance in the intricate repeating pattern of the cloth; but the faces of the two were un-Byzantine in their human and individual quality. It was a beautiful ikon. Maisie had no doubt that it was authentic, probably early twelfth-century and Russian. Maisie had enough stored knowledge to let her instinct guide her – she felt the uniqueness of this ikon. She did not doubt it was the Steppes ikon.

Maisie worked silently for nearly an hour, Denisov watching her without one word. The old woman quietly cleared away the remains of the little feast. Michael and Menshikov talked in low voices like old companions who had known each other for many years – it was as if some alchemy had been at work between them.

At last Maisie put her things away and closed her case. She looked at Denisov's yellow old face, and smiled.

'That's all I can do for today,' she said. 'I shall have to do some research. Make some enquiries. Tomorrow I am going to Kiev to attend a conference, and I hope there I will be able to consult Professor Werner who is a world expert.'

'We wish to trace all its journeys. We want to know the craftsman who made it. We want to discover its history as fully as possible. We wish the ikon to be authenticated in the interests of our cause. We are willing to pay well for your work, Dr Shergold, and we wish you to accept this first payment.'

The old man held an envelope in his shaking hand. A little taken aback by this straightforwardness, Maisie thanked him and put the envelope in her case.

Again the moth-like touch of old flesh as he kissed her. 'Kiev, you say,' said the old man in his tired voice.

'Yes,' said Maisie.

'Ah,' said the old man.

# PART TWO

*Kiev*

# I

MAISIE saw the lights of the airport runway pierce
the night with fairy-like beauty as their plane
approached.

She took Michael's hand. As they flew softly on to the
runway he covered her mouth with his, and the kiss and the
quivering landing became one thing. She thought of a
painting she had seen somewhere of Leda and the Swan, the
dark bird covering Leda's white thighs. Who had painted it?
Etty? Sometimes she wished the art historian in her would
take itself off.

'I'm scared of landings,' Michael said, 'that made it
better.' Maisie laughed and kissed him again sweetly.

Another smaller Russian aeroplane flew them quietly
over the Ukrainian steppes to Kiev.

'Welcome to Byzantium,' he whispered in her ear. She
was surprised. What had made him say that? The words
should have been hers.

Later that night as they lay in bed, she asked him why he
had said it.

'I just felt it,' he said. 'It came into my head.'

She could feel him smiling in the dark. 'You're lovely,'
she said.

'So are you. Ever so lovely.'

She switched the light on. They were both slippery with sweat.

'Can't you settle down?' He looked tired, deep circles under his eyes. She was remorseful.

'I'll try. Wasn't it beautiful, flying over the steppes and – everything?'

'I thought you meant making love.'

'That too.' She sat on the edge of the bed and looked at his wrist-watch on the little table; was it really still the same night?

'Come back to bed, you'll get cold.'

Maisie picked up the cotton shirt he had been wearing from the chair and put it on, mopping her body with it. Then climbed back into bed.

'Take that thing off.'

She took it off and threw it out of the bed.

'You're tired.' She began kissing his fingernails, fingers, wrists.

'Dead tired.'

But before they slept they made love again. Though she pitied him for his tiredness. Then they fell asleep. Falling. Just as they were, tangled in each other's arms and legs, like soldiers fallen on a battlefield.

Maisie woke first. It was still dark, but she sensed it would soon be light. Patiently she lay completely still until the slow light began to seep into the room. This room which held her sleeping lover; who slept as if drowned. She turned her head very slightly so that when the light got stronger she would be able to make out his features.

Lapped now in light – the look around the nose and mouth reminded her he had once been a boy. But also sleeping there, something she was afraid of. A wilfulness of its own, a looking inward to its own dark centre. And the black hair and eyebrows – he came from a different tribe. Leo had been of her own tribe. Michael was other. Strange, she had only lately become aware of this, of his darkness.

Strange. It was as if he was changing from the 1.
first met.

She could never grasp him, have him for herself.
she killed him now, as he lay sleeping. But she would
destroy him, for she already loved him in another way
well – dispassionately. Perhaps it was another part of her
that loved him like that – loved him for himself and saw the
child and the old man in him and wanted him to be free. It
was *her* dark self that wanted to swallow him. She knew
this.

Her scrutiny woke him. He opened his eyes.

'Hallo,' he said. 'Hallo, Maisie.'

Gently she put her fingers over his eyelids and closed
them.

'Go back to sleep,' she said. 'It's not morning yet.'

'Yes, it is,' said Michael, his eyes still closed. 'Listen.'
They could hear the sound of the radio, someone was getting
up and moving about behind the thin walls.

'I don't have to turn up until three o'clock for the
reception.'

'We'll stay in bed until three o'clock, then.' And he went
straight back to sleep.

Maisie slithered gently out of bed and went to the
window, wrapping herself in the bed-cover. They were on
the fourth floor and their room was at the back of the hotel,
looking over an enclosed space, a kind of courtyard. Everything was covered with a thin sprinkling of snow. Birds
hopped in the solitary leafless tree. It looked iron-cold. Who
said the first day of Creation wasn't like this? Iron-cold.
Leafless. Before God had practised with everything else. Just
a tree trying to live in the bitter cold and trying to give
shelter to small birds who wanted to survive in this new-
made world.

Even as she watched, it began to snow. First a flake or
two. Then more and more. She drew back the lace curtains
and watched until this other curtain of incredible purity hung

om the sky. Maisie watched it for several minutes before she turned away, half-hypnotized.

Quietly, she sat on the floor – there was no comfortable chair – and opened her briefcase.

Sitting there on the floor, she realized there was something about the room. It was an odd shape, small but high-ceilinged, giving the feeling that the room had been turned on its side. The hotel itself was nineteenth-century, and its large rooms had been partitioned off and adapted to its modern use.

Sudden sounds of water-pipes and ablutions in other rooms could be heard, and Maisie could still hear the sound of a radio. If she strained her ears she could almost catch what the newsreader was saying. It sounded like something going on in Bashkir.

Shipwrecks, famine, earthquakes, bloody wars and coups. They streaked the world with misery and blood.

All that mattered to her was this one man, his sprawled shape under the light-as-a-feather duvet. One of his feet was sticking out of the cover and she resisted taking it in her hand, holding it. He filled up her mind and her imagination.

Very quietly she took her papers and notes and a couple of reference books from her briefcase. She was working on some notes about Andrei Rublev. If there was time, she might be asked to give a paper. But it would be towards the end of the conference. One or two people had been asked to prepare papers to be given if there was time or if anyone dropped out.

When Michael stirred in his sleep, she stopped writing and watched him. Dark stubble on his chin made him look older.

After a time she went back to her notes.

When he did awake, she wasn't aware of it, and he had been watching her writing for some time before he said, 'If I don't get up I won't get any coffee. And if I don't get any coffee the day won't happen. It's as simple as that.' And he leaped out of bed in a ferocious display of fake energy.

Maisie laughed and kissed him and put away her papers, as he dressed with unfussy, spare movements. As he shaved, she said, 'It's probably too late for breakfast, let's go out for coffee.'

As they went out into the corridor a girl passed them, a plain little chambermaid, round-shouldered, almost hunch-backed, carrying a pile of linen.

'Do'braye oo' tra,' said Michael turning round to her. He was practising his Russian. The girl broke into a huge, beautiful smile, showing big teeth.

'Do'braye oo' tra,' she replied, clutching the pile of linen close to her.

Another older woman sat impassively at the head of the stairs as if waiting patiently for the end of the world. Maisie put their room key into her dreamily outstretched hand. Would all the keys be finally gathered in before the Apoca-lypse? It was doubtful.

As they went out of the heavily grand main doors into the freezing air, Michael turned up the collar of his coat and put on the Russian hat that Maisie had bought for him at the airport. She nearly told him how wonderful he looked in it but the words wouldn't come. She found she couldn't say these easy things to him. It was something to do with a sort of magical loss of power.

They were getting their bearings, standing at the top of the hotel's flight of granite steps. It was still snowing, but not heavily now.

Two young women turned to watch them, the young man and the woman in her red coat with a long swirling skirt almost brushing the ground – a striking-looking pair, standing at the top of the great flight of steps as if on a stage, arm-in-arm. They were unaware of the rest of the world. And obviously foreigners. A pair of foreigners in love.

Maisie's clothes did make heads turn in Kiev. She always wished that everyone would dress in beautiful clothes so that she wouldn't be noticed, but she wouldn't give them up for anonymity in spite of her reticence. She used clothes as a way of cherishing herself. At least, that was one of the ways she cherished herself through the quiet years after Leo. And she had the habit of dressing well.

They made their way to the Kreshchatic. They chose a dim corner of the café and sat down at the starched white-clothed table to have their coffee. Instinctively they made for a table where they could be only with each other – they did not want to sit by the window and watch the citizens of Kiev go by.

'Are you glad you came?' she said.

'You know that,' said Michael, smiling. 'I've left every-thing and followed you.'

'Left your music.'

'Yes, my work.'

'How will you live if you have left your work?'

'You will keep me.'

'Yes.' She looked firm and solemn.

'I'm teasing you, Maisie. I've brought plenty of money.'

'Do you make much money with your music?'

'Sporadically. When I do make money it tends to be a lot, and it keeps me going. And it dribbles in from the records. And I write a bit for music magazines – odds and ends like that.'

'Have you let people down coming with me?'

'Yes. There was a recording session tentatively fixed up in London – but it doesn't matter. Nothing matters.'

'I know.'

But she wondered if she would have given up the conference for him. It was a real question in her mind.

'Would you have dropped all this – and come with me to New York or wherever?'

'How do you know my thoughts?'

'Because my mother is a witch, I told you, and she has taught me some of her secret powers. You will never be able to think anything without my knowing it. So be careful what you think.'

There was a little vase on the table with two red carnations in it. He pushed it towards her.

'Well? Would you have given it up?'

'I would give up people for you.'

'Yes, but other things. This conference.'

'I'm not sure. Why talk about it? I asked you to come, and you came. And we must be happy and not question each other.'

'All right, Maisie. Rare beast.' He kissed her fingers. 'What shall we do now?'

'Don't pull the petals off!' He was plucking the red petals from one of the carnations and dropping them on the table-cloth.

'I've already done it,' he said. He had pulled the head off a whole flower and had a handful of petals.

'You're a vandal, Michael. A destroyer. A—'

He scattered the petals over her hair and paid the bill.

'Come on,' she said as they went out into the street – she was shaking the red petals out of her hair. 'I'll show you Kiev.'

'Come on, then. Show me.' He put his arm round her and kissed her.

'Well, I'll have to go back briefly, to the hotel – but we've got an hour or so.'

'What will you take me to? Churches, I suppose – there seem to be a few.'

'I'll show you the best thing of all in Kiev.'

'Come on, then, show me the best thing.' He tightened his grip, squeezing her thin shoulders. 'I know what it is. It's Maisie Shergold. The best thing in Kiev – my beautiful, sexy Maisie.'

'Yes. I'll show you the next best thing.'

'That's me,' said Michael.

'Yes, well, after that.' They were, it was true, by far the best things in this splendid, glorious city. She longed to put her arms round him, hold him forever close to her. Closer.

But she started to run, pulling him, her skirts flaring out, threading through the passers-by. They raced down the street, which was as wide as a river, tree-lined, bare-branched against the giant grey buildings; they were flying past everyone, running out into the road to avoid the people and back on to the pavement to avoid the traffic. Then they were leaping up broad steps to a park.

Suddenly Maisie stopped and pointed down.

'Isn't it wonderful?' she said, out of breath. 'Have you ever seen such a sight?' They were looking down from Maisie's chosen vantage-point, on the Dniepr.

'It looks like the sea,' said Michael. 'You would think it was the sea. I've never seen a river like that. I really thought it was the sea.' Another sea came into his mind; the grey-green, silver-crested sea of his boyhood, leaping with fish.

The great swollen river looked alive. It looked like a live thing. A wonderful, shining, powerful creature that some-times leaped and danced and sometimes lay as still as a sheet of steel, and now heaved and swelled and rippled its great body.

Behind them lay the city with its golden domes and tall modern buildings, and below them, across the great expanse of water, the power stations and chimneys of industrial Kiev, and then beyond, the Black Steppe reaching out to the horizon, as if drawn by a dark finger against the sky.

People stood along the embankment of the river and stared into the water – as if it were a god, or might be the home of a god.

'I'd rather look at a river than a cathedral,' said Michael.

'I'm getting cold,' she said.

'Come against me, then,' he said. He stood behind her and folded her inside his coat. 'That's better. Lean against me.' She leaned back against him, his body and the river, the sky and the domed city behind them all rocked together in her perceptions.

'Different gods here,' he said. 'The older gods of water and forest and earth.'

'The older gods are in the cathedral too,' said Maisie, 'at least the mother goddess. The Russian Mother of God is the Mother from which everything in Nature flows, all fruitfulness – and to which everything returns. Mother of God, *Bogoroditsa* is the Russian word.'

'Why did you decide to love me, Maisie?'

'Do people decide?'

'Sometimes.'

'I don't think I decided. I don't think I wanted it like that. It just ran into me – like an accident.'

'You make it sound like a catastrophe.'

'Perhaps it will be.'

'No. We won't let it be that.' He kissed her hair, then, turning her round to face him, still inside his coat, kissed her mouth.

At last he released her, and they started walking, then, back the way they had come.

'What happened with you and Leo?'

'We became too friendly. Too easy with each other. There was no friction.'

'He seemed so suitable for you, Maisie. Just right for you.'

She hated him saying that, but only answered, 'You liked him?'

'I thought you would have suited him – more than Irene. What do you think of her?'

They had come to an iron seat and sat down.

'I've hardly met her,' said Maisie, 'but I wouldn't have thought of her for Leo. I think he's intrigued with her more than anything. She's so different from him and he's never met anyone like her.'

'I've met quite a few women like her,' said Michael.

'You and Leo have moved in different circles.'

'Do you still care for him?'

'Well – I still care *for* him.'

'Didn't you feel betrayed by him?'

'I've forgotten.'

'You don't want to talk about it.'

'It's not that. It's just that whole time – I can't really remember what happened, how I felt.'

'Cut yourself off from feeling about it?'

'Well – perhaps that was it.'

'I think you would do that. Just slip away. I feel that about you – that you could just slip through my fingers.'

Maisie could not understand him talking like that, when every shred of her now was wrapped up in his being.

'Why did you love me?' she asked. She knew she should not ask this, but expected him to say because of her fascination, her sex appeal and beauty, her honesty and directness. Things that Leo had once said about her.

'Because you loved me first,' he said simply. That truth brought tears to her eyes and she turned her head away. She pretended to look at her watch.

'We'd better go,' she said, 'I mustn't be late.'

'Are you crying?'

'No.'

'We'd better go.'

'Yes.'

'Come on,' he said, 'now I'll show *you* Kiev.' Pulling her up from the seat, he began to run. Then they were both running, running down a wide street. This time he was pulling her along.

'This is October Revolution Street!' he shouted, looking up at the street name. He was getting good at translating the Russian alphabet. They ran and ran. They whirled round a corner.

'This is – this is another street,' he said, unable to read

the name. She couldn't go any further, and pulled away from him, panting. He pinned her against the wall. One arm each side, a prisoner.

'You are my prisoner,' he said.

# 2

'I REALLY loathe conference receptions,' said Maisie in a low voice. 'I'm inflicting this on you.'

She had changed into a simple dress and complicated jewellery.

'I'm enjoying myself,' said Michael, 'I love it.' He had his name label on upside down.

'I love you,' said Maisie, and drifted off.

The delegates were being welcomed in what had probably been the ballroom of this pre-Revolutionary palace. The huge room still had splendid sad bones. It was completely bare of furniture, not a chair in sight, and people tended to range themselves in little groups round the walls, so they had something to lean on. This left the centre of the beautiful, immense wooden floor in a pool of light from the chandeliers, empty, except when the space was occasionally crossed by a distracted delegate looking for someone. Chandeliers with pieces missing dripped like broken stalactites from the ceiling and gave the room, with its peeling walls, a cave-like melancholy and grandeur. You felt that, looking up, you should see a hole in the ceiling, letting in the light. But grey wintry light, unlike the glow from the chandelier, came from long windows, cloister-like down one side of the room. That side of the room retained its former elegance and looked on to frozen grass and statues of gods and goddesses mantled in snow. One of them was headless.

An obstinate-looking young woman with a blankly pretty face seemed to be in charge. She made sure everyone on her list was introduced to their hosts.

'This is Aleksandr Pavlovich Ivanov from the Bureau for Cultural Exchange,' she said to Michael. 'Which party are you with?'

'That party,' said Michael, pointing to Maisie.

When everyone was suitably drunk they were all shooed into a lecture theatre for the introductory talk.

This was given by an intense little woman who was at pains to impress on her polyglot assembly that the purpose of the conference was to do with cultural roots, not religious faith, the churches and monasteries, even the ikons themselves, she said, if regarded correctly, symbolized the people's struggle. They had been fought over, much blood spilled. They were, in a way, trophies of war.

Maisie pricked up her ears, though, when the speaker went on to mention the 'ikon about which we have all heard various rumours . . . sacred duty to procure it for the people . . . to occupy a central place in the Museum of Russian Art'.

Maisie was surprised to hear such open reference to what she had thought had been generally regarded as an almost fable-like account of a miracle-working ikon put about by credulous and superstitious elements. Apparently she had not had her ear to the ground of late. She imagined Denisov's alarm.

The little woman made no mention of the fact that the Orthodox Church had a claim on it which it was unlikely to give up.

'This conference,' she was saying, 'showed the strength of new cultural ties re-established with Europe and the world, since they were systematically eradicated.' She paused, then went on.

'It was delightful to see scholars from so many countries

with so many diverse talents and views. For so long the intelligentsia had been despised, deprived of oxygen, of free exchange of ideas. Now it could begin to breathe again.'

There was faint polite applause as people shuffled their transcripts.

Maisie put her hand on Michael's thigh.

'It won't all be like this,' she whispered. 'Once the individual speakers start it will be fascinating.'

Michael looked at the programme. 'Ikons and Ikonography of the Romanov Dynasty'. After a coffee break, 'Early Russian Wall Painting'. He pulled a wry face. Maisie's fingers pressed the sinewy muscle of his inner thigh. She smiled.

Sitting in the lecture hall with Michael she felt the loneliness of the past years seeping away like a gradual thaw, like pack-ice thawing after a hard, deeply sleeping winter. She hadn't even known, until now, that she had been lonely. Lonely did not describe what she had been. Lonely. What did the word mean? she pondered. She had not felt lonely. She had thought herself fulfilled. At the same time calm and still. She had needed those years. The being alone had been right. Under the ice something was happening, protected and hidden. In a way those frozen years had been happy. Happy. What did the word mean? And the breaking-up of the ice was not painless. But she couldn't go back. There had been something frozen, she now knew, as she felt the movement of something in the depths of her. A stirring that was now out of her hands. It had come of its own accord. Perhaps her defences had been down that evening; tired off the train, open to anything that might happen to her, she'd relinquished control and it had happened.

A babble of conversation among the delegates broke into her thoughts. The speaker now told them, above the din, about hotel arrangements in the city, apologized for any mix-ups; dining arrangements were to be in the ballroom where the delegates first met. Were there any queries? There weren't – people were already streaming out. The woman's

54

voice rose somehow over the noise. There would be a special banquet the next day to welcome guests. (The next day was Christmas Day in Europe and for Catholic Russians, and the banquet would be by way of a Christmas dinner.)

As they made their way back to the hotel Maisie said, 'I must telephone my mother. I'll do it in our room.'

'Do you want me out of the way?'

'No.'

She sat on the edge of the bed to telephone, and he lay beside her looking at a sheaf of brochures he'd picked up from the Intourist desk – he'd made a mistake and shortsightedly picked up Chinese instead of Russian ones.

'I'm trying to learn Russian, not bloody Chinese,' he said. He had rolled over towards her and put his arm lightly round her waist. She got through at once and her mother's voice was as clear as if she had been in the same room. He felt like a husband this evening, thought Maisie. It distanced her mother's clear tones.

'It's a wonderful line, Ma. You're as clear as a bell.'

'I'm glad you rang. Rose has arrived but she's out at the moment. That man has been telephoning ever since she got here. He's driving down for Christmas lunch. A long way to come for lunch. A very peculiar relationship. How are you, my dear?'

'I thought I'd better telephone today – they've laid something on for tomorrow. I'm fine,' said Maisie.

Michael had moved away from her, and was looking through his little Russian-English dictionary and phrasebook, his glasses on the end of his nose.

'Well, it doesn't seem like a good relationship to me,' her mother was saying. 'She speaks of him as if he was the biggest fool. The whole thing horrifies me. I'm surprised at you, Maisie.'

Not a husband, she thought, a stranger, really. A stranger husband. Yes. That exactly.

'Well, it's not me that's having the relationship with

Glantz.' There was a small silence. What was her mother getting at? thought Maisie.

'There was something to be said for girls marrying before they were twenty and having a couple of children to give them a sense of reality.'

Maisie looked at her watch – this would be an expensive call if her mother didn't stop soon, but she couldn't resist saying, 'It didn't give you a sense of reality, Mother. You dumped me with a nanny and went on the stage. Rosalind at Stratford.'

'Yes, I know. But at least I knew who I was.'

'Did you?'

'Of course I did. We did in those days.'

'Well, have a lovely Christmas, Ma. Make Rose and that man wash up, and put your feet up.'

'I had a call from Leo – wishing me a happy Christmas and everything, checking on Rose. He doesn't like that man either.'

'Which man?'

'Glantz.'

'Well – have a splendid Christmas, Ma, and thank you for my present. Just right.'

'Well . . . goodbye, then, dear.'

'I knew a psychiatrist,' said Michael, looking up the Russian for the word in his dictionary, 'and all he did – he ran a sort of private madhouse – was pair up the men and women. It was the only treatment. No drugs. Never used drugs. Said it was better than drugs.'

'Sounds quite a creative approach – if you believe most of these troubles stem from frustrated love. I wonder if he followed up the results of his treatment to see what happened, though.'

'I shouldn't think so. What's the worry about Rose, anyway? She seemed perfectly sensible to me.'

'She is sensible.'

'Seems to be coping with life.'

'Yes – but she's not happy.' It occurred to Maisie that Michael was getting to know more and more about her and the relationships that surrounded her – and she knew no more about him than when she had first met him. Was it just women who were barnacled about with so many indissoluble relationships?

He had a look about him – of freedom. She had been aware of it from the beginning. Perhaps it was that she had fallen in love with. Perhaps that was it. Did she want to *be* him – because he was free?

It was in his eyes even now, however loving, however interested in everything about her, behind them, a light of non-attachment. But his voice was kind, intimate, caressing.

'Well, that's a lot to expect – happiness. Until you've made up your mind that's what you'll be, that is.'

'You mean we choose if we are to be happy or not?'

'Oh, yes. It's a decision we take – one way or the other. I'm sure of it.'

'What have you chosen?'

'I've chosen to be miserable,' said Michael, smiling. 'It's better for my art. What did your mother give you?'

'A book I wanted,' said Maisie.

'I've never asked about your father. Is he alive?'

'No,' said Maisie, 'he is dead. Damn – I haven't any shampoo.' She was rummaging through her things.

'For long? Has your father been dead for long?'

'Quite a few years now. I was seventeen.'

'He died young.'

'Yes. He died – he died, well, it was alcohol that killed him.'

'Were you close?'

'Earlier I was. I suppose I was in love with him. And then things got mixed up. Well – it was pretty awful at the time. And for my mother.'

'I can't imagine your mother being married to anyone like that.'

'Well, she was.'

'Which book did she give you?'

'Oh, just an art history book.'

'What's it called?'

'Why do you want to know?' She laughed a little short laugh. She would not tell him.

He put his arms round her. 'Tell me,' he said.

She was laughing more now. 'No,' she said, laughing until the tears began to come. He tightened his hold.

'You're hurting,' she said.

'Tell me,' he insisted, not smiling, pretending to be grim-faced.

She gave in. 'Oh, *Origins of Christian Iconography* – it's a paperback, I had it before and lost it. It's out of print. My mother must have combed the Brighton second-hand book shops for it.'

Stopping the flow of words, he kissed her.

'Don't you want to know who wrote it? The publisher?'

He kissed her again, tenderly. She began to feel dream-like. Perhaps he felt a little out of his element at this conference, she thought. They were not the sort of people he was used to, she guessed.

'This is when I feel you will slip away from me,' he said, holding her away from him now. 'I feel that about you sometimes. You look so – you look as if you don't need anyone. Don't want anyone.'

Maisie was bewildered. She groped in her mind towards trying to understand his words. But she was too shocked by them. It must be that whatever was happening inside, the thaw, did not yet show on her face. She looked in the little mirror on the cheap dressing-table. She touched her face. 'Do I look like that? Is that how I seem?'

'Yes.'

'I don't feel like that,' she said. 'I think I am in love with you.'

'Oh, Maisie.'

He was standing behind her, both now seeing the other's reflection. 'Be careful.'

Maisie felt the blood drain from her face, and her pale reflection in the mirror, the only colour her brilliantly lipsticked mouth, against her lover's dark features, became blurred to her. She almost felt she might faint. She felt she had been dealt a fatal blow to the heart. She felt her life's blood flow from her.

She said nothing and fought to recover herself, but the voice inside her was saying over and over again – 'Be careful.' Careful. Why? Be careful. Why be careful? Careful. Careful.

Why had he briefly felt like a husband? No. He was a man she had known for two weeks and with whom she had fallen in love. She felt afraid. She began to tremble.

'Are you coming to bed?' he was saying. Casually. Like a man who might have picked her up a couple of weeks ago. Picked her up in a railway station or somewhere like that.

'Not yet,' she said. 'I want to check something at the desk.' She was walking down the long corridor. The hotel was like a huge ship adrift on a vast, cold sea, its tunnelled passageways opening out on to the stage-set of velvet-curtained, potted-palmed, turn-of-the-century spaciousness. A heavily carved staircase spiralled down, curling round an ornate iron lift shaft, the elaborate and splendid cage of which moved slowly up and down. Maisie flew lightly down the stairs, round and round again. She hardly knew she could not see for unspilled tears, her feet scarcely touching the ground in a feeling akin to ecstasy.

The girl at the Intourist desk looked up, but Maisie turned away to scrutinize the notice-board with unseeing eyes. She was still shaking slightly.

Had nothing changed since she was twenty years old, then? After all the years of taking thought? Did they count for nothing? The placid walks in the park, watching, without pain, the seasons change. The daily rituals of life; the pleasant stress of work. The whole thing. Her life. What she had made of it.

It had fallen apart. The white bone laid bare.

No longer her own woman, then.

When it came down to it, where was the sense of her own reality as a person alone in the world? Had he taken it from her already, was it so fragile a thing? The self-sufficient Maisie Shergold – was she his prisoner?

She scanned the notices about exhibitions and concerts as if she might find the answer to her desperate questions. She hardly knew him. Her quick-grown delicate trust shattered like glass by two words of warning – 'Be careful' – and pierced her with bloody splinters.

Be careful. Why? Why be careful? Why careful? For the first time she wondered if there was anyone else in Michael's life. She had never thought to ask him. She knew nothing at all about him except that his mother was a witch. And even something that had not troubled her before began to trouble her, as she wondered fancifully if this might be true, and not a light-hearted joke. She saw Michael's witch-like mother, tall and commanding, standing behind them both, reflected in the dim, cheap little mirror on the dressing-table.

Maisie took the lift up to their floor. Inside the cage there was plush velvet, and mirrors all the way round it. Maisie's side-view, her neat head and pale high forehead, her softly shadowed eyelids; the elegant bobbed hair showing off finely drawn ears with the cornucopia earrings. Maisie front-view, feathered eyebrows, delicate, fine long nose, neck clasped about with a triple-banded Mexican silver plaited necklace. She had had enough of mirrors. She closed her eyes.

When she got back to the room Michael was reading in bed. He looked about eighteen years old. At once her feelings changed, like the sudden lifting of a fever.

What did it matter if he left her? What did *she* really matter in the whole sum of things?

This young man – so young, his dark hair fallen over

his forehead, his gold spectacles rakishly on the end of his nose.

'What are you reading?' she asked gently.

'*Origins of Christian Iconography*,' he said. He had really been absorbed in it. 'It's interesting.'

'Good. I'm just going to have a shower.'

'Oh – don't wash off all your smells.'

'Don't be silly.' She unclasped the heavy necklace and took out the earrings.

'Oh, I found your shampoo – it was in with my things.' He went back to his book and forgot her until she came in beside him smelling of her favourite sharply haunting perfume.

'It's not silly,' he said. 'Attraction is supposed to be based on smells.'

'It's all chemistry, then.'

'No, of course not. It's everything. Everything about you. You.'

'You don't know everything about me. You don't know much. Only what I tell you.'

'I know you. I *know* you.'

'I don't know myself,' she said.

'Perhaps we are figments of the other's imagination.'

'Yes, I think we are.'

'My little figment. My sweet little figment. I'm going to call you that. My little fig. Fig.'

'I don't like that name. I'd rather be "rare beast".'

'No, you're a fig.' And he began licking her. His body was ice and fire. Nothing else mattered at all. Questions and answers, unable to be apprehended by touch, taste or smell, retreated.

His eyes were closed; that cold, clear light, like the light over the sea, was shuttered over. Hidden away. Only his touch. And her passion for this chance-encountered man.

# 3

A BRILLIANT red cloth overlaying a white one ran down the centre of a long narrow table. This was the cave ballroom, set for a feast. The statues outside the window peered in from the darkening snowy garden. They whispered to the one that had lost his head telling what they saw; what rich splendour had returned. Crystal dishes filled with pears and a centrepiece of a many-branched candelabra, like a little tree with flames.

Everyone was skirting round looking for their place-name. Maisie found her place: Professor Werner on one side and the poet Lozinsky on the other.

Michael was sitting opposite her, partly obscured by the candelabra. An Irish academic from Cork, a woman in her early thirties with masses of auburn, Rossetti-like hair, was taking her place on his right, and the obstinate-looking hostess with the flat pretty face sat on his left.

'I've never seen champagne decanted into jugs before,' said Maisie. She was watching fascinated as two of the staff – young students from the university by the look of them – busily uncorked bottle after bottle and poured the champagne into tall glass jugs. Everyone was having their glasses filled before any food appeared, as if there was no time to be lost.

'I think it means we are supposed to drink deeply,' said Werner.

Different from abstemious conferences she had attended in England, thought Maisie.

She was wondering how she would broach the subject of the ikon she had promised to investigate for Denisov. If anyone knew anything, it would be Werner. He seemed to be concentrating on his soup, which had just arrived.

She turned to Lozinsky. 'Have you a special interest in some aspect of the conference?' she asked politely, in Russian.

'I am a poet,' said Lozinsky. 'I am interested in everything.'

She had never much liked bouillon, and sipped her champagne, nibbling bits of bread. She smiled across at Michael. He looked relaxed and happy, wolfing down his soup in an heroic way.

The uncertainties and doubts of the previous day had gone. She had recovered her poise and was in possession of herself once more. What had she been about – trying to make something unassailable out of their relationship? It was like trying to capture fire and imprison it. It was the way to put it out, she knew. Freedom was like oxygen to a love affair. Today she accepted this and felt strong and powerful. She saw Michael say something to the Irishwoman which made her laugh, throwing back a lovely white neck. Seeing this only made Maisie feel more powerful. Nobody was any sort of rival to her. Michael was her lover. No woman was strong enough to take him away from her, however beautiful the red–gold hair in the candlelight.

'Philip Larkin is a very good poet,' Lozinsky was saying. Maisie nodded; she could see that Larkin might appeal to the Russian mind.

'But poetry changes so much in translation,' she said. It was rather pleasant to find a poet at this conference. There seemed to be a sprinkling of such people, members of the

63

intelligentsia, perhaps they were all keeping an eye on each other and on the conference. Perhaps it was policy from above.

'I am afraid I do not know your work,' said Maisie. 'Is it like Larkin at all?'

She had asked for it. As the soup plates were cleared and the next course was placed before them, he began reciting in a slow, deliberate voice:

> *'I tried to break my way out of the chrysalis*
> *I used hatchets and every means I could*
> *But all I could hear in the commotion*
> *Was the sound of my own breathing.'*

'It is about the breaking of the systems of order,' he explained.

'Politics?'

'Of course politics. This conference is politics. The ikon, the image – it was a system of order. Sometimes the image is human – Stalin, a tsar. My poetry is about the breaking of images.'

'Do you think Russia could ever have a tsar again?'

'Nothing is impossible. Russian people cannot stand freedom. They are afraid of their own inner chaos.'

'Perhaps you could let me have a copy of your poem,' she said, 'later in the week, there's plenty of time.' Something about the man's eyes had moved her. Who knows what his life had been?

'The fish is very good,' she said. It was some sort of pike, or carp, perhaps, stuffed with sultanas and celery and other things in sour cream. The poet beamed at her and tucked into his meal, elbows all over the place.

She turned to Werner. 'I enjoyed your book on Byzantium so much,' she said.

'Yes. It is an important work,' he admitted.

Maisie smiled and ate her fish, it had some faint delicious spice in it. A musician had started to play a balalaika. It all reminded Maisie of when she had been taken as a child to Lyons Corner House; she had had the same sense of opulence then.

'I have been interested lately,' she said to the German professor, 'in the miracle-working ikons and in those carried into battle. The ikon as a magical helper.'

'Like the Ikon of the Steppes that one is hearing about.'

'Yes,' said Maisie, trying to keep the eagerness out of her voice.

'That is a most strange case,' said Werner. 'It seems to have suddenly disappeared again from the face of the earth. Perhaps that is part of its miracle-working properties – the ability to disappear.'

'It must have a most fascinating history.'

'I have not made a study of it,' said Werner, gulping down forkfuls of food. 'Someone should make a special study of it. Perhaps you.' He wiped his mouth with a huge white napkin.

'I think they must be left from before the Revolution,' Maisie said, fingering the thick damask of her napkin and smoothing the tablecloth.

'Indeed we are living like tsars. Is your hotel comfortable?'

'Oh, yes. And yours?'

'It is clean – but very hot. At night I cannot sleep – it is too warm. And you cannot regulate the heat at all.' He drained his glass and looked around for it to be refilled. 'But we must not complain.'

It looked as if Michael might be doing just that. He had fixed their hostess with his gaze. Maisie wondered vaguely what he could be saying to make her look so stern.

In fact he was telling her of his difficulties with her language. 'I want to learn Russian in ten days,' he said.

'That is quite impossible,' she was saying severely.

'I have been working very hard at it, I sit up at night and work.'

65

'Yes. That is good,' she said. 'But you must have a teacher.'

'Ah, yes,' said Michael, 'that is what I need. A teacher. I would get on much better if I had a teacher.'

His hostess looked pleased with herself. 'I studied English for many years,' she said. 'You cannot learn a great language in a few days, you are too impatient. Which party are you with?'

Michael pointed with his fork to Maisie, who caught his eye and blew him an imaginary thistledown kiss from the palm of her hand; the champagne was getting to her. Their hostess looked disapproving. She herself had a tremendous capacity for sobriety as well as study.

'I think our hostess would agree to give you lessons,' the Irishwoman whispered in his ear. 'I feel it in my bones.'

'I think I'll stick to my own method,' said Michael.

'Which is?'

'I try to switch off my own language. And switch another on. It's like listening to a different sort of music. Listening is the key to it. Really listening hard. You start to pick it up.'

'It's nice to hear another Irish voice. Where do you come from? You sound Dublin.'

'You're not far out. Between Dublin and Wicklow – I've spent a lot of time in Dublin, though. I was brought up on a farm – chicken droppings in the kitchen, holy pictures on the wall – you know – but we used to bring back fish for supper that tasted even better than this. Straight from the sea. And you live in the fair city of Dublin!'

'Do you ever go back?'

'Oh, I still live in Ireland.'

'Still with the chicken droppings and the holy pictures?'

'Yes.'

'You never got away, then?'

'Well, you could say I lead a nomadic life, but the old farm is still somewhere I always go back to. It's still my home, I suppose – at least, I haven't any other. Only homes I make here and there for a time. At the moment I'm living in London with my lady love. That's her – Maisie Shergold.'

'I've heard of her, I think. I love the way she dresses. Most academic women have an extraordinary way of dressing, eccentric but doleful as well. She looks elegant – and interesting.'

'She is a very nice lady.'

'What is your subject?'

'I'm a camp follower,' said Michael. 'I shouldn't really be here. Eating the food. Drinking the booze. They had some spare places – a whole delegation from Czechoslovakia dropped out – some wrangle. Look, they're just about to pop a few more corks. Have you ever seen champagne poured from jugs before? I never have and I've seen some queer things. I wish it was draught Guinness.'

'You sound homesick.'

'It's talking to you. You didn't tell me your name.'

'O'Grady – everyone calls me Philomena.'

'And is it your name?'

'Of course.'

Maisie sensed they had been talking about her, she wondered what they were saying. The woman was the professor from Dublin – Maisie was looking forward to her paper that evening.

'Just the smallest taste,' she said to the girl with the platter of pheasant, 'please – one piece only.'

She watched amazed as Werner piled his plate. She imagined him dying of a surfeit of pheasant and thought she had better get some information out of him before that happened. Without preamble she plunged in.

'Do we know anything about the origins of the Steppes ikon?'

'Both its origins and its present whereabouts,' he said with his mouth full, 'are equally mysterious.'

Maisie decided to leave him to eat.

'You are speaking of the Mother of God of the Black Steppes ikon,' murmured the poet Lozinsky.

'Mm.' Maisie turned to him. 'I suppose it does follow that its beginnings should be so obscure – it's a feature of miracle-working ikons that they were miraculously discovered.'

'You are interested in this ikon?'

'Yes,' said Maisie carefully, 'but I think the furore around it at the moment has got out of proportion.'

'All at once,' said Lozinsky, 'everyone wants to claim it for different reasons. The Church. Moscow. Even the Ukrainians.'

Werner leaned across to join in. 'It is said to have been miraculously found,' he said, 'by a young peasant girl who had been raped by Tartars. She had been left for dead by the soldiers who raped her. She had a vision of the Mother of God walking towards her over the black earth of the Steppes. She recovered and found her vision made into matter – in the shape of this ikon. It came from nowhere. Not made by human hand. Or so the story goes.'

'It is almost,' said Maisie, 'as if somehow we are expecting another miracle from it.'

'Yes, I think we are,' said the poet, 'it is a time of crisis. The people are looking for something to pull them together, to save them from chaos. Ironic that a religious image is involved.'

'Even more ironic that it is, apparently, a missing image,' said Maisie.

'Of course it has disappeared before,' said Werner. 'More than once. If you really want to find out more about it,' he said to Maisie, 'you should speak to – let me see – I'll write it down for you.' He wrote a name on a piece of paper. 'He is an ikon painter and works at restoring old and damaged ikons. He is the last documented person to have seen it.'

Maisie was overwhelmed with gratitude. She felt elated.

Perhaps she would have some real information to take back to Denisov.

'Will you have a marzipan cake?' she asked, passing him a dish of little decorated cakes in gold paper. He took three.

The red cloth had gradually become wrecked with crumpled napkins, spilled wine and nutshells. The uncurtained windows looked out now on a starry night sky.

Catching Michael's eye, and in response to his signals, Maisie carried her coffee into the library. Michael and Philomena followed, Michael playing an imaginary balalaika, and the poet scuttled after them. They sat on old wooden chairs with narrow high backs, which Michael drew into a little circle for them.

A sense of camaraderie had quickly sprung up among the four and they chatted for a while contentedly.

'You must come to Ireland,' Philomena said to Maisie. 'I have a house in Dublin which is empty often. You would be welcome to use it. Though I should like it if you visited while I was there.'

Philomena looked hard at her with a kind of boldness, singling her out. But Maisie turned away then and leaned over to Michael, taking his hand.

'It is Christmas Day,' she said, 'and you haven't given me a present.'

She knew in some obscure way that she had rebuffed the Irishwoman. And now she wanted to get away.

'Shall we walk to the hotel?' she asked Michael.

'You won't miss my lecture?' asked Philomena. 'I shall be devastated if you aren't there to hear it.'

'Nothing would make me miss that,' said Maisie. 'But we have time. Our hotel isn't far.'

They all stood up, except Philomena O'Grady. Michael and Maisie left, and the poet sat down again to try a very halting conversation with a now slightly bored Irishwoman.

Michael and Maisie walked back in the moonlight, which

picked out glittering diamonds in the hard-packed snow. When they got back to their room, Maisie said she would have a little sleep, she was tired after the festive luncheon.

'I'll play you to sleep,' said Michael. 'I'm sorry I haven't anything to give you. I really couldn't find anything in the shops. But I'll play you to sleep.'

He played soft carols on his flute. Some sweet, some sad, some she had never heard – folk carols. She could tell he needed to play.

'Well, I never got anything for you,' she said sleepily.

'No, you are very bad and you don't love me or deserve me to play to you. But I will.'

She smiled and slept. When she woke he was still playing quietly.

When it came to his flute, he was left-handed. He had explained to her that the Brothers at his school had managed to make him right-handed in everything – except his flute-playing, which they knew nothing about. The left-handed-ness made him hold his instrument a little differently from usual; the slight awkwardness about it made her love him with a great desperation. I love him because of this sort of thing, she thought, how he can make something graceful out of something awkward.

When he saw she was awake, he stopped playing.

'I am stopping you sleep,' he said.

'No, I like watching you play. It's marvellous. Just by blowing air across holes in a pipe – all those ravishing sounds.'

'There's a bit more to it than that,' said Michael. 'I've been playing since I was nine or thereabouts – starting with a tin whistle.'

She loved his flute, because it was part of him. It was a wooden flute with eight keys, and she guessed it was an old one, at least nineteenth-century, probably older. It's funda-mental tone was strong and mellow. She loved it.

He stopped playing and began cleaning it with a bit of

rag and a stick, breaking the instrument down, blowing through the pieces, spitting on the pads and blowing across them. When he had finished he wrapped the flute in an oily, slightly dirty red silk handkerchief. She caught a faint whiff of almond oil as he stowed it away at last in its old leather case.

'You don't want to miss the lecture,' he said, 'especially as Philomena has taken such a fancy to you. Come on, you've got half an hour. Just over.'

Maisie put her arms round him sleepily.

'No time for that,' he said, pulling her up.

She washed her face and put on a warm woollen dress with a patterned scarf round her neck. She coloured her lips with fresh bright lipstick.

'Ready,' she said. 'We'll have to hurry.'

When they got there Philomena was shuffling her notes and fiddling with the slides. Someone was giving out transcripts of lecture notes.

'Oh, good,' said Michael, 'a slide lecture. I can go to sleep in peace – it's my turn.'

They need not have hurried, no one else did. The afternoon banquet had slowed everyone up and Philomena began twenty minutes late.

'There is something special about a Christmas Day lecture,' she began. 'I hope it will become a tradition, as I hope this Kiev conference will also be.'

'I want to consider', she went on, 'not the devotional repose of the older ikons, but the narrative and didactic elements to be found in the later religious works. And I want to start with the late-seventeenth-century so-called "Burning Thornbush Mother of God". Would someone lower the lights, please?'

Someone lowered the lights and for a moment nothing happened. A picture of Christ, protected inside a mandorla like a seed-pod, and descending into Hell, flashed up.

'Sorry,' said Philomena.

Another picture came on to the screen, hovered about and settled down. It was the Mother of God inside a large eight-pointed star. The central four-pointed star enclosed the Virgin with the Christ Child on her arm, and a tiny Man-Christ, carrying a ladder, situated in the region of her heart.

The other points of the star contained various angels. Scenes from the Old Testament stories formed a border round the panel.

'Look first at the Old Testament stories which fore-shadow the coming of a Redeemer,' Philomena said. She dealt with each of these in scholarly detail.

'And now I turn to something which may seem external and of small account, but does have an important bearing on our subject of study – I refer, of course, to the inscription.'

Michael had gone to sleep, his head on Maisie's shoulder. She settled down to enjoy the lecture.

'As you know, the proportions of the figures are sym-bolic,' Philomena was saying in her clearly enunciating Irish voice, with the faintest trace of accent. 'The tiny adult Christ-figure stowed in the region of the Virgin's heart points our minds forward to future events; he is holding a ladder in one hand – the ladder to Heaven, made from the Tree of Life. We are reminded of the tree on which he died.'

Another ikon flashed up on the screen.

'Again seventeenth-century, again Russian,' said Philo-mena. '"The whole of Creation rejoices over thee."'

Maisie felt very happy.

# 4

'I T IS a highly stylized art,' murmured Maisie, as they watched the young bearded monk at work.

'It is full of rhythm,' whispered Michael. 'I am intrigued and amazed.'

'It is a form of prayer,' said the young monk, clearly, in English, looking up from his work.

The three fell silent then. The ikon painter went on with his work as if alone in his workshop, the silence broken only by the brief sound of birds squabbling in the garden, by the occasional bubbling sound of glue being heated on the stove. The smell of resinous glue and chalky plaster and paint mixed with wood was not unpleasant.

The monk, his dark hair almost shoulder-length, prematurely thinning on the crown of his head, and with a straggled beard, looked as if he was strong and peasant-built under the flowing black robe. His face was slightly pockmarked, his hands strong-looking. He held the brush with workmanlike dexterity; the palette in his other hand was a piece of broken pottery smeared with earth colours, ochre and burnt umber and black.

All around the workshop were ikon panels in various stages of restoration. The merciful Christ with cruciform nimbus, open book in hand, the metal casing badly broken.

Beside it an impassive Christ the Judge. The Mother of God of Pity, one of the Eleousa type of specifically Russian ikons with its peculiarly tender quality – almost black with the years of candle soot. But the monk was engaged now in painting a new ikon. It was one depicting St George and the dragon, a favourite Russian subject. As Maisie and Michael watched in silence, they saw how the painter was using strictly laid-down rules in his work. He was in fact using a pattern-book as he coloured the dark coils of the serpent.

'A painter's manual,' whispered Maisie. 'Every line, every colour and gesture has a symbolic significance – it's all in his manual.'

'Individuality', explained the monk, speaking Russian now, 'does not come into it. The manuals specify even the stance of certain figures, how they are dressed and even what is in the background. An ikon must be able to convey its specific message even to an illiterate person.'

Michael was as intensely interested as he had been bored by the lectures. Maisie explained what had been said. She felt pleased that his boredom had lifted. She could sense the instant sympathy and rapport he had with many men. He looked as if he would have taken up a brush in his hand and helped with the painting, given half a chance.

But the monk's next words explained the seriousness of the ikon painter's occupation. He was doing something more than a painting, he said. He was translating matter – wood, water, resins, paint – into prayer, a means of salvation, a 'window to heaven'. He prepared himself for his work by prayer and regarded the making of the ikon, the carving of the wood, the making of the plaster, the painting of the subject matter and even the sweeping-up of the wood chippings from the floor as part of the same prayerful activity.

'Every man that comes into the world is stamped with the image of God,' said the monk, 'and every ikon should have God's seal on it.' He carefully washed his hands in the corner before beginning to apply gold leaf. All three again lapsed into silence.

Michael really wanted to handle the tools, stir the glue; as it was, he brushed some wood shavings into a corner with his foot and picked up a piece of wood.

'What kind of wood?' he asked.

'Birch,' said the monk, 'but we use other woods. Oak, alder.' The two men had an easy naturalness between them, an instant bonding of some sort. What was it? Just that they were men, perhaps, thought Maisie, and felt jealous, and curious as to why she should. Her bond with Michael was not easy, it was full of awkwardness and tension. She envied the uncomplicated, unalloyed camaraderie of men. They could become brothers quickly, with no questions asked, in certain circumstances. Men. Doing any job, any work. St George's vermilion cloak fluttered out behind him as his horse pranced over the dragon.

After a while Maisie said, 'I have come looking for someone.' She showed the monk the piece of paper with the name on it that Werner had given her.

The monk crossed himself. 'He was my teacher,' he said. 'He died one week ago. He was a very old man. He died just sitting there in his chair, as if he had gone to sleep. I was his apprentice.'

Maisie's heart sank a little. How would she now ever find out about the ikon Denisov set such store by? She was standing in the very workshop where the Mother of God of the Black Steppes ikon had been restored. If she had been here only a few days before, she might have been able to speak with the old monk. Her disappointment was keen; but she wondered if his apprentice would be able to help her. She brought up the subject of the miracle-working ikons.

'Then the Ikon of the Black Steppes', she said, 'was restored in this workshop. Did you hear anything of its history, or what happened to it afterwards?'

'I heard about it, of course. I heard about it many times.

My teacher spoke of it, his methods of restoration and so on. Yes.'

Somewhere the plangent sound of a bell began, calling him to prayer.

'That ikon', he said, 'had been hidden for many years in the catacombs here. It was brought up during the time of the German advance into Russia. It had deteriorated in the catacombs and needed careful restoration.'

'Afterwards,' asked Maisie, 'what happened to it?'

'It disappeared,' the monk said gravely. 'Perhaps it had done its work. The Germans were beaten back, Kiev survived. No one knows what happened to the ikon in the chaos of war and later in the persecution of the monasteries. It was a terrible time.'

'Was it ever replaced in the catacombs for safe keeping?' asked Michael.

'I do not think so,' said the monk. 'The catacombs are now much visited. We would have discovered it.'

It was time for him to go. He held the door open for them, blessing them gravely. They watched him, like one of the black-hooded crows on the snow-covered grass grown large, flapping his black wings as he hurried down the hill to join his brothers.

They began walking across the stiff white grass; it crackled under their feet. Pale winter light washed over everything – the sprawling monastery, bare trees, blue-black crows.

'I was hoping to have more to tell Denisov,' said Maisie. 'There is a gap between when the ikon was last seen in Kiev and when Denisov acquired it. I suppose that's the penalty for trying to investigate miracle-working ikons.'

'Do you know how Denisov came by it?'

'He bought it in a Paris sale room,' said Maisie, 'just after the war. It was before the fashionable revival of interest in ikons and he got it for next to nothing.'

'Our monk would be horrified to think of an ikon bought and sold. Wasn't he impressive? Single-minded. His life so orderly and deep.'

'I wonder', said Maisie, as they walked around, hardly knowing where they were going, 'whether, if you had to choose a companion – one companion, you are on a desert island, like Robinson Crusoe – you would choose a man or a woman?'

'That's a strange question, Maisie.'

'No. It isn't.'

'All right, it's a perfectly ordinary question. Coming from you I will take it seriously.'

'Well?'

'I'm thinking.'

'You have to think?'

'Well, of course, I would want *you* on a desert island.'

'Yes. But that's not quite my point. Imagine a whole life. Your whole life, into old age, death, everything. I don't exist. Another man or a woman?'

'It's a very searching question.'

'Yes.'

Michael hesitated. 'I think it would be a man,' he said slowly.

'I thought you would say so.' Strange that her heart was beating so fast.

'Because ultimately,' said Michael, 'I would find it more interesting.' He looked at her, a little taken aback at his own words, and tried to explain. 'Well. A man has a sort of *thereness* that a woman has not. She merges into things. A man doesn't do that. He's *there*.'

'What about sex?' she asked.

'Mm,' said Michael. 'I wonder what Robinson Crusoe did. Why are we walking round in circles?'

'This conversation is getting unsuitable for a monastery.'

'Very suitable, I'd say.'

'You're very weird, Michael.'

'Well, you asked me. What about you? I suppose you'll say now you would take a woman.'

'No, I would take a man.'

'Why? Apart from the obvious.'

'Because a man has a sort of thereness, of course.'

Michael laughed and drew her very close, so now they were walking down the white slopes of the grassy banks, joined like one creature almost – a man-woman. Walking, then nearly running.

'I want to see those catacombs,' Michael insisted. Maisie had seen them before and had not enjoyed the gruesome experience. But with Michael's warm loving flesh pressed against her, thigh on thigh, hip on hip, she felt brave. It had after all been the time of her break-up with Leo and perhaps she had been more sensitive than usual. She thought it would be a test of Michael's love if he could protect her psyche, down there in the catacombs, from horror. And there she was again, always wanting to test things in such ways. Or was this now just the child in her, wanting to be protected from harm?

As he led her into the catacombs she felt she should not have come. Stacked with mummified cadavers and skeletons of centuries, it was a grisly place, there was nothing there to relieve the atmosphere of horror. Only Michael's presence in front of her now, and sometimes the touch of his hand as he helped her down steps slippery with dripping water. She did not examine what was around her, but sometimes a bony hand or broken skull leaped out at her from the half-dark as in a ghost train – except these ghosts were real.

Some of the skeletons were dressed.

Half-way through, claustrophobia seized her. She knew from last time that she was half-way through the dreadful, labyrinthine place. While in the grip of panic she fought against it silently, breathing slowly, though, with nostrils tight against the smell of the dead air.

She kept her eyes down and said nothing. It would make things worse if she spoke, asked Michael to hurry, admitted her predicament. She must contain the panic herself, she knew. It is always like this, she thought. When it came down to it you are alone. Childbirth, extreme terror, going into battle, sickness, death. You are alone.

Momentarily taken out of herself, Maisie noticed and pitied an old man, thin, fur hat pulled down to the eyes, worn old black coat too short in the sleeves, purplish cheeks and watery eyes. She wished he had not come down there. Among the skeletons. And mummified bodies. Some dressed.

And as they emerged and the panic seeped back into the catacombs from whence it came, Maisie's first thought as she surveyed the world again was that Michael had not been able to help her.

'You didn't like that, Maisie,' said Michael. 'How I love you. Sometimes, how I love you. You look so white. It is an awful place.'

'Yes.'

'Oh, Maisie. We'll go back to the hotel and go to bed.'

'Now?'

'Yes. I want us to make love.'

It was enough that he had understood how she felt. If he had not been able to protect her down there in Hades, at least he understood where she had been. It did not matter now if they did not make love. But they made their way back anyway, stopping for a bowl of steaming bortsch at a rough little bistro.

Back in their hotel room, they undressed quickly and made love for a long time with a sort of determination, as if it would conquer death.

'Sergei told me that the peasants used to cover their household ikon with a cloth when they had sexual intercourse,' Michael said.

'How sweet,' said Maisie. 'Who is Sergei?'

'This bloke I met, he's a musician. I asked him where I could buy a present for you and he took me to one or two shops but it was hopeless.' He was laughing quietly to himself. 'And you are an expert – a consultant, forsooth – and you didn't know enough to advise your clients to cover their ikons before sex.' It amused him that he was able to tell her something she did not know about her subject.

But she was not listening, still seized by a ravenous physical hunger and wishing he would stop laughing and pay attention to it.

Instead he said, 'I am going now to resurrect myself. Have a shower. And we are going to hit the town.'

But he knew there was still something to expunge and he tried words, as he smoothed her body with his hand. 'Think of it like this – it's all the same creation. This – your lovely body. Wind, flowers, snow, all the same, blood, entrails, bones.'

Maisie remembered the litter at Paddington Station with its aura of glory. But the cadavers in their dreadful grave clothes had not been glorified for her. Death and decay. What was it?

'You get dressed up in your jewels and everything, and I'll go down to the Intourist place and see if they can fix up tickets for something or other.'

'The ballet,' said Maisie.

'Oh, God, all right,' said Michael.

He left her trying on different earrings and came back to find her naked except for pearls in her ears, but he took no notice.

'No seats for the ballet,' he said, looking pleased, 'but there's – would you believe it? – a version of *Hamlet* in Russian, and with music! The poster looks as if it's more like a circus than a Shakespeare play. What about that? Might be fun. Or a boring concert.'

'I don't mind,' said Maisie, beginning to dress. 'You choose.'

'*Hamlet* it is,' said Michael.

There had never been a *Hamlet* like it, nor ever would be again.

The actors were athletes and probably circus performers. They leaped and twirled and danced about the stage with that special laconic verve and energy Russians have, making incredible feats look easy and natural.

The story had been pared down to the source story on which Shakespeare had based *Hamlet*: the murder of a king by a usurper to the throne, aided by his paramour, the queen. All of Hamlet's soliloquies were cut out, along with much else of the dialogue, but if the play was short on dialogue, it was long on sword fights of incredible acrobatic dexterity. The travelling band that came to entertain the royal impostors included fire-eaters and trapeze artists. The whole play was accompanied by wild percussive music. It was fast, noisy and exciting, and very colourful. The curtain came down on a stage littered with corpses.

The audience had loved it and applauded enthusiastically as the corpses got up and re-enacted sword fights and fire-eating by way of an encore.

'But is it Shakespeare?' laughed Michael, clapping wildly.

'I think Shakespeare would have loved it,' said Maisie above the din. 'It was very exciting theatre!'

'Well, I must say I preferred it to any Shakespeare I've ever seen,' said Michael as they made their way out of the theatre.

'Better than rotten old ballet,' he said as they got ready for bed that night.

'What a day it's been,' said Maisie. 'I'm completely exhausted.'

They were both exhausted and that night fell into bed and into each other's arms and into sleep.

But later, Maisie started out of that sleep with a horrifying nightmare.

'It was those bloody catacombs, I expect,' said Michael. Maisie switched on the bedside light, and they lay looking at each other.

'I can see little nightmare pictures in your eyes,' said Michael. 'Tell me, it's best to talk about it.'

'Not yet.' They lay quiet for a bit, then she said, 'A picture I once saw. I can't remember who painted it. Yes, I think it is a real picture I was dreaming about.' She pressed her fingers together and began to wring her hands, but Michael gently stopped her, holding them.

'These skeletons,' she said, 'skeletons, dressed up in clothes.' She shuddered. 'Lying and sitting around . . . a warm lighted stove. They had horrible attitudes, I mean the way they were propped about the place, like broken dolls.'

'It was the catacombs. I found it a perfectly ghastly place . . .'

'But it didn't really worry you?'

'No.'

'I remember now. There is a picture. It's called *Skeletons Warming Themselves*. I've seen it somewhere.'

'Well, I don't blame you for having a nightmare about it all. I thought making love would get rid of it. Tell yourself this . . . bones, decay . . . it's all part of the same creation. Mud. Rotting things. All a part.'

'Maggots?'

'Yes, and bloody bandages. Pus. Everything.'

'Matted hair on a corpse?'

'Yes, matted hair on a corpse in a grave after it's been raining.'

'What about the stink?'

'All God's creation. Millions of wonderful, invisible bacteria . . .' Michael's voice was sleepy.

Then, like children, they talked themselves to sleep.

# 5

SERGEI PEROVSKY was in his late twenties, around the same age as Michael himself. Slim, with the body of a dancer and the sort of face you never see in the West – a face where emotions and thoughts flitted across the mobile features with extraordinary transparency. He looked completely alive. But the sensuousness had a subtle austerity about it too, making it a strong, nearly cruel face, for although his mother was Ukrainian, Sergei had inherited his father's Tartar blood.

He and Michael had liked each other on sight when they had met on the Kreshchatic, literally bumping into each other. And to Michael the scene inside this old empty wooden house on the outskirts of the city, where Sergei had brought him, was meat and drink.

'This is what I'm about,' he thought to himself. 'Now and always.' And in his heart he made his vows again.

It was like nothing he had ever come across before in his musical world. This was a rock band. Raw, absolutely bloody raw. Like a new-born creature lying there in the straw.

They played on anything they could get. They made music out of bits of steel and wood, a shovel and a piece of tin, even what looked like a dustbin lid. Someone played the saxophone. Someone else a wheezy cello. Among them all was a girl fiddler, standing, her feet a little apart, in a brown dress that swirled around her calves to the movement of her body as she played a precise, uninhibited and glorious top harmony above and over the cacophonic rock sound. She swirled like a bird over it, dipping and rising.

Sergei took off his coat, and offered Michael a chair with a broken back. Sergei was the one who held this lot together, Michael soon realized. He didn't conduct in the usual sense, he sort of danced the music. And he became the embodiment of it. He controlled it.

Michael's mouth went dry with excitement. This is what he'd come to this country for, he had known there was a reason. The music tore through his brain. He realized some part of him had been dead.

Watching Sergei and listening to the throb of the music, he thought this man was probably the most free human being he had ever met. There was an extraordinary wit there too. Both Sergei and his music were filled with wit. There was absolutely no naïvety about this harsh, exciting sound which was new to Michael. The excitement he felt was like a potent drink. He longed to be part of it all.

There were half a dozen musicians besides Sergei and the girl who played the fiddle. And there were a dozen or so people hanging round, listening and smoking. A couple danced in the corner, their whirling dance becoming a sexual display for each other. One painfully thin, huge-eyed man stared into space; oblivious to the cold, he was naked from the waist up and his torso was decorated with musical notes – clefs and minims, either tattooed or painted on, Michael wasn't sure. His ribs stuck out like a famine victim's.

The music throbbed through everyone like a heartbeat. The old wooden house vibrated and shook. It was fortunate that it stood in an isolated place, in a little clearing in a wood which was really the remnants of a village and had an abandoned air.

When the musicians finally packed up, Sergei took Michael's arm and they wandered outside. Sergei, who was bathed in sweat, put on his old coat which came down to his ankles – it looked like an old military coat and had red insignia on the sleeves. The snow crackled under their boots.

They had wanted so much to communicate with each other, but neither had much command of the other's language. Michael was saying, 'Good, good,' in Russian, and Sergei was slapping Michael on the back instead of using words.

Sergei stopped then and threw back his head, breathing the freezing air. 'Come,' he said to Michael, and led him to a battered old truck. 'Come,' he repeated.

Michael had all day to fill in. Maisie was at her lectures morning and afternoon. There were even lectures some evenings, he had noticed on the programme. He was going to be at a bit of a loose end. Though somehow, he thought, perhaps he wasn't now.

Sergei was driving the rackety truck hell for leather down the rough track which led on to the main highway back to the city. He lived in a small flat in a crumbling modern block, with his wife Annya, and two little boys.

Annya smiled shyly at Michael, and the two boys sitting together in one chair looked at him gravely and intently, as they might a flamingo or polar bear that their father had brought home. Their intense stare became so fixed that Annya shooed them out of the room, afraid they would seem rude. But they soon came back.

Michael looked round the little room, a characterless box that had somehow been given life and warmth by the kind of people who lived in it. There was colour everywhere. An embroidered table-cloth, orange enamel dishes, a pot of shiny green leaves, a heap of little red and yellow apples, bright posters on the walls.

Annya was dishing up some sort of meatballs for their

dinner. She pointed to a chair for Michael to sit with them. Sergei had brought home several bottles with foil tops which turned out to be vodka.

'Thank you,' said Michael in Russian, accepting the plate of food and the glass of vodka. '*Spasseba.*'

Sergei drank his vodka from the bottle. They ate with nods and smiles, but few words, Michael watching Annya and Sergei unobtrusively. Both parents were thin and agile. Annya had beautiful hooded eyes, blue as cornflowers, and a wide mouth. She had thin delicate wrists and long brown fingers and quick movements. They really looked rather alike in some ways, but Annya looked more dreamy then her husband – and kinder. Sergei, for all his wonderful good humour and obvious wit, had that cruel look to the mouth – at least, it could have been cruel. But not now, as he tenderly fed the younger child who had lost interest in his meal because of the strange flamingo at the table with him.

On his way back to the hotel, Michael saw Maisie and ran to catch up with her. She said she had been looking for him. He kissed her.

'Good lecture?' he asked.

'Sort of,' she said. 'Werner on Byzantine ikon painting – the last phase. It was excellent material but he is an awful speaker. He has that way of making interesting facts sound incredibly dull.'

'I'm glad I wasn't there.'

They held hands as they hurried up the flight of steps to the hotel and he held the heavy door open for her.

'Where did you get to?' she asked.

'I met Sergei – he asked me to his flat to meet his wife. He's got two little boys.'

He didn't mention the out-of-town music session. It occurred to him to tell her about it, perhaps he would later, but he realized suddenly that he could not convey to her properly what it had meant to him, so he might as well keep quiet. It wasn't that he hadn't the words, wasn't articulate enough, it was that he knew Maisie would not really understand what he meant, couldn't plumb the depths of all that. It wasn't her world.

He watched her take off her flamboyant coat. Under the layers her slim body in the black woollen dress looked wistful.

'Don't you wish I was a professor, a scholar?' he said, 'An authority on Byzantium or something?'

'Why should I wish that?'

'Then I would be part of your world. We could talk about all the things you are interested in and spend our spare time in museums and art galleries. We would never be lost for words.'

'You feel different,' she said. 'I suppose it's because we've spent the day apart.' She kissed him, trying to make him what he had been before.

'Let's go out, this room is beginning to get to me,' he said.

'We've only just got in.'

'It's such a queer shape.'

'Mm. The proportions aren't right, I must admit. They are not right for the human body in some way. The eighteenth century had it right. People feel right with it. It's all a question of proportion.'

'Come on,' he said, picking up her coat from the bed and holding it open for her.

'Where are we going?'

'Just for a breath of air. I don't want to analyse the architecture of this room. It's got a bed in it, that's all that matters.'

Outside, their breath smoked in the street lights. Passers-by huddled up to the eyes hurried past, boots clacking like iron on the icy pavement. Lowry-like against the tall buildings.

'They build on such a scale,' said Michael. 'It makes you

feel like Gulliver in the land of the giants.' He had a sudden longing to be in the kitchen of the farm in Ireland, womb-like, dark and warm.

'Now you are analysing the architecture. Anyway, what exactly did you get up to today?'

'Nothing that matters,' said Michael.

The words froze in the air and fell to earth at her feet.

'Let's go back,' he said.

'We've only just come out.'

She longed for him to be happy, or more truthfully, she longed to be the one to make him happy, to be the agent of his happiness. When he was apart from her, she wanted him to suffer and be miserable.

'We'll go back,' she said. 'I've got some whisky and some caviare – we'll eat it in the queer-shaped room.'

He kissed her, his cold lips on hers, even colder.

'You're good at putting things right,' he said.

The female of the species offers food, thought Maisie grimly.

Later that night, as they lay on the bed, Maisie took one of his hands and, holding it still, outlined his fingers with one of hers, drawing round his splayed-out hand in the air. Then he told her about what the day had meant to him. It frightened her and, although she tried to listen carefully, she only half-heard what he was saying.

He was talking about a great raw sound splitting the air. She heard him say it was the most exciting thing he had ever come across. And he was trying to interest her by telling her how physicists could produce sound on matter, the shape of the sound would make patterns, exquisite spirals and repeat-ing wave patterns, and shapes like the markings on butter-flies' wings. And he wondered what shape Sergei's music would make, perhaps it would make a whirling cosmic shape like a comet. Then he was talking about the wonderful Sergei and a girl like a swallow.

Maisie gave a small smile. She leaned across him and

switched on their little radio and began to undress, sitting beside him on the bed.

'I'll find some music,' he said. He began helping her to undress with one hand as he changed stations with the other. 'Keep that on,' she said, listening intently to the snatch of late night news. The Russian voice spoke too quickly for Michael to try to make out what was being said. He stroked Maisie's back and waited while she listened.

'They have sent troops in,' she said. 'It must be serious.' Michael was running his finger down her backbone, from neck to coccyx.

'I love backbones,' he said. 'Shall I find some music? An Orthodox service? Yes?'

'The whole thing is fragmenting,' said Maisie. 'It needs an Ivan the Terrible to hold it together.'

'Don't let it all worry you. I love you.'

She was quiet, letting his words hang in the air. But he had said it quite lightly, she knew. It was not in the least a vow.

He began to undress. 'I've got a present for you,' he said. 'Get into bed and I'll give it to you.'

Maisie sat in bed, her thin shoulders hunched, breasts half-covered, her knees drawn up under the duvet. She watched him standing naked. She was fascinated watching him shave, she could have watched this for hours. The way he stood, his body planted there in front of the washbasin. She loved to see the practical movements as he drew the razor across his cheek and under his chin, the muscles in the back of his shoulders moving just slightly. He had a nice body, she thought, compact and strong. Leo had been a bit overweight, which made his body ever so slightly feminine and smooth. This man's body was for her a kind of perfection in that she did not want to change anything, even its imperfections. The slightly thick neck, the brown birthmark on the thigh. Its imperfections were for her what perfected it.

He turned towards her, drying his face with the rough towel. How strange and complicated was the male sexual organ, having a life of its own, like a separate thing. It was like something fabled, not real, you would never have dreamed of it being like that. So curiously made. Like a sea creature which should have a shell.

'Shut your eyes,' he said.

He hadn't wrapped her present. It was in a large paper bag. It was a book of Russian fairy tales.

'This is no ordinary book,' she said, opening it with delight. 'Did you know it was made just after the Revolution? It's hand-printed – look at those lovely rich dyes, the thick paper. The government set up workshops just after the Revolution, and they produced this sort of thing. But this is lovely. Where on earth did you get it? Look, the Frog Prince – how green he is! And Babayaga – oh, she's horrible, isn't she?'

'Trust you to know all about it. I thought you'd like it, though.'

Underneath her genuine pleasure in his gift, she felt secretly that she did not want him to give her things. For if the affair ever ended, and they parted, and she lost him, the things that he had given her would become unbearable. These same beautiful glowing pictures in her book would take on a different aspect.

'Put out the light,' she said.

'I want to see you.'

'No. Let's put out the light.'

She switched out the light and the darkness swallowed them up. But in the dark she could see the bright edges of the Princess, and the Frog Prince and Babayaga and the horrible fence of bones round her house.

'Will you come to the lecture tomorrow?'

'I said I would meet Sergei. He wants me to try something out with them, wants me to sing. He's heard me on record.'

'Your fame has run before you.'

'Sergei is the sort of bloke who would know about me if anyone would.'

'A lucky meeting. Are we going to chatter all night?'

'No.' He drew her close to him and began kissing her with moth-like kisses.

Next morning they slept late, having spent half the night making love. Maisie was going to miss the beginning of a much-awaited lecture on Andrei Rublev, and she hardly said goodbye as she left on her own.

Michael went back to sleep, until Sergei thumped on the door, having created quite a lot of consternation at reception. Outside the hotel he had left the engine of his old truck running. When they got to the wooden house where the musicians met, everyone was having a break, messing about with their strange instruments. One of them had a file and was bending his piece of tin into a different shape and filing patterns on it, experimenting with the different sounds it made. The man with the notes painted on him had a seaman's jumper on covering them up; he was asleep, curled round a car tyre. He looked dead.

Michael wondered what to sing. His music was so unlike Sergei's savage rock sound. He hummed one or two things to himself. He had been working on a poem. It was Donne, he had set it to music – and over the last day or two had even tried, with Maisie's help, to translate it into Russian. The language, new and exciting to him, was now part of his feeling about the song.

He began singing, eyes closed, almost to himself, in English.

> *'Sweetest love I do not go*
> *For weariness of thee . . .'*

The girl with the violin was listening and picking up phrases. They worked together, like blind people feeling each other, a touch on the cheek, hands brushing against each other, groping towards something.

He sang a verse, inclined his head to the girl, who played a contrapuntal phrase and bowed to him as he took up the words and melody again.

Then he sang in Russian. He tasted and held the strange and beautiful and harsh sounds on his lips and tongue and in his throat. The sound of the words was like a love affair in itself.

And in the middle of it all Michael remembered her for a moment, remembered Maisie, remembered his lover. He was amazed at what she had done to him. He had thought it was just the music – but there was something else battering his heart. Careful, be careful, he thought.

# 6

MAISIE tried to open her letter from England with a pen; she made a mess of it. Michael handed her a knife from the breakfast table and poured them both coffee. Maisie started to read to herself, biting her lip. 'It's from Rose.'

*Dear Mummy,*

*Did you have a good Christmas with the Irishman? I thought him a little too much, you know – almost glamorous. A bit flash. I prefer ugly men.*

*I am writing this from Granny's. Daddy asked me for Christmas – if Irene had backed up the invitation perhaps I should have gone, but she doesn't like me. I can't say I blame her in the circumstances. But she's a bit wet. It can't last with Daddy. Pity about the offspring, she's already beginning to look blurred – you know, like pregnant women do. I don't ever want all that. No thank you.*

*Anyway, it's nice to get out of London. I bought Granny an absolutely huge bunch of mixed-up flowers – they're all over the flat, she didn't have enough vases, we had to use milk bottles. She said it reminded her of when she was in the theatre.*

*I don't think Granny is very well, though she never
says. She takes so long to do things now, and she looks
awful without her make-up. A man calls on her all the
time, he was there for Christmas lunch. I hope he's not
after her money. He's a mathematician, a professor,
Hungarian and very peculiar, and probably poverty-
stricken. I'm not sure Granny should be mixed up with
him and I'm very worried about her. And if I may say so
you are really the one who should care and keep an eye on
her.*

*But I expect you are too busy.*

*Your loving daughter
Rose*

*P.S. Daddy thinks I ought to begin to specialize a bit – in
Russian furniture, there is no one else in that field.*

'How's the Glantz business going?' Michael helped her
to rye bread and apricot jam.

'She doesn't mention him . . . at least . . .' Maisie started
to read the letter again.

'What lectures have you got today? Anything fascinating?'

She looked up. 'I'm going to stay in the room today and
work on my paper. What about you?'

'This morning I'm going to stay and distract you – later
on I shall go to sing my songs and play my flute and
carouse.'

'Sergei?'

'Yes. He knows someone with a recording studio – he
wants to record my song.'

'"I do not go" – that one?' She had a feeling it would be,
she had helped with the Russian translation.

'Yes. He knows everyone in the music business, apparently.' Michael hesitated, then said, 'He wants me to stay on
for a few days.'

94

'Do you mean stay on after tomorrow?'

'Yes.'

'Well, it's not that easy to stay on. You won't be able to.'

'Sergei says he can fix all that. He knows a fixer. You're angry.'

'No. Yes, I am.'

'Don't be angry, please, Maisie. It's only a question of a few days, it's such an opportunity. The music scene here is interesting. I want to do it.'

'Well, I *have* to go back.'

'Yes, well . . .'

'Where will you stay? Here? Oh, I forgot – Sergei knows a fixer. You should be careful of people like that.'

'I *can* take care of myself, Maisie. I expect I'll stay with Sergei – anyway, it doesn't matter where I stay. It's only a few days.'

'You keep saying that.'

'Let's go.'

In the lift he held her tight, and neither of them spoke. Back in their room, Maisie got out her notes and books.

'Michael, I don't know what you're here for. I can't work with you here. Why don't you go out for a walk or something?'

'I want to spend some time with you. There's only tomorrow. Only two more nights. I'm going to miss you like hell.'

'Yes, well, you can't just pick the time that suits you. I've missed you quite a bit this week. Now you're just a distraction.'

'Is that what I am?'

'Are you going to go and let me work?' She felt driven to say these things, although she longed for him not to go.

'No, I don't think so.'

'What is this?'

'It's the beginning of a quarrel, I think,' he said, 'and it's because I'm staying on for a very short time.'

'I suppose that's it. Because you're letting me go back alone.'

'You're a very unreasonable person, Maisie. You expect everything to revolve around you and your work. You just expect me to fit in. I've got work.'

'What's that?'

'I'm a musician.'

'Oh, yes. I forgot.'

'You are a bitch, Maisie. I'm going out.' And suddenly, without saying another word, he picked up his coat and left. When he had gone Maisie tried to read through what she had done of her paper. She looked up one or two things. Changed a word here and there.

'Damn,' she said aloud. 'Damn everything. Every bloody thing.'

She wished she had a cigarette, but she had given up a year ago. She got up and looked out of the window, holding back the stiff lace curtain. The courtyard below was deep in snow which blurred the outlines of everything. Nothing moved or stirred. It could have been an oubliette. She shivered.

Then, damning every bloody thing again, she got to work and finished her paper.


And then she wondered how to fill in the day. She really wasn't in the mood for the summing-up that would take place all afternoon. But she decided to wander over to the conference centre anyway and have a glass of wine in the bar.

When she got there the bar was crowded. She thought how insufferable intellectuals were en masse. The sort of people who would rather talk than listen; to whom it was important to have the last word, who would rather win an argument than have any real feelings about anything. She supposed that she might be like that too; she was one of them, she thought with disgust. She longed for something simpler. Longed to be simple.

She wondered how she could bear to go back to London without her lover. She drank her white wine and hoped it might dull the feeling she had of splitting in two. The babble of voices round her felt like a physical pain; she wouldn't be able to stand much of this.

'Dr Shergold.' It was Werner. 'We all have to part soon,' he said.

There was something odd about Werner. About the way he looked at her. Either he was mentally undressing her and trying not to let it show, or he wasn't doing that, but just trying to hide something else. Or both. She ought to thank him again for the information about the ikon she was investigating, but she didn't. She didn't feel much like talking. Weakly she let him buy her another drink, and then she had to listen to him going on about his life, his life history, at least his version of it. Apparently he and his wife spent a lot of time apart – they had this arrangement. Maisie gathered he was looking for someone to sleep with before the conference concluded. He had probably been looking round all week without success and now his desperation made him bold. There were only two nights to go.

She felt slightly annoyed that Michael was not there to fend off this sort of thing: what was the use of having a lover? Werner was settling himself closer to her. Was it that men did not pick up the fact that a woman wasn't interested, or did they not really care whether she was or not? Werner was asking if she was going to the summing-up or would she like to spend a quiet afternoon with him. She wouldn't miss the summing-up for anything, she said, and made her escape as a delegate from the Crimea, a solemn young woman, flew into Werner's sticky web. She decided to go back to the hotel and have a bath.

The hotel was practically empty. It was like having a huge house all to oneself. Her footsteps echoed down the long corridors.

The bathroom was cold, but the water gushing from the tap was boiling and hissing with steam. Soon Maisie could hardly see across the room. The combination of the cold air and warm steam as she took off her clothes was pleasant. She turned on the cold tap and poured some carnation-scented oil into the water. Too much. The clovey scent was overpowering.

She lay in the bath and wondered if she was a bitch.

Perhaps she should try to sort out her feelings for Michael. She was beginning to realize that they might be in charge of her, and that she was likely to behave irrationally. For instance, she felt she could easily make a ridiculous fuss to try to get Michael to go back with her; or that she might foolishly try to stay with him, a course that would complicate her own life, even if she could manage it.

As the warm clove-scented water lapped round her, she tried to unfold her true feelings and inspect them.

She thought back to her first meeting with Michael. She felt the same now as she had then. That first unsought magnetic pull was as strong now as it had been then, it had not weakened its hold at all. So how did you inspect that? It was like trying to inspect an electric shock, while you were still having it.

He had entered her life and immediately taken up the position of the only man she was interested in – although the world teemed with men. She was in love. Yes. She showed all the signs. The heart beating quickly when she heard his step. His voice and touch imbued, for her, with magical quality. The sense of loss and desolation when they quarrelled, as they had now. How when he left something died in her. It was all in the love songs that came over the radio all day. Except it felt as if she had been under the surgeon's knife and put back together differently. Especially her stomach was in a different place.

She splashed her feet about. She was taking a fearful emotional risk with all this. He could go at any time. Should she, could she . . . step back, let him go hang a bit, rearrange her feelings a little? Rearrange her feelings, care just even a small scrap less? She knew she could not. It was not in her power.

Neither was he in her power. She could not make him do exactly what she wanted. Had she thought she would – a younger man, putty in her hands? The nasty thought appeared and left in a flash. But it had been *she* who had seen him first.

Now he would not let her be the prime mover. If he had, would she have lost interest in him?

She began washing her feet. Sometimes she looked back on her marriage with Leo and wished things had gone differently. It had not hurt like this. And Leo would always be a part of her. Their brief happy love affair had been nothing like this. It had settled quickly into a pleasant marriage, give and take, everything they said should happen for a successful marriage. Neither tried to dominate the other, both looked after the other's interests, unselfish, putting the other first. All of that. They had liked each other immensely. But in the end the life had gone out of it.

She didn't know if she liked Michael or not. She did not know him in that way. Well, sometimes she liked him but that was by the way. Liking didn't come into it. Overwhelming attraction came into it – not just sexual; she was attracted to the whole of the personality of the man, inexorably drawn to him.

It was no good. She might be able to behave rationally, but inside she felt as if in a kind of hectic fever. It was like a sickness in some ways. Sometimes in a feverish sickness there is a heightened awareness, a fresh way of seeing things, a clarity emanating from a narrowed-down vision.

Maisie washed her underwater limbs and belly and breasts. She thought of Irene's expected child. What was Leo doing – fathering other women's babies? She had been so surprised when she heard, as if in nature the thing was impossible.

She began laughing quietly at herself.

She had loved being pregnant. Now Irene was beginning to show. Well, that was all over for her. All she wanted was Michael. Just the two of them. What about his feelings? If she could hardly unfold and inspect her own, how much less could she fathom his? She wondered if she really wanted to know his most secret inner thoughts and feelings towards her, to have them laid bare. In their inevitable vicissitudes. It might crush her.

One thing she would cling to in all of this. She would not let go of her work. She should have gone to the summing-up. She must siphon enough energy from this love affair still to work. It had been her raft in life before and she would not abandon it. She lay back in the water. The carnation smell in the hot water was beginning to make her feel sick. She flicked out the plug with her toe and ran cold water.

She got out gasping with cold and rubbed herself dry. That bit about the Marxist view of art history wasn't really right. She'd have another look at it. She worked on and off for the rest of the day.

And that night Michael did not come back.

A coldness began to seize her heart. She lay in bed sleepless, angry and bereft.

She fell into a restless sleep in the early hours and woke an hour before she was to give her paper.

She felt numb, and still angry. Coldly, quickly, she began to get ready for the day. She would wear her blue dress. It was a quiet dress, it didn't distract. She would snatch herself something to eat – she did not want to faint in the middle of her paper.

And she had managed not to think of Michael for several minutes. Though he was there at the back of her mind.

There, that morning, underneath her thoughts of what she was to speak about. There, a shadow over her heart, as she took up her position on the platform. Hers was the last paper, some people had already left to travel home, so she would address a smaller audience, for which she was quite thankful.

She looked for him along the slightly depleted rows of delegates. People tended to keep the seats they had first taken up, but he was not on the end of the second row where he and she had sat together at the beginning of the conference. If he did not come, it meant he did not care for her at all. That was it. If he did not come, it would be like a sign to her that it was over.

Over. It was over. The seat where he should have sat was empty. She wished he would come so much that she thought she almost saw his shadow-figure taking his place, sitting there, waiting for her to begin. She must be going mad.

She put her notes out in front of her in order, had a sip of water, and plunged in.

'I want to talk this morning,' she said, 'specifically about *Russian* ikons, and I want to try to trace the Russian roots of Rublev's vision, and the way it changed how we view ikons for ever.'

And then she saw Michael slip into his place. She wanted to harangue him with angry words from the platform – that dark unshaven man, flopping, graceful, tired . . . his coat with the astrakhan collar flung on to the seat in front of him.

'Where have you been through the night? How is it you dare behave with this appalling lack of consideration. Lack of love. Didn't you think of me, didn't you care that this morning I had to give my paper?'

She pressed her fingernails into the sides of the wooden lectern. 'Our knowledge of very early ikons is lamentably scant. This gap must necessarily leave much to conjecture. We cannot trace Rublev's artistic roots to their very first source but we must endeavour to do our best.'

If only she could sit down. But she would not look at him again. 'I don't want to feel this. Why must I feel it? Why am I broken down by you, Michael?'

She felt, although this did not surface as thought, that he had let this incident happen purposely in order to keep their affair in check, a way of telling her to come no closer. A way of saying she was close enough for his liking.

Michael watched her and her words flowed over him. 'This ikon was perhaps used to decorate an early version of the later Russian iconostasis.'

'How beautiful and clever and cool she is. She does not try to devour me. True, she had not wanted me to stay without her, but I would have felt the same. It's not significant.'

He knew he admired her because she seemed to have autonomy. At first he thought her vague, elusive, and it bothered him that he could not grasp her in some way. Now he saw it as a strength in her. Her central mystery was intact for him, he thought. He no longer reached out for it. But he wondered a little if she just fancied him like hell. She knows nothing about me. But I like not to be known after all. Kate knows me through and through, what she did not know my mother has told her. Through and through to the point of claustrophobia.

'The first canonized Russian ikon painter – Alipi – may well have been an inspiration. The miracle-working aspect of certain ikons must have influenced Rublev's mind and become woven into his perceptions. I come now to his individual view of divine light.'

'There are dark places in my love for you, Michael,' she thought, 'perhaps better kept dark.' Michael closed his eyes.

'Last night the music and the wild excitement. The fact that I was *working*. I feel released. I have been emptied and filled. There is a part I must never give away – that is how it is and it is for the best. Perhaps she does not realize that I am the same as her – I have my central mystery too.'

'The white highlights created the effect, a marvellously ethereal effect as if the soul's light shone through the body. It was a technique that Rublev perfected.'

Maisie turned to the last page of her notes.

'I have not, you notice, taken up the Marxist position which is so prevalent in art history today – because that has been already considered fully by others and because I think it leaves out too much, of an indefinable nature, and perhaps blinkers one to the intensely spiritual nature of the ikon painter. It leaves out man's relationship with God. At the very least it gets the balance wrong.'

She looked up. The bloody man looked as if he was nearly asleep.

'But saying that will, I am sure, call forth some comment from delegates with different views. We have a few minutes for questions.'

Predictably, one of the Marxists asked a rhetorical question about the didactic purpose of ikons in maintaining social and economic order. Then Philomena asked a question about the nature of Rublev's so-called divine light.

'Is not this perhaps a theory that has been superimposed by later critics? Something fabricated?'

'In a way that could be said to be true,' said Maisie. 'Rublev's work was lit by prayer, and it shows – to call it a theory is perhaps wrong.'

Maisie was interested in the questions Philomena raised, and the rest of question-time consisted of a two-way conversation between them.

Afterwards, as Maisie was gathering up her notes and shaking hands with various people, Michael came up to her. Immediately, rudely almost, she left the little knot of people around her and went to him.

He said casually, warmly, 'Darling Maisie, I'm sorry I

didn't make it back last night. It was late and I thought you'd be asleep. I didn't want to disturb you.' So lightly he said it.

'That's all right.' She spoke carefully, casually. 'How did it sound?'

'It was . . . good, Maisie, as far as I'm a judge. They were all on the edges of their seats. It was good. No one went to sleep, anyway.'

She took his arm. Lightly. Casually flirtatious. Not feeling quite safe with him. 'Our last night in Kiev,' she said. 'How shall we celebrate it?'

'You choose,' he said, kissing her cheek lightly, their quarrel still unmentioned.

'We'll go to church,' she said, as they made their way out into the street. Michael looked a bit startled, but only said, 'What, now?'

'Well, not exactly now. We have time for a drink, something to eat.'

'Am I allowed to have a shave?'

'If you must. You look rather nice like that.'

'I don't feel rather nice.'

'Did you enjoy your carousal?'

'I did. I really am knocked out by Sergei's lot. It's given me so many ideas about my own music.'

'Oh, good.'

'Look, Maisie, I am sorry I didn't get back.'

'I think you said all that bit.'

'It's not right between us, though, is it? It won't be, I suppose – what we ought to do this afternoon is go to bed.'

'No, we're going to church.'

'But it's a weekday.'

'There are services every day at the cathedral.'

'Well, perhaps I ought to go and do penance, or are we going to get married or something?'

A wintry sun was shining. They jumped on to a tram going to the Kreshchatic. It was full and they had to stand.

People stared at them as they stood, holding on in the swaying tram.

'They're thinking you're an anarchist,' said Maisie, thinking how very good-looking he was, even – or especially – in his tired, unshaven state.

'It's you they're staring at,' he said. 'They're wondering where you get your clothes, who cuts your hair, where you bought that beautiful shade of lipstick. They're thinking, who's that frightful looking old tramp she's with?'

'This is it,' she said, and they got off. 'Promise to leave the flowers alone.' It was the bistro where Michael had deflowered the carnation.

They had huge bowls of bortsch with hunks of rye bread and some splendid smoked cheese. The carnation on the table was white this time, with a little sprig of fern.

Maisie felt happy and light-hearted. Her paper had been delivered. Michael was looking his most vulnerable and touching. She loved him. The wine had an interesting edge to it. So had life. She was enjoying the small rift between them. It distanced them as if they did not take each other for granted. Strangers again in a way, like it was at the beginning. She liked the feeling. It was light and exciting and anything could happen. Now, in a strange way, she was glad she was going back on her own.

The cathedral was full. Michael and Maisie stood pressed about by a motley crowd of people. Everyone stood stoically, no one sat or knelt, even the ancient black-garbed women – so lost in their giving of themselves to prayer, their frail bodies forgotten. And every so often they crossed themselves, not in the way it is done in the West, but backwards – forehead, right side, left side, breast, with a quick instinctive movement as birds might ruffle their feathers; it seemed a bodily movement not connected to a thought process.

This was essentially a drama, a ritual one watched and

partook of by means of the senses. There was an overwhelming sense of the numinous. The bearded priest, his eyes yellowed with the fumes of incense, his robes richly encrusted with symbolic embroidery, wheat and grapes and flowers, the black-gowned monks, the warm glow of the tiers of candles, marigold-bright. Gold everywhere one looked. Gold set on fire by candlelight. And the rich dark colours of the ikon screen which screened the sanctuary from the nave, the sanctuary being a view of heaven on earth, shielded in its radiance from the human eye by the ikons, windows to heaven. The choir, sonorous, floating, bearing one along and aloft, the words of the service reverberating through the priest as if he was God's sounding-board. The smell of candle-wax and incense.

Maisie, pressed into a corner with Michael standing behind her, slightly taller than most around her, had a good view of the iconostasis. It was rich with ikons and provided Maisie with a great deal for her mind to work on throughout the long service. It told the story of Christ's sojourn on Earth and his Resurrection. Here were ikons showing the Nativity, Baptism, the Entry into Jerusalem, Descent into Hell and Ascension. The gleaming gold Royal Door pierced the iconostasis.

She could identify the workshops where most of these ikons had been produced, which schools of ikon painting they represented, and all the nuances they conveyed. There was one almost like the famous black Madonna, where the Virgin's face was so darkly olive-coloured as to be nearly black. Maisie knew that, as these ikons of the Mother of God had been so revered, and so discoloured over the years with smoke and grease from the candles, it became the practice to paint the faces very dark to begin with. This Madonna was full-length frontal, ornamented and probably late thirteenth-century of the Yaroslavl School.

Now the Procession of the Book of the Word – a jewelled, gold-bound book covered in small ikons – was being enacted by the priests. The crisis of the liturgy was approaching. The Song of the Cherubim. The richness of this Orthodox liturgy represented Heaven, this was the meeting of Heaven and Earth. Incense, the odour of Heaven.

Now the priest was spooning sacramental food as though feeding his flock of birds, mouths open trustfully.

Neither Maisie nor Michael received the Sacrament. Onlookers again, they saw the worshippers filing past devotional ikons on lecterns, kissing them in such natural, unaffected ways, almost as if they might be revered members of their own family.

More than two hours had passed since they entered the cathedral and the service was drawing to a close. Michael took her hand as they emerged into the dark, foggy street.

'We forgot to get married,' he said.

'I went to an Orthodox wedding once,' said Maisie. 'Very beautiful – the extraordinary way of elevating human life, holding things up to Heaven, as it were.'

'Did you notice,' said Michael as they walked away from the cathedral, 'there was a point in the liturgy when the whole atmosphere changed?'

Maisie, who had been brought up as a sceptical Anglican, if anything, was certainly not entirely without a religious sense – she needed it for her work in any case – but she kept it under control; if it raised its head too much she picked up a heavy volume – Freud or something – and banged it firmly on the head.

'Where do you mean?'

'Just before the Sacrament is offered – you feel the invisible world about you. Heaven watching. Time stopped.'

'The Song of the Cherubim,' said Maisie. 'Let us now lay aside all earthly care, while we, invisibly escorted by the unseen armies of angels, receive the King of all things. Something like that. Wonderful, isn't it?'

'Yes, you really feel the invisible world about you,' he said.

'You could almost hear the fluttering wings of angels with us there.'

'You have kept your religion, Michael.'

'I don't think much about it usually,' he said. 'I suppose it's there in the background.'

'But obviously you believe in an invisible supernatural world.'

'Oh, yes,' he said simply. 'Of course. Well, it's there, isn't it?'

Maisie laughed. 'I don't know,' she said. 'Why are we walking so fast?'

He slowed down. 'We'd better find a taxi,' he said. 'It's like this,' he went on suddenly, stopping. 'Have you ever looked down a microscope and seen the teeming world invisible to the naked eye? Well, you can't think that is the only hidden world. It seems likely that there is another world all around us that we can't see.'

Maisie could see the priests at his school talking; she could just picture them, with their bony wrists and eyes as grey as an Irish sky.

'Did the priests at school tell you that?'

'Yes, but I knew it anyway.'

'From your mother's knee?'

'Yes, that's right. She's a good Catholic witch.'

'If you believe all that, why don't you practise your faith?'

'I let all the monks locked up in monasteries do it for me. That's their job. I'm too busy.'

'Can someone do it for you?'

'No,' said Michael, signalling to a taxi. 'Get in, lady.'

Time was beginning to run out very fast. That night they said their farewells with their bodies and spoke very few words.

Maisie caught the first flight to Moscow. She would be back in London by nightfall.

Invisibly escorted by angels.

# PART THREE

*Brighton, Walsingham
and London*

# I

As MAISIE paid off the taxi, she looked up and saw there was a light in Rose's living-room. She let herself into the house quietly. The hall and stairway were dimly lit. There was a pile of post for her on the hall table.

Leaving her luggage in the hall, she picked up the letters and made her way upstairs. There was that characteristic smell of the house – the beeswax polish Rose used on her antique furniture and the smell of soot some London houses still have, lingering from the past.

There was a crack of light from Rose's door, which was ajar, and Ella Fitzgerald was singing 'Every Time We Say Goodbye'. Maisie felt like someone in a fifties film. It was all such a cliché. But that didn't stop it hurting, if anything it made it worse, feeling the weight of all those who had suffered before.

She tapped on Rose's door and called out, 'I'm back, Rose.'

Rose took a long time to answer but Maisie hardly noticed. She was tired from travelling and the song had taken possession of her as she stood there in the half-dark.

'Every time we say goodbye I die a little . . .'

Then Rose was there. 'Hallo, Mummy. I expected you back yesterday.'

'No. Today.' She gave Rose a kiss and wondered why it always felt like kissing someone she'd wronged.

As she sat down on Rose's huge white hessian-covered settee, Glantz appeared from the bathroom.

'Mummy's back,' said Rose. 'Put the kettle on, Bernard. Have you met? No, of course not. Mummy, this is Bernard Glantz of ill-repute. Bernard, my mother, just back from foreign parts.'

'Kiev, actually,' Maisie said.

'Every time we say goodbye I wonder why,' sang Ella Fitzgerald, the words clear and painful. No one attempted to turn down the volume.

'Happy New Year,' Glantz said, holding out his hand.

'Oh, yes – a happy New Year to you both,' said Maisie.

'Would you bring up Mummy's things?' said Rose.

'Please don't bother,' said Maisie. 'They'll be all right there. I'll see to it in the morning.' But Glantz was already on his way.

'I'm putting him up temporarily,' said Rose. 'This is much nearer his practice than his own flat.'

'Oh, I see,' said Maisie.

Nothing she had heard about Glantz had prepared her for the instant liking she felt for this ugly, intelligent-looking man with the awful yellow knitted waistcoat.

'I'm clearing out the swan room for him,' said Rose. The swan room had a stained-glass window in it, of a swan on a lake surrounded by bulrushes. Usually it was full of bits of furniture.

'Oh – the swan room – yes.'

'How was Kiev?'

'It was a good conference.'

'Where is the Irishman?'

'Oh, Michael – he's staying on for a day or two on some business. Thanks for your letter.'

'Tea?'

'No thanks, darling. I'm really tired and all I want to do is get to bed. I can never sleep travelling.'

Bernard Glantz was at the door with her bags.

'Upstairs,' Rose ordered him. Maisie wondered if she always spoke to him this way, she hoped not.

'I'll come now,' she said, and led Glantz up to her room.

'It's a nice house,' said Glantz, as they climbed the stairs.

'I hear you are going to be in the swan room.'

'Unless you object.'

'Of course not. Here we are, and thank you.' It felt rather nice having someone else in the house – they said goodnight and Maisie opened the door. She knew she should have probed Glantz. But Maisie had a certain reticence about such things. Somehow she never felt she had the right to go heavy-footing about in other people's lives. She watched instead, with a loving fearfulness, and also a sense of fate.

It was odd to be back in her own flat. She hadn't thrown away the flowers before she'd left and there was a vase of withered, blackened stalks on the table.

Before doing anything else, she threw them into the waste disposal. They had drunk all the water before dying – she washed out the vase.

She put on the immersion-heater for a bath and found herself a nightdress, and then poured a glass of mineral water. She tried to work out what time it would be in Kiev and thought it might be afternoon, but she wasn't sure, she'd never quite grasped time zones. Perhaps after a while she would begin to feel whole and the sore, grieving feeling in her solar plexus would go away. Perhaps one day she might even feel as she had before she met Michael, living so calmly in this room which she had made her own, but which now seemed to have very little to do with her. It was full of emptiness, as if emptiness could be a palpable presence.

He wasn't there.

Everything in the place knew he wasn't there. The table and chairs, the shrouded, empty bed, even the cold knives and forks in the drawer knew of his absence, and were drained of meaning. How was she to live through the days until he came back? And supposing he never came back?

She bathed and found a book to read in bed. But she fell asleep over it with the light still on.

She was wakened by the telephone. Wondering for a minute where she was, she picked up the receiver automatically.

There was the click of an international call before Michael spoke.

'Hallo, darling,' he said. 'Hallo, Maisie.'

'Michael.'

'Just wanted to know if you got back all right and if you're missing me. If you still love me.'

'I've been back, let me see, three hours. I was asleep.'

'Sorry.'

'No, I'm glad you rang.' There was a pause.

'Well, don't forget me, Maisie.'

'When do you do your recording?'

'I'm not quite sure yet what the plan is.'

'Well, I hope it goes all right.'

'You're in bed?'

'Yes.'

'I should be with you.'

'Yes.' There was another pause, she didn't know what to say.

'Well, go back to sleep. Goodnight, Fig.'

She held the receiver in her hand for a long time, then very slowly she replaced it and lay down again. She switched off the light and lay wide awake. She wished she had said more to him, told him how she longed for him, that she loved him.

She wondered where Michael was going now, after he had telephoned her. Was he still at the hotel? Sergei probably had no telephone.

Restlessly she switched on the light and picked up her book. The words seemed strung together without meaning. She got up and went over to the window. It was the kind of neighbourhood where there was always someone awake, even in the small hours – a party, an insomniac, someone working through the night, always a light in one or two windows.

It had been raining and the street gleamed in the lamplight as if wrapped in cellophane. A lone figure of a man wandered up the road with an aimless air about him. Somewhere a dog barked.

Maisie wondered if her daughter and Bernard Glantz were sleeping together and supposed they were. It had to happen sometime. She wished them well, guessing Rose to be a virgin, but thought them probably unsuited. Rose was going to bully him. She imagined he had had a string of unsuccessful affairs and was probably already resigned in advance to the failure of another. But you could never tell with people. Sometimes the strangest alliances worked.

She closed the curtains. It was no use going back to bed, she wouldn't sleep.

In a day or two she would have to go down to Brighton, she thought. After she had caught up with some of her other work.

She started to look through the pile of letters on the table. A few late Christmas cards. One or two New Year's cards from clients. Catalogues. A note from a bookseller in Cambridge to say he had found a book she wanted. Junk. A request for her to view a reliquary for a prospective buyer at auction and value it. A belated letter from the conference she had just attended, welcoming her and sending a list of events in Kiev which coincided with the conference. And a letter from Denisov. She recognized the thick hand-made paper, the large wavering writing.

> Dear Dr Shergold,
> The matter becomes pressing.
> Vladimir Dimitrivich Denisov.

She would telephone in the morning.

She went to bed then, and lying there in the dark, trying to remember what Michael looked like, fell asleep. And woke once more to the sound of the telephone. She had overslept but felt better for it.

It was her mother welcoming her back.

Maisie made a sudden decision that she would go down to Brighton that day, and told her mother she would see her soon. Then she rang Denisov and left a message that she would be there in the early afternoon.

She squeezed the juice from a couple of dried-up-looking oranges and made coffee, packed an overnight bag and telephoned for a taxi. While she waited, she made up a pile of things to go the cleaner's and another pile for the laundry. The flat needed dusting.

When the taxi came it was late, and she was out of it into the train with no time to buy a sandwich. But she was only eating because she should, she felt she could have lived on air.

As the half-empty train rocked swiftly to Brighton, Maisie closed her eyes and took herself back to Kiev, to the dark cathedral, the orange-tongued candles licking the darkness, the seamless chanting rising and falling, and the feel of her lover's body when she leaned back against him. She still could not remember what Michael looked like, could not recall his features in her mind's eye, but she remembered exactly the feel of his body, and his scent was still in her nostrils, it had never left.

She imagined herself as Michael's male companion, his comrade, on that desert island they had talked about. He was her lord and friend, she his squire and his heart's companion. Thus she would be able to explore that part of him closed against a woman, reach him as no woman ever could. But then she wanted to be both man and woman to him, everything to him, complete. She wanted every bit of him and wondered what he and Sergei were doing.

It was still raining when she got to Brighton. She took a taxi round to her mother's house. Someone was standing outside pressing her mother's bell. She waited with him but there was no answer. Maisie surreptitiously scrutinized the man. He was very thin with a gaunt, interesting face, shabbily dressed; he had noticeably beautiful hands.

'She must be out,' said Maisie.

'I expect she's in the town,' said the man. He had an accent. Central European.

'Can I give her a message?' asked Maisie. 'I'm her daughter.'

'I can see some certain likeness.'

One of her mother's odd friends, no doubt. Foreign, slightly shabby, sophisticated. Interesting. There were her conventional Brighton friends, church and bridge friends, and then there were her occasional odd-ball friends.

'Imre Thèk, please call me Imre.'

'I'm Maisie,' she said, remembering the Bonnard card on her mother's mantelpiece. 'I'll come back later. If you see her, would you be kind enough to tell her I've gone for some lunch and will be back?'

'I know a nice little place. Not expensive. Please let me show you – it's newly opened.'

'All right,' said Maisie.

So they ended up having fried sprats and brown bread and butter together.

'How is my mother?' asked Maisie, remembering Rose's reference to her health.

'She seems very well.'

'You met my daughter Rose at Christmas. She said you are a mathematician.'

'I am retired. I taught mathematics and logic in London for more years than I like to think. Ever since I came from Hungary.'

'At the time of the uprising?'

'Yes, that's right. I came over then.'

What else could Maisie find out about him in defence of her mother's interests? She could feel Rose urging her on. She was interested, anyway.

'Are you one of Ma's bridge friends?'

'No, I'm afraid the only game I play is chess and your mother isn't very good at it.'

'I thought perhaps you had met her through her bridge group.'

'No, I met your mother in the Lanes. She was raising money for Amnesty. I gave her all the money I had with me. We got talking, we just took to each other at once. I happened to tell her I had been imprisoned as a political prisoner in Hungary. She said, "You poor man, you must be hungry, so am I. I shall buy you some poached eggs on toast." I told her that I had not recently been released from prison. In fact already I had lived in England for many years. And I had been teaching at the University for over ten years – where the food is not too bad. But poached eggs sounded like a good idea, if she would buy it as I had put all my money in her tin.'

'All that sounds typical of my mother. She has a streak of recklessness about her.'

'It is that about her I most admire. She has a certain ladylike wildness – I find it very attractive.'

Maisie laughed. 'That describes it very well.'

'Your mother and I,' he said, 'we find we have much in common.'

Maisie watched him curiously as he took their coats from

the coat-stand and paid the bill, carefully counting the change. These sorts of people had always drifted through her mother's life, she had a deep interest in and sympathy with certain sorts of people, often on the fringes of the seemingly conventional life she lived. Though that conventional core to her mother was just as much a true part of her, giving the wildness a certain stable centre and saving her from eccentricity.

'That was delicious,' said Maisie. 'Thank you. Tell my mother I shall be along later. I have to make a call this afternoon.'

They shook hands and went their separate ways.

# 2

MAISIE stopped off on her way to Denisov to buy a pot of white hyacinths for her mother and some groceries. As she rang the bell, she breathed in the flowers' perfume, faint in the cold air.

She was not shown to the same room where she had seen Denisov before. The old man was in bed, and she was taken to his bedside.

The Steppes ikon was on the wall at the foot of his bed, and underneath it a small sanctuary lamp burned. The old man had undergone a change since Maisie last saw him. She was aware of the skull beneath the almost transparent flesh; the bony old hands waved her to come close with a strange grace, a gesture beautiful in its utter exhaustion.

But Denisov's mind was sharp and clear.

'You see why I have called you. I have the holy image with me now, it will accompany my last days on this earth.'

He smiled. 'What did you discover for me?' he whispered.

'Only part of the story,' said Maisie. 'There is a crucial gap.' And she told him what she had been able to uncover of the ikon's past travels.

The old man listened, sharply attentive as she spoke. 'When the time comes,' he said, 'we must have our facts ready. There must be no doubts. It must be clearly shown that the ikon is the original authentic Mother of the Steppes.'

Suddenly he was asleep.

Maisie kept very still, her eyes drawn to the ikon and the bright look between the Madonna and the Child, and then to the old man's face, closed in sleep, and then inexorably back again to the ikon. There was an extraordinary aliveness in the way the Mother and Child regarded each other; the longer Maisie looked, the more alive this remarkable gaze became.

'Where is your companion?'

Maisie was startled by Denisov's question; he had woken as suddenly as he had slept. 'The gentleman who came with you before. Michael Curran.'

'He is still in Kiev,' said Maisie, surprised that the old man had remembered his name. 'For a few more days. He will soon be back.'

'I trust you both,' he said clearly, strongly.

Denisov seemed not to be worried as he had been before. He spoke deliberately, calmly, not wasting his words but making sure Maisie got his meaning. He seemed to have given himself up to his death with an almost joyful recognition of what was happening to him. He seemed to be resting in tremulous hope, half-way to Heaven – almost blithe in his very weakness. It was as though this giving up to death had given him a trust in life. He trusted Maisie.

'I want to ask you a special thing,' he said.

'Yes?'

'I will want you later to have care of the ikon. I want you to put it into the hands of a certain gentleman. His name and address I will give you before you go. Will you do this?'

'Yes,' said Maisie.

She decided to tell him, as he seemed so calm, something of the interest the ikon had stirred up in certain quarters.

He listened intently. 'Will you have some tea?' he asked.

'Yes, thank you,' Maisie said, watching his expression. He seemed unruffled. He pointed to the tasselled bell-pull for her to call the old woman to bring them tea.

'The ikon's place is in the cathedral,' he was saying. 'When the time comes, it will be there . . . at last.'

As the old housekeeper brought in tea, he drifted off to sleep again. He looked like a fish skeleton, lying there.

Maisie sat and sipped her tea and wondered if she would ever see Michael again. Always her mind went back to that very first meeting with him. Always her heart turned over as she remembered it. If he did not come back to her, she would not be able to bear it. Her life would stop.

When the housekeeper came back to clear away the things the old woman saw that Denisov had not touched his tea. She pulled him out of his light sleep in a matter-of-fact way, propped him up with pillows and held the cup to his mouth. The tea dribbled down his chin. His body had little use now for food and drink.

'I shall arrange for you to collect the ikon,' the old man said to Maisie. 'It won't be very long now.' He handed her a folded piece of paper. Then he smiled, a sweet, ecstatic smile. 'What a beautiful smell,' he said. 'Bring the flowers closer.'

'They are for you,' Maisie said on impulse. 'I'll leave them on the table for you to catch the perfume.'

'What are they called?' he asked.

'Hyacinths,' replied Maisie, and she kissed him goodbye.

Downstairs in the light of the hall as she was being shown out, she glanced at the name and address on the piece of paper before folding it and putting it in her bag. The name was Russian, the address was Walsingham.

It was dark as she made her way to her mother's flat. The sea was rough and threw small pebbles up over the promenade. It roared and threw itself against the beach. She walked quickly, carrying her bag of shopping in front of her like a baby. There were few people about on such a wild night. Once or twice Maisie could hardly stand against the wind which came in sudden gusts.

Imre Thèk answered the door, and she followed him into the big sitting-room. The velvet curtains were drawn to shut out the winter night and Maisie's mother and her new friend had obviously been reading peacefully beside the fire. A tranquil scene.

They both fussed round her, taking her coat, offering her a drink and a place near the fire. Maisie could see at once that her mother and Imre Thèk loved each other. As she sipped her sherry she began telling them a little about Denisov and the ikon she was investigating.

'I thought at first I was simply authenticating an ikon,' she said. 'But I seem to be getting drawn into something else.' She stopped, cautious of saying too much in front of a comparative stranger.

'You must be careful,' said her mother.

'Don't worry,' answered Maisie.

'You meet such a funny lot in your line of work. How was the conference? And what have you done with that young man you brought here last time?'

'I left Michael in Kiev in the clutches of an extraordinary chap called Sergei. They are supposed to be making a record. I think Michael's just enjoying himself with his ilk.'

'What are his ilk?' asked her mother.

'Footloose musicians,' said Maisie shortly. She turned to Thèk. 'Do you know Kiev at all?' she asked.

'When it was Soviet Russia it was somewhere where one avoided going,' said Thèk. 'It was somewhere where if you went, you were probably never seen again. The sound of the language – everything – still fills me with fear and hatred.'

'Imre was imprisoned for a time in Hungary as a political prisoner,' said Mrs Sharpe.

'Yes, I know. We got to know a bit about each other over the sprats,' said Maisie. 'But things are different now, things have changed since those days.'

'Time will tell,' said Thèk. 'I am not hopeful.'

'Imre was in solitary confinement for a year,' said Evelyn Sharpe. 'They took away his glasses.'

There was a silence.

'Perhaps they will find another tsar,' said Maisie in a small voice. 'Perhaps the monarchy will return anyway to Russia itself – it had such a strong hold before the Revolution – if an heir to the throne were to be found – perhaps such a one exists.'

Thèk threw his head back and laughed.

'It is a romantic and amusing idea,' he said, 'though perhaps slightly more feasible than the idea of Russia becoming Europeanized. No – she will always be enigmatic, Eastern, and confused and volcanic beneath the surface. Shambling, eccentric, wild – terrible.'

'I think it is you who are romanticizing now,' said Maisie. 'You speak as if Russia is a kind of Caliban – a sort of chaotic subconscious area of the world.'

Thèk shrugged and held out both hands in a characteristically Central European gesture, meaning, 'You said it.'

'Anyway,' Maisie went on, 'strictly speaking, the idea of kingship is anti-romantic. That is, if romantic ideas are about freedom, revolution, the primacy of the individual and so forth – if they are against hierarchies.'

There was another little silence.

'Did you bring something for our dinner tonight?' asked Mrs Sharpe.

'Yes – and I'm going to make it,' said Maisie.

'Well, don't you believe in the primacy of the individual?' asked Thèk.

'I'm not at all sure,' said Maisie. 'Romantic freedom has a hell of a lot to answer for. One small step and we're into chaos.'

'I'm glad you realize it,' said Mrs Sharpe.

'But life is worth nothing,' said Thèk, 'if the individual cannot be true to himself. He is not a clone, not a serf, not a number on a wall. You have to shout out your name. I am the one and only Imre Thèk.'

'Mm,' said Maisie. 'I like to think I'd do the same, but suspect I might not. I might just fade into my appointed fate, without a word.' She stood up, picking up the bag of groceries. 'Spaghetti all right?'

'I remember my father talking of the old Tsar,' said Mrs Sharpe. 'He used to sail off Cowes. My father met him on board his yacht. Spaghetti is fine – a nice change. Do you want any help?'

'No – you two just sit there and let me do all the work. Go back to your books.'

The telephone chirped and Mrs Sharpe picked it up. There was a pause.

'It's for you, Maisie. It's Michael, I think.'

'I'll take it in the kitchen,' said Maisie.

Michael sounded slightly drunk.

'How is it all going?' she asked, a little too briskly.

'Christ, Maisie – stop being so bloody offhand. I love you. I've been ringing your flat all day.'

'I love you too,' said Maisie.

'Shall I come back today?'

'Have you finished the recording?'

'No.'

'Well, stay and do it. I thought you were so taken up with it. You must finish things you start.' She could hear her mother in her voice. 'I thought it was so important.'

'It is important. But I miss you. I'm a weak man, Maisie, you should have stayed with me.'

'I had work to do, Michael, I just can't go on like that – anyway, I'm glad I came back, Denisov is dying, I saw him today – he wants me to take the ikon to – to somewhere. I've agreed. Have you heard any more talk there of the ikon, or anything?'

'The sort of people I mix with aren't interested in such things. Well, Sergei's fixer friend might be, he's got a finger

in all sorts of pies. He has got a sort of trade going in ikons
– it's illegal to trade in them, he loves anything illegal, it's
like a magnet to him. But I don't want to talk about that, I
just want to tell you how I feel. I want to be with you,
Maisie.'

His words sounded sweet to her.

'I'm making spaghetti carbonara,' she said.

'I love you.'

'Ma has got a lover.'

'To hell with your mother, and spaghetti whatever it
was. I love you, Maisie. Tell me you love me.'

'I love you, Michael.'

'Say it again.'

'I love you.'

'Goodnight, then, Fig.'

She put the telephone down and started grating parmesan, melting butter, making a sauce. She was glad he was a
weak man. She smiled to herself to think he was a weak
man.

She began to sing to herself, she danced around the little
kitchen, the grater in her hand. She put the bread to warm,
started the sauce, uncorked the wine and poured herself a
small glass. She began to wonder if she had been too offhand
and worried a bit that she had sounded cold.

When the food was ready, she carried it through to the
other room where her mother had laid the table by the
window and lit the lamp in the dining end of the room. Imre
Thèk was polishing the wine glasses.

Maisie felt strongly motherly towards both the Hungarian and her mother as she brought in the plates of food, the
crisp warm bread. She felt motherly to the whole world.
Her mother and Thèk, Rose and Glantz – everyone with
someone else. Arms encircled round each other, clinging to
each other, like partners in a dance. And sometimes one
danced alone, and sometimes one changed partners.

'Parmesan?' She offered the grated cheese to her mother.

Thèk poured the wine into his sparkling glasses. They helped each other to food and drink as they drank and ate. Maisie thought the two of them had a settled little air of suitability hovering over them.

She and Michael had no such settled little air. Michael and she, chance met, as were her mother and Thèk. But however unsettled their relationship, however unsuited they might be, she would never give up this man. She loved him and wanted him. If he did not come back soon from Kiev, she would fly out again and bring him back. If he would not come she would drug him with a secret drug and bring him back. If he stopped loving her, she would find some love potion and put it in his marmalade. Maisie's face had a fierce look about it, but she was not far from tears either. She felt wounded by love. As she lay in bed later that night, her wounds hurt and bled.

# 3

SHE thought she might feel nearer to Michael once she was back in London. She was glad to be back. Quietly she put the key in the lock and opened her front door. The smell of warm olive oil wafted from Rose's room, with the muffled tones of Ella Fitzgerald's haunting, inexorable voice. Rose had got into the way of playing the record all the time as if she had got it on the brain. The smell and the sound found a connection in Maisie's mind.

As she passed Rose's door she heard voices, but did not stop. She made her way up to her room, her shadow sliding up the wall of the stairway.

She felt like a shadow-woman without her lover to give her life and blood.

She wished passionately that she had never met him.

No, not that she had never met him.

For she had met him, and now he was her love-shadow, her darker self, she could no more get rid of him than she could her own shadow, and she carried the knowledge of him everywhere.

This separation from him was like something that had come unhinged in nature. Being back in London did not help at all. Only part of her took off her wet trench-coat, made herself a cup of coffee, opened the window to let in a little fresh air to the still room, pulled a harebell-blue mohair jumper on against the chilly air and started to get out paper, books, writing things. All the while she was doing these things she felt as if she was bleeding from her central nervous system; she felt sore and raw. Separation from him was like a physical wound that weakened her and left her bruised and bleeding. His absence was a palpable thing. A presence. I do not go, my love, for weariness of thee, but every time we say goodbye I die a little.

She unfastened a portfolio of prints. The draught from the window riffled the heavy paper and she got up to close the window.

Rose and Glantz were waiting by a taxi, its engine running. Rose got in, and then Glantz. She wondered where they were going. It was good to see Rose going anywhere.

Maisie went back to her prints. She laid three prints side by side on the table. All of them were of the Virgin of Vladimir, but centuries lay between them. The first was a reproduction of the original and most famous of the ikons – Our Lady of Vladimir. This ikon had been taken from Constantinople to Kiev in the twelfth century, and later to the city of Vladimir so that its miraculous powers might help the town. It had not, like the other two, come from a Russian workshop. In it, the Virgin's gaze was forward and not on the child, who pressed his cheek against his mother, his arm round her neck.

Maisie compared it with the second print – this one attributed to Rublev. This Virgin and Child was very different, though derived from the twelfth-century ikon. This was fifteenth-century, and unmistakably Russian. Something had been added to the balance and harmony of the Greek influence of the original.

Maisie pondered what this difference was. It looked – the Russian Virgin and Child – more of this world, the faith that informed it more human and earthy, more rooted in nature. The colours were deep, full, and spoke of the earth too. It was very tender – the attitude of the child, clinging like any young creature to its mother, the two bonded, the Virgin's gaze veering more to the child in her arms.

The third print was of a much later ikon – seventeenth-century. This was more decorative and formal, the heavy use of gold made it glow distinctively. The Virgin looked abstracted in this portrayal. Maisie carefully put these Vladimir Virgins to one side, and went through the other prints one by one.

A Nativity, in which Mary floated in the centre of the ikon on what looked like a carpet, the exact colour of a scarlet pimpernel, surrounded by the iconography of the nativity.

Christ's Entry into Jerusalem.

The Washing of the Feet.

Maisie began to write down her observations and reflections on each of these prints. She was not making notes with any particular purpose in view, it was just her habit to write things down. And for a few years now these ikons had gradually taken a hold on her. She was beginning to become addicted to them. She wanted to see them often. They spoke to her.

With Maisie it was the visual sense that came first, and meant most to her. It was what she looked at.

This was how she had fallen in love. She had just looked at Michael. It had been the sight of him.

Packing the prints away, tying up her portfolio, she longed to see him. If only she could see him now – and she would just be content to look and look. Perhaps that would be enough, just to look at him, all her delight.

Most important, it was his face. But it was not just the face, she loved beyond sense and reason his innate grace, even the very way his clothes arranged themselves and draped on his body. And yes, she perceived with sudden delight and almost a sense of relief to have hit on it, yes, he had that earthy realism, that immediacy that so appealed to her in Rublev's work. How near, she thought, were religious and profane love. The thought gave her a sense of delicate joy – and made her laugh, too.

She longed to see Michael in his own setting, his natural background, in Ireland. It was the first time she had wanted that. But when she went to bed, still seeing pictures with her inner eye, they were of Michael, in a dark red cloak, walking in the Russian steppes.

She slept.

When she woke, startled by something, she thought she saw Michael's shadow-self sitting on the bed beside her, so like flesh even in the dim light. It was a split moment of eternity after they had reached out to each other that she knew he was real. They just held each other. A longer time before he spoke; and she was sure.

'Life tasted so thin without you,' he said. 'We'll stay together now.'

As she felt his human warmth, his sweet breath, life and blood began to quicken in her, and the shadow-world gave way to the dimensions and colours and sounds and smell of a real, urgent, incredibly, vividly present world. She was part of it and knew her place in it.

She touched his hair, his mouth. Her mouth opened under his lips.

They lay against each other, touching everywhere they could touch, their whole bodies embracing each other. Unable to get close enough, to feel close enough, wanting to live inside each other, gradually they undressed each other until, with a subtle shock, they were naked.

'Come closer,' said Maisie.

And still they were not close enough until he had opened and entered her body. Then, whole and strong, they became that thing – a man-woman. Whole.

And they kept still for a long time, he hardly moving at

all. They were one flesh. Then the man raised himself on his elbows and looked into the woman's eyes. He saw in them the light of love, and she saw in his eyes the same light.

And then the man began to move inside the woman. Now his body was strong and powerful like any male animal, like a tiger or an eagle. Only he was more, because he was human, and had a human heart and brain. His powerful loins and hands were human, and his tongue was a man's tongue.

And the woman was silk and milk. It was easy; it was right.

And Christ, with what joy she hurled into the sea all the false glitter of trying to do this or that. She hurled all that away with one easy throw. And loving her, he let go with hungry fierce amazement wanting this or that, or let's try it this way. They knew each other. It all came easy. And they both came easy.

Afterwards, feeling his sleepy blood throb through his veins, through his warm body, now almost baby-like in its warm soft limbs and heavy eyelids, like a baby who has fed on its mother's milk and is full, Maisie wept a little, and Michael drank her few salty tears.

'Did you have a good journey?' she whispered, on the edges of sleep.

'That last bit of my journey was the best,' said Michael. 'Now I am home.'

'Home?'

'You are my home, Maisie.'

'Yes,' she said.

Even as her whole being was in bliss, she knew it would soon pass. Nothing could be grasped and held. Let it go – but not yet. She folded down the edges into sleep so as not to let it go. And in her little pocket of time she slept in Michael's arms. He was already asleep.

# 4

WHEN he woke, he was alone in the bed and red winter sunshine was pouring through the window, lighting up the lace flowers of the bed-curtains.

The next thing he saw was the Steppes ikon. It lay in a pool of sunlight on the table amidst a pile of straw, newspaper, cloth and corrugated cardboard in which it had been wrapped. It looked as if there was a fire in the straw.

Maisie was in the kitchen making coffee. She brought a tray of toast and coffee over to the bed.

'We have to go to Walsingham,' she said. 'Denisov is dead.' She nodded towards the ikon. 'It was delivered by hand this morning.'

'Walsingham?'

'Yes. Do you know it?'

'No. I don't think I've heard of it.'

'It's a village in Norfolk. A place of pilgrimage connected with the Virgin Mary – in medieval times it was of great importance.'

'And we have to take the ikon there – it seems an out-of-the-way place. I might have known it would be somewhere outlandish.'

'There has been an enclave of Russian monarchists there for years, apparently.'

'I don't want to go to Walsingham. I want us to stay here and just go out for food sometimes. I don't want us to leave this bed and go anywhere.'

'I made a promise,' said Maisie. 'We must go today.'

'May I have some toast first?'

'Yes, all right.'

'Is there an egg or something? I don't see myself going on this pilgrimage fasting.'

Maisie made him two poached eggs and brought them to him on a butler's tray.

'When you've had this you must get up,' she said. She kissed him but slipped quickly away.

Michael drank his coffee and ate his eggs, looking at the straw which looked as if it had caught alight in the sunshine.

'We must go,' said Maisie.

'Come back to bed.'

'I want to start now – I love London in the early morning before the traffic really gets going.'

'How are we supposed to get there? Horseback?' He flung back the bed-cover and lay there spreadeagled and naked.

'I've hired a car,' she said. 'It's outside the house.'

Michael got up and looked out of the window.

'Oh, good,' he said, 'it's a Merc.' He dressed quickly then and grinned at her cheerfully.

'I'll drive,' he said.

'We'll take turns,' she said.

'I'll drive first,' he said.

Maisie laughed. She was wrapping the ikon in its straw, pages of *Le Monde* and blue cloth, and then binding the thin wire round the corrugated cardboard.

'Let's go,' she said, putting the swaddled ikon into Michael's arms. 'It's all yours,' she said. Downstairs, she ripped open a brown envelope and shook out the car keys.

The silver Mercedes was waiting for them, its windscreen flaming red. Maisie locked the ikon in the boot of the car and gave the keys to Michael.

'All yours,' she said again.

Michael took off his jacket and threw it on the back seat. He looked different. He was wearing a simple dark sweater, the sort worn by merchant seamen; he pushed up the sleeves as he turned on the ignition.

As they drove through early-morning London, laid out calmly in the morning sun, Maisie asked him, 'Are you the same man I met at Paddington that day?'

'No, I am much changed,' said Michael. 'You have changed me. Knowing you.'

'I want you to be the same man I met then.'

'We can't stay the same. We affect each other, change each other. Nothing stays the same – life is all flux.'

'But I fell in love with that particular man.'

'Oh, Maisie, I'm sorry. I'm not that man.'

'Take the Cambridge Road, I have to stop there briefly.'

'We could have lunch there.'

'Yes, we could. Tell me about Kiev,' she said. 'I mean, after I had gone.'

'It's all a bit of a haze.'

'You did the recording?'

'I think I did.'

'Did they try to make you stay?'

'Well – yes. I may go back one day. With you.'

Unsaid things began to travel with them as the Mercedes slid out on to the motorway, and Michael switched on the radio to disperse them. Then switched it off again.

They were beginning to travel very fast.

'We'll be in Cambridge before you know it,' said Michael. 'This car will make short work of the journey. Who have you got to see there?'

'I just want to pick up a book.'

'Did you go to university there?'

'No. Rose did – Fine Arts.'

'Does she paint?'

'She's very good, but she never does any.'

When they got to Cambridge the town looked as if it had been carved sharply against a now sunless sky. There was a raw wind. The leafless trees shivered over the Cam. They found a dark warm pub and had coffee and sandwiches, and Maisie left Michael guarding their precious parcel while she went off on her errand.

When she came back, he was reading the paper and drinking beer. He handed her the newspaper.

'Some poor sods have tried to blow up the Kremlin. Sort of Guy Fawkes stuff. Got caught. Do you think they can be some of Denisov's lot?'

'I shouldn't think so,' Maisie frowned as she read. 'They're all so high-minded. I don't think murder comes into their scheme of things. It is a religious quest.'

'Religion never stopped people killing before. I don't think we should get mixed up in it all.'

'I'm not getting mixed up in it. I'm just delivering something for a client.'

'Yes. I suppose so. A client who happens to be dead. It's heady stuff.'

'You're not very adventurous.'

'I've learned to keep out of things.'

'Oh – yes. You never talk much about Ireland.'

'I'll take you there, Maisie. We'll go soon – you'll like it. I think you'll love it.'

'I'd like to go there. See where you come from. Your home.'

'You're my home, I told you.'

Maisie touched his face and he kissed her fingers.

'Let's go,' she said.

This time Maisie drove – more sedately, they had time to notice the countryside. Dark rushes shredding in the wind and wide, pale skies, grey and turquoise.

She wished the journey would last for ever. They were as if encapsulated; time and space became eternity and infinity, as they travelled through it. She tasted joy like a good wine, it sang through her veins. Her mind and heart lay down with each other, she did not know one from the other.

Seeing some wild duck flying over, Maisie stopped the car to get out and watch them. They flew fast, and were soon overhead.

'Teal,' said Michael.

'I love the way they stretch out their necks as if they really mean to get where they're going,' said Maisie.

The raw wind whipped round them as they stood.

'That wind comes straight from Russia.'

Maisie smiled at him. 'It's always cold on this side of England,' she said, 'but I love it. I think it's my favourite part.'

'I haven't kissed you properly for two and a half hours,' said Michael, and he kissed her properly standing there, the sound of the wild duck in the sky, the sharp little wind, cars whipping past them. Someone sounded a horn in appreciation.

'Doesn't take much to make you blush,' said Michael. 'Come on, let's stop making a spectacle.'

Back in the car he got out the map and put on his glasses. 'Which way now?'

'All roads lead to Walsingham,' said Maisie, starting up the engine.

> 'As ye came from the holy land
> Of Walsingham
> Met you not with my true love
> By the way as you came?'

'That's nice. By the way – is the ikon insured?'

'In a way it is uninsurable – but yes, it is insured.'

'For a lot?'

'Yes.'

'They didn't trust to its miracle-working properties?'

'It was doubtless insured for more because of them.'

'God and Mammon get awfully mixed up sometimes.'

'I've noticed it.'

She switched on the radio and found some going-to-Walsingham music.

'Going-to-Walsingham music,' she said.

'Exactly right,' he said.

Maisie was enjoying driving the car – it was a while since she had driven, it didn't seem worth having a car in London. She felt that everything was in its right place, she felt young and a bit wild and full of splendid courage. She felt pleased with her strong, young-feeling limbs and steady heartbeat, and amazed at the beauty of the man who was her companion and lover.

Up ahead an odd-looking hitch-hiker lunged forward. He had a notice which said 'Swaffham'.

'You're not going to stop?'

'Why not?' said Maisie, slowing down. She was not reluctant to stop.

'Well – why? Stop worrying about people.'

'He is a fellow pilgrim, perhaps,' said Maisie.

'He'll pinch the ikon and then we'll have to spend the rest of our lives looking for it.'

'It's cold out there.' She stopped the car beside the hitch-hiker. The man was probably in his forties, he was dressed in a once-good tweed jacket which had belonged to someone a couple of sizes bigger, his collarless shirt was ragged, his hat shapeless, its band stiff with dirt.

'Chuck your notice over the hedge,' said Michael, somewhat unreasonably. The man took no notice, and with some difficulty wedged it in the back of the car with him.

'Perhaps he's deaf,' Michael spoke under his breath.

Maisie frowned and turned to her new passenger. 'There's a seat-belt,' she said, smiling at him.

The man had one of those faces that have gone down the

centuries. His heavy eyelids hooded eyes either stupid or shrewd, you couldn't tell, he had large coarse ears, and a slightly dopey-looking half-smile which said God knows what. He looked equally capable of good or evil. He stank a bit of rotting sacks. He made no attempt to fasten his seat-belt.

'All the way to bloody Swaffham,' sighed Michael, as Maisie pulled out on to the road again. They drove in silence then, except for the radio music, for several miles.

'It's a very wonderful thing,' said the man at last, 'to listen to such beautiful music along the road.'

Maisie glanced at Michael, and they smiled a bit at each other.

'A privilege,' added the man.

After a while, Michael said, 'Stop when you can, Maisie – I'd like to drive for a bit.'

When they had changed over, Michael drove very fast to Swaffham, where they said goodbye to the man. They watched him as he went off, shouldering his placard as if it were a rifle. He didn't look back, intent on something.

'Let's get some tea,' said Maisie. But before they had tea she went into an ironmonger's and bought a rucksack.

'We'll have to do the last couple of miles on foot,' she said, 'like the old pilgrims. There was a relic, you know – some of Mary's breast milk – brought back by the crusaders, and even Henry VIII went barefoot, the last bit to Walsingham. So we must at least walk it.'

'How did I come to be keeping company with a madwoman?' But he tried the rucksack on, altering the straps and stowing the ikon inside it.

'You look like something out of my Russian fairy-story book,' she said.

'It's your fault,' said Michael. 'My appearance is a direct result of my knowing you. My Russian hat, my heavy rucksack with precious contents, my hangdog expression – all of it because of you. Because I love you.'

He stooped and kissed her. 'I really love you, Maisie,' he said. He put his arm round her. 'Let's go and have some tea.'

They sat for nearly an hour, drinking tea in front of a coal fire. It was a pleasant tea-shop, the table old and round, polished and rickety on the uneven floorboards. The waitress, old too, with thin, mousey hair and swollen ankles in their thick stockings, had a sharpish, direct way of talking, which left one refreshed and strangely soothed because of its lack of sweetness.

'You're not from round here,' she said. 'Neither am I.' There seemed very little to eat in the place, though the huge pot of tea was fresh.

'The buns are yesterday's,' said the woman, 'and they're better toasted. I'll bring you some jam.'

So they lingered on, enjoying the emptiness of the place.

'I'm not surprised no one comes here – there's nothing to eat,' said Michael.

'Have some jam,' said Maisie.

'Are you happy?'

'Yes,' she said. 'Very.'

'Doesn't take much to make you happy, does it?'

'Well – it takes being with you.'

They left the waitress a huge tip and made their way back to the car. On the way they passed their hitch-hiker outside a chemist. He was holding up his notice which now said, 'God is not mocked'.

'I told you, he is an iconoclast,' said Michael, 'protesting against graven images and medieval goings-on. Which road do we take now?'

'Take the Fakenham road.'

'No more hitch-hikers.'

'No more hitch-hikers.'

When they had passed Fakenham, Maisie asked Michael to look out for a good place to leave the car.

'We must walk the rest of the way,' she said.

'It's going to rain,' said Michael. 'Look at that dark cloud.'

'You're allowed to keep your shoes on, then.'

'Thanks.'

He parked the car by a bridge and two or three cottages.

'Now,' said Maisie, 'let's get to Walsingham.'

They set off at a good pace, the rucksack with the ikon on Michael's back. It was about four o'clock and the winter's day was beginning to come to a close. As they made their way along the country road, a strange greenish light shone from behind a dark cloud. Before long there was a brief sharp hail-shower, like cold hard grain flung into their faces. Soon after, a rainbow hung in the sky, gradually becoming brighter and more intense. It stayed fitfully for most of their walk.

Birds hopped in the dry leaves that filled the ditches, a few hard catkins shivered in the hedge. Everything smelled cold and earthy.

They got to Walsingham just before dusk.

The first person they saw as they came to the market square was a hooded monk carrying a plastic carrier bag with 'Jollife's Emporium' written on it in red letters. He was just standing there in the dwindling light.

'I've got a feeling it's all going to be like this,' said Michael. 'It's addictive, one begins to want everyone to be odd, and the odder the better.'

And when they knocked at the Georgian house that was their destination and were greeted by a Russian who must have been nearly seven feet tall, and who embraced and kissed them both, it did seem as if it was all going to be like that.

Although he was dressed like an Englishman, it did nothing to disguise his foreignness. His long grey hair fell about a face that was hypnotically attractive, dark eyes that missed nothing, a large bony nose, cavernous cheekbones. Nevertheless, the room to which he led them was very

English too, understated and comfortable. A bright log fire burned in the grate.

They were offered vodka or whisky, but did not accept. Michael began, at once, to unwrap the ikon. Carefully he folded the newspaper and the cloth and brushed aside the straw, to reveal the image. A piece of straw fell on to the immaculate carpet and Maisie picked it up.

They were all looking down now at the exposed ikon, still lying on its bed of straw. The Russian made no attempt to hide his tears.

'If this were the only image in the world,' he said, 'we would need no other.'

Maisie found the complexion of her thoughts much changed by the meeting with the Russian, as they walked back to the car.

'It would be easy to be drawn in,' she said. 'I find it difficult sometimes to distance myself – his emotions and beliefs are so compelling. They could be infectious.'

'It's a job you have done. And now it's over,' said Michael.

'It is not really completed yet.'

'Leave it,' said Michael. 'I wish you would just leave it now. How far is the car, would you say?'

'A mile or so, not far.'

'I hope to God it's still there.'

'Of course it will be. Don't worry. Let's enjoy the night.'

They walked on. Sometimes a car passed them, but no one else was walking out on that moonlit night, although it was nearly as light as day.

When they reached the car Michael said he would drive. Neither of them spoke much as he drove all the way to London, but the silence between them was like a conversation. And as the car sped south, the moon sped with it, lighting the clouds as it travelled.

# 5

'WE can stay in bed, and just go out for food,' said Michael the next morning.

He had flung back the duvet, so that he could see Maisie's nakedness. He stroked her thigh, then kissed it. Maisie turned on to her stomach.

'I have to go to an auction preview this morning,' she said.

Michael groaned. 'Where? Newcastle? Portsmouth?'

'Knightsbridge. Will you come?'

'Oh, just down the road, that makes a change. Yes, we'll go together.' He slapped her on the behind and then kissed her in the same place.

'I can't get enough of you,' he said. 'I want to eat you.' He pretended to eat her, starting with her little finger. When it got a bit rough, Maisie pushed him away, laughing.

'You know where all this will end,' she said. 'Get up.'

'You're always ordering me about,' he said, but he got up, and they showered and breakfasted and got dressed between bouts of larking around. They were both happy.

When they emerged into Kensington, it was drizzling with rain and they got on a bus to Knightsbridge.

'It won't take long,' said Maisie. 'I've just got to look at something for a client.'

'Another ikon?'

'A reliquary,' she said. 'My client is very excited about it.'

And it did turn out to be a very beautiful and arresting piece of work. Made of plain and beaten gold, it was a round, flower-shaped casket about the size of a man's head. In the catalogue it was described as a French double reliquary with an unusual locking system, decorated with angels with wings folded over their breasts.

Maisie showed Michael how the thing opened and where, once, it would have hidden relics. (According to Maisie's research, these were a fragment of cloth from the swaddling clothes of the Christ-child and a thorn from the crown of thorns.)

'The relics were probably stolen at some point,' said Maisie. 'It was the relics themselves, not the reliquary, that would have been prized.'

This reliquary did not look like a receptacle or container but more like a burnished flower: its beautiful fretted border was like the rays of the sun or the petals of a flower. A sunflower, perhaps.

Michael smiled at Maisie's serious face. Everyone – there were quite a few people in the big echoing auction room – spoke in a low voice as if taking part in a conspiracy. Time ticked by slowly.

When they came out once more into the street it was like moving into a speeded-up film. Everyone was suddenly rushing about. Dark-coated men with long legs and large black umbrellas. Old women with lipsticked, wrinkled mouths and Harrods bags. Indian women floating along, their bright saris like wet tissue paper trailing along the pavement.

'Home,' said Michael.

'Not yet,' said Maisie. 'I want you to amuse yourself in a pub or something. I have to see someone – one of Leo's friends. I won't be long,' she added.

'Don't be long, then. I'm not safe left alone.'

'Don't be childish,' said Maisie sharply. He was threatening to get drunk, she supposed, if left to his own devices for too long. Michael raised his eyebrows at her tone, and she apologized for it but seemed suddenly abstracted.

'I'll see you in about an hour in the pub on the corner,' she said, and she walked briskly away, leaving him to wander off to the Golden Lion.

Maisie walked for ten minutes or so, arriving at a fine terraced house with railings and a bronze plaque. She rang the bell and picked a bay leaf from a neat potted tree by the door.

She waited for a few minutes in a room with bowls of dried roses and delphiniums, copies of yachting magazines and a single original Matthew Smith on the wall.

Quentin Freeman kissed her on the cheek. 'Hallo, love,' he said, 'come in and sit down.' He led her to an easy chair in his surgery.

'Sitting comfortably?' he asked.

'Is it as bad as that?'

'Depends,' he said. 'It's a positive result, Maisie. You're definitely *enceinte*.'

'Oh, God. I can't believe it,' said Maisie.

'You must have had a good idea that you were.' Quentin Freeman looked at her curiously, kindly. 'What does Leo think?' he asked.

'Leo? Look, Quentin, I don't want Leo to know about this.'

'All right.'

'Promise?'

'Of course, Maisie, you have my word. Is it a willed one, a wanted one? Do you want to keep it?'

'No. No. I don't know.'

'It's early days – but the sooner you make up your mind . . .'

'Yes, I know. Of course.' She began tearing the bay leaf

into pieces. Quentin Freeman watched her quietly. At last she said, 'Did you mind my coming to you?'

'Good Lord, no.'

'Well . . . Leo and, well . . . you know. But I thought you wouldn't mind.'

'Good Lord, no . . . what are friends for? How is Leo? I haven't seen him since the summer.'

'He's . . . the same. Unchanged, really. You know Leo.'

'What about you?'

'Well, I'm having an unsuitable love affair.'

'Why unsuitable?'

'Well . . . too hectic.'

'Sounds good. Better than being bored.'

'Perhaps. I wasn't bored, though.'

'You probably were without knowing it.'

'Jessy all right?'

'Oh, yes, Jess is fine. Look here, Maisie, no need for us to lose touch. Why don't you come round – if you can find time in the midst of your love life?'

'Thanks. I might. I'd like to,' said Maisie, but knew it was unlikely, anyway while she was with Michael. She wanted no one else; she wouldn't care if the world emptied. Just her and Michael and the birds and the fish, the creatures which inhabited Adam and Eve's world. No human babies to mess up Paradise.

'Goodbye, Quentin,' she said, 'and thanks.'

'Good luck, Maisie.'

Walking back down the street she had walked up only a short time ago, she carried a new knowledge with her. She was pregnant. The world had changed. It was now a different place. And she was different. Nature had her in its maw.

Soon a sort of panic would set in. She remembered.

By this time the winter afternoon had begun to thread its way through the streets of Knightsbridge, switching on the lights in windows.

Michael was drinking beer with a tot of whisky beside it. He stood up as she came in.

Without waiting to sit down, Maisie said, 'Michael, I seem to be pregnant. What am I going to do?'

'Is that what you've been to find out? Why didn't you say? Why have you kept it to yourself? Sit down, for God's sake.'

But Maisie wouldn't sit. 'Oh, what shall I do?' she said, as if to herself.

'Isn't it we? What are we going to do?'

'I think it's me that's pregnant,' said Maisie. She looked at him. 'It's my life that's falling in ruins about me.'

'Let's go,' said Michael, finishing the whisky and leaving the beer.

'Where?'

'I don't really know. Home, I suppose.'

A feeling of strangeness lay between them as they walked to the tube station.

I am lashed to nature, thought Maisie.

She has done this magic thing, thought Michael. How fearful a thing is a woman.

How dangerous his seed is, thought Maisie, as their train slid towards them out of the darkness. How does life come from that strange sap, that milky juice?

The train jolted away.

'What are you thinking about, Maisie?' he asked quietly, his face white in the eerie light of the underground.

'Pomegranates,' she said.

'Why pomegranates?'

'They are the most beautiful of all fruits. When you cut one in half, think what the seeds are like. Their shape and colour, and the way they are fitted together like a mosaic.'

He squeezed her hand and turned away, thinking he was near to tears. They changed trains like sleepwalkers.

'Earls Court,' he said, 'we get off at the next stop.'

The next two days were spent for both of them in a state

of unreality. Neither could absorb the fact of Maisie's pregnancy. Neither knew what they felt or what to do, if anything, about it. There was also uneasiness about the question of Maisie's age, which, for the first time, occupied their thoughts.

Their love-making was changed. Maisie hoped against hope that the physical traumas of sex might deter the foetus from settling down comfortably in her womb. She wanted their sex life to become more violent to this end. Michael, secretly and illogically, felt that his love-making would reinforce the fact of Maisie's pregnancy.

And they were at odds with each other at some deep level that neither could define or express.

Often, though, they forgot the problem, and things were as they were. Until one of them remembered – usually Maisie.

Then one of Michael's musician friends telephoned.

'I'll only be gone for two days,' said Michael. 'I want to get this thing over, it's been hanging about long enough. It'll make some money and I need to.'

'Must you stay overnight? It's only a stone's throw – Shepherd's Bush,' said Maisie.

'I want to get it done in one go,' said Michael.

He knew the timing was wrong. Just when Maisie had discovered her pregnancy, he was about to go off. But she was sensible, he thought, not the sort of woman to get into a state. Capable. Intelligent. That was what he liked about her, he thought, as he held her, kissed her, told her he would miss her and would be back soon.

It was a wrench to part with her. But once outside there was a kind of relief. Guilt is part of being a man, he thought.

As he jumped on to a bus which was slowly making its way up Kensington Church Street in the heavy traffic, Michael had the fleeting thought that it would be possible to disappear into London's seething, changing life, and never see Maisie again. He was startled and sickened by this thought. His emotions ricocheted against each other as he sat there, looking out of the steamy window, seeing nothing. He felt relief at being anonymous, packed in a crowd, alone; himself for himself only. He felt guilt. He felt a tender love for Maisie. He felt fear. Fear of being pulled into the web of family again. It was as if all that was going to happen again: he saw his mother's dark face as she sat in the corner in the best chair, the suffocating pull of home, its roots buried deep like black threads under the skin, in the flesh, around the heart.

But Maisie was different; she did not hold him, only touched him with a light touch that made him want her to stay for ever.

But a child – his and Maisie's child – it was somehow an uneasy and impossible idea. In its impossibility, its uneasiness, it dissolved, like a mirage, in the reassuring familiar atmosphere of the recording studio. The boys were sitting around on pieces of recording equipment, smoking. Someone was playing a piece of Segovia on the guitar.

An older man with a crew-cut and an earring offered Michael a can of beer. 'Hell's job to get the boys together,' he said. 'How's life, Mick? Kate?'

'She's well.'

'That's good.' The man looked round vaguely.

'I've worked out the backing, it's slightly changed,' said Michael. 'Let's get going.'

'It could end up spot-on – or junk.'

'It won't be junk, it'll be superb. Let's go.'

'We're waiting for the engineer,' said the man.

'Oh, Christ, don't say we're waiting for the bloody engineer again.'

'He's here,' someone said.

Michael aimed the empty can at the corner, where there was already a pile of them.

'How's Jilly?' he asked the older man.

'Gone and got herself pregnant again. Can't for the life of me see bloody how. I think she does it on purpose.'

'All women do it on purpose,' said Michael.

'You know, you're bloody right there. I've just realized. It's a fucking plot.'

They both laughed, watching the engineer trailing wires everywhere, but a strange little spurt of anger flared in Michael, taking him by surprise. Then he put it out of his mind.

'We'll do it straight through,' he said. 'No pauses. If it goes wrong we'll bash straight on. But it'll not go wrong. It's going to be great.'

The engineer made a thumbs-up sign through the glass, and Michael cleared his throat and settled into himself. The first piece was a gentle, straightforward love song backed by a very soft rock sound.

> 'She opens her eyes like flowers in the morning.
> Margaret in her tower, her high hiding place.'

The passion was muted, gentle, like morning mist. It was coming just right.

Michael grinned, pleased, and then looked down, collecting his thoughts, drawing a cloak around him, as it were, a cloak of dark, melancholy cloth, shutting out the world. For the next piece was bitter, and had a cruel cutting edge. He sang these words clear as freezing snow crystals, still quiet, but his words drew blood from the shrivelling heart:

> 'She has pierced me with small words, words and kisses
> And carried away my joy for ever.
> A long way off where I can never find it again.'

Watching him, it was as if a shadow passed over his dark features. And that song had been right too. It was going well. The mesmeric backing filled in the pauses between the lyrics. Now he was lost in it, too far to go back.

For the next song was throbbing, full of passion, using his voice to the full.

> *'Call me back to the sweet flesh of yours*
> *Which charms and craves me,*
> *Oh, cool and lily flesh of my lover.'*

Maisie's flesh was like that. Suddenly he wanted her. Suddenly he remembered how she would have his child – and something quickened in him, like a hare turning its head all of a sudden, in an open field. He sang the last song on the track, a song of farewell and parting. It was his latest song and he sang it unaccompanied:

> *'I do not go my love*
> *for weariness of thee.'*

Afterwards they all went to the top room of the Fiddler's Cat and did some serious drinking.

It was a mistake to go back to Maisie like that. But he needed her that evening. He wanted to get away from everyone. And he felt so tender towards her. She seemed vulnerable, he was seeing her with different eyes. Really, she was a vulnerable woman, not cool, not all those things he had been thinking. He wanted to look after her. Shield her. And the baby she would have.

That was what he was trying to do as he unfastened the heavy lace bed-curtains round her bed, as she lay there roused out of her sleep. Gently he was drawing the curtains round her, shielding her from the world, from all harm.

Maisie was furious. 'Why come back here,' she asked tightly, fiercely, pushing back the folds of the lace curtains and fastening them up with shaking hands, 'like that? You're drunk. Really drunk.'

'Why do you say that?' asked Michael, hurt.

'Because you can't walk straight. You're swaying about. You're drunk.'

'Well, I came back because I love you.'

'Oh, for God's sake,' said Maisie. She was frightened. Not of a drunken man: but that she was pregnant now, trapped, and her lover, the father of her unborn child, was showing himself in his true colours. This man, who had wreaked her new state upon her, was unknown to her. It suddenly terrified her.

Michael wondered if this could be the same woman he had known up till now. White-faced, her fists clenched, kneeling in the middle of the big bed, she looked wild-eyed, slightly crazy. Her sleek, straight, ivory-coloured nightdress was slipping off one shoulder, showing her breast and brownish-pink nipple.

'Can I come to bed?' asked Michael, taking off his shoes. He felt he had to lie down very soon.

Maisie hesitated. She really did not know how to take this. She pulled up her shoulder-strap and muttered something Michael couldn't hear. He decided to take it as an invitation. Half-undressed, he lay down. Maisie got up and put on her robe.

She went into the kitchen and began making tea.

'What are you doing?' asked Michael, his eyes closed.

'Making a cup of tea.'

'Come here.'

'Go to hell.'

Michael quietly digested this. Then something like a black cloud of fury began to darken his mind. What did she say to him? Go to hell? Hell? She'd have him go to hell. That dreadful place. There was no peace or rest in any part of it.

He opened his eyes, his head throbbed. 'What did you say?'

'Go to hell.' The small, crisp voice came from the kitchen.

Somehow Michael got off the bed and went into the kitchen. He stood there, swaying slightly.

'That's a strong word to use.' He spoke in a slow, exact way, trying to control the slur in his voice.

'What – hell?' She was not looking at him, she laughed.

'A bad place to send me, Maisie.'

He made to put out his hand, but Maisie shrugged it off. He reached out to her roughly. Angrily he took her by the shoulders, shook her from side to side. His hands were on her throat.

Without a single thought, acting entirely from instinct, Maisie slid to the floor, feinting like an animal in danger, and lay there quiescent, harmless at his feet.

As Maisie slid through his awkward hands and lay there before his baffled, drunken gaze, he started laughing in a sudden release of feeling, a sense of the ridiculous. What was he doing? he wondered. He wasn't much good at this sort of thing – he'd certainly make a bit of a hash of trying to strangle a woman. It was so funny. He was on all-fours, bent over her, his head down, laughing and laughing, helpless in the grip of his shaking laughter.

Maisie was still. Somewhere there was a deadness. She was coldly afraid of what had happened. She felt abandoned in some deep, deep sense. And at last Michael saw that although he had not really hurt her, she was in some way badly hurt. He knelt at her side, his laughter all gone.

'I'm sorry, Maisie,' he said. 'What have I done? Be all right, please be all right. Are you all right, Fig?'

He lifted her from the floor, and, cold-sober now, carried her to the bed.

Dreamily, Maisie opened and closed her eyes. She had distanced herself from all rational and intellectual thought and was acting directly from instinct. No thoughts went through her head. Her mind was empty.

Her eyes closed, she felt Michael undress her. He pulled both the shoulder-straps of her nightdress down, and kissed her breasts. Then she felt him pull the sheath of her satin nightdress from her, she felt it as a snake might feel its skin sloughed off. She lay there quiet, half-asleep almost, relaxed, and let him do what he wanted without responding, but

153

without struggle. She lay as if curled in the warm sun under a leafy tree, whose heavy fruit was ready to drop to the ground.

But soon his touch began to shiver through her: how strong nature is and how it subdues everything to its will! With stronger and stronger insistence, like the undulating waves of childbirth, her whole body became suffused with feelings that sprang directly from the deep wells of nature, and involuntarily, she cried out.

But underneath, or rather beside her, aloof and somewhat cold, some part of her appeared, seeing all this, and thinking, analysing what had happened, and what might follow from it.

# 6

I RENE was dressed in the fashion for pregnancy – not an attempt to hide it, but rather to show it off. She was wearing a long pink tee-shirt which clung to her ripening, swelling belly, and made the most of it. She wore a string of hand-made beads and no make-up, and her long hair was freshly washed and flowing like a shampoo commercial.

Maisie had previously only glimpsed her. Now Leo introduced them. He did it very nicely. 'I'm so glad you've met each other properly at last. My dear girls.' And he kissed them both.

Maisie was wearing a short black dress she had often worn before, it suited her, showing off dark-stockinged legs and her pretty red shoes tied with ribbons. She had a small bruise on her throat. She and Irene nodded to each other, their smiles managing to miss each other just slightly.

Rose came up and brushed her lips against her mother's cheek. 'Thank you for my present, Mummy.'

'Do you like them?'

'They're lovely – I'm wearing them.' She fingered the earrings – gold star clusters hanging down from her neat, flat, small-lobed ears. She was wearing a sari with a gold border.

'Happy birthday, Rose,' said Michael. He was looking

very handsome in his dark way, serious, older. Somehow very correct. A little withdrawn. He was wondering how long it would be before he was offered a drink. He needed one. He still felt a bit shaky.

'I have to go soon,' Leo was saying, 'and meet Evelyn's train.'

'Oh, shall I go instead?' Maisie put her hand over her glass. 'I haven't had a drop yet, anyway it's mostly tonic.'

'No, I'd like to. Come if you want, Maisie.'

Maisie hesitated, trying to distance herself from Irene's hostile vibrations. 'All right. I'll come with you,' she said.

They went quickly, before anyone could stop them, or join them.

'I've been wanting to talk to you,' said Leo, as they drove off.

'It's really nice to see you,' said Maisie, 'but if you wanted to talk about Rose and Bernard Glantz, I shouldn't worry. I don't think it will last.'

'I very much don't want it to last,' said Leo. 'I am suspicious of that man's motives.'

'Motives?'

'I think he's making use of her.'

'Well – I suppose you could say he is, in a way. Don't we all make use of each other, though, Leo, in one way or another?'

'Stop being oceanic, Maisie, please. I get enough of that. This is Rose we're talking about. We don't want her to make a mess of things.'

'My view is that at this point in her life almost any relationship is better than none.'

'I don't agree. I don't agree at all.'

'No,' said Maisie, 'but you're being selfish.'

'What the devil do you mean?'

'You know how she feels about you, Leo.'

They were waiting at traffic lights and Maisie turned and saw the look on his face, as reflected lights crossed and recrossed his bland, handsome features. His expression was inscrutable, alarmed, smug, confused and watchful all in one. Maisie sighed and dropped the whole thing.

'Ma's got someone with her, I expect you know that.'

'The Hungarian philosopher chap.'

'Yes. Thèk.'

'What's he like?'

'An exceptionally nice man.'

'Oh, that's wonderful. We never get to talk,' said Leo, glancing briefly at her. 'How are things, Maisie? Are you happy?'

'Sometimes. Are you?'

'Sometimes.'

'Irene looks well.'

'She's in fine fettle.'

'Anyway, don't worry about Rose – it's probably on its way out already.'

Leo smiled at her as he parked outside Waterloo Station. The smile was charming, tender. 'Well, let's go and collect these two old things,' he said.

As they made their way into the station, he put his arm round her shoulder. Maisie was wryly, bitterly amused to realize it made her feel safe. Mrs Sharpe and Thèk had seen them and were waving.

'They look so full of life,' said Leo. 'Thèk's face looks familiar.'

'Ma said he was in a television series on philosophy – perhaps that's where you've seen him.'

'Yes, I believe that might have been it,' said Leo. He threw up his arms in actorish ecstasy and hurried towards them, embracing Evelyn Sharpe and then shaking Thèk's hand warmly.

'Oh, this is so lovely,' said Mrs Sharpe, as they packed into the car. 'It's ages since I've been up to town.'

'Shall we stop off at the gin palace and have a quick one before we go back?' said Leo.

'Better not, Rose will think the train crashed or something.' And when they rejoined the party, Rose came up to them and said how long they had been, and Irene gave Leo a rather stony look from eyes that had begun to bulge a little, before she resumed her conversation with Glantz, between sips of orange juice. Glantz was looking earnest but slightly puzzled.

'And this cheers you up?' he was murmuring.

'It gives an experience of wholeness,' said Irene. 'Of spiritual wholeness and a realization of woman's mythic place in the universe.'

'Have you never caught cold doing it?'

'Oh, no, it gets rid of colds.'

'Well, I think you are very brave, in this climate, to go through all of that. Making a shelter of sticks and twigs, heating the stones over a little fire, pouring on water to make steam. Crawling inside and then, oh dear, jumping into the freezing water. Where does all this go on?'

'In our garden,' she said. 'We use the swimming pool.'

'You could go to a sauna.'

Irene looked at him pityingly, and gave a snorting little laugh. 'How do you think you would learn to work with the inner wisdom of the body in a sauna?' she said.

'No, perhaps not,' said Glantz. He hesitated. 'But it would be less trouble, more convenient.'

'Or listen to its subtle messages,' she added. She took a long sip of orange juice.

'Another juice, darling?' asked Leo, taking her glass. He had caught the end of all this.

'She's losing her sense of humour, Bernard,' he said lightly. 'I expect it's hormones, don't you know.'

'How men patronize us,' said Irene. 'What on earth are those marks on your neck, Maisie? Has Michael been trying to throttle you?'

'Oh – yes. He will keep doing it. I think he's really a werewolf.' Maisie touched her neck, and looked at Michael, who was sitting by himself. She went over to him. She longed to touch him, but would not. She spoke lightly. 'Go and be nice to Rose, she's got that look – and it's her birthday. I want her to have a nice party. Go and flirt with her or something.'

'She's having some sort of row with Glantz, I think,' said Michael.

'Yes, I know, go and talk to her.'

'What about?'

'Oh, anything. The Book of Kells. Anything.'

'Put some music on,' said Leo in a loud voice. 'Bring on the dancing girls.'

Rose put on Ella Fitzgerald, and Leo began dancing with her. He was a good dancer, she wasn't.

'I'd rather talk to you about the Book of Kells, anyway,' said Michael. 'Better than that – we'll go and see it.'

'I'd like that,' said Maisie, sounding absent.

'I know you would, I know. I want us to get away. Out of all this – London.'

'To Ireland?' she said, flippant, almost mocking.

'Yes. I've got the staleships.'

'Staleships? What a word!'

'It's what the gipsies get when it's time to move on.'

'Perhaps you want to move on – away from me.'

'No, I want you with me. Always near me.'

'What was last night about?'

'I don't know, Maisie, I'm a bloody fool. It's not you – it's me. I want you to know everything about me.'

'Is there a lot I don't know?'

'Yes – but I want to show you everything – the Irish part, if you like, I want you to know all about me.'

Oh, God, she thought, every look – every gesture – every move he makes. Perhaps they should go to Ireland. She had to give a paper in Dublin some time quite soon; perhaps she could take Michael, though she had intended flying back the same day.

'Do you still love me?' he asked, knowing that she did. 'I wouldn't blame you if you didn't.'

'Love,' she said, 'what is it?'

'It's what we feel for each other,' he said, touching her lightly with one finger on the cheek. 'For better or worse. I'll go and chat up Rose later on, she's happy with Leo.' They watched the two dancing in the middle of the room. Leo caught their glance and steered Rose towards them. He looked at his watch.

'The restaurant's booked for nine-thirty,' he said, 'but it's only round the corner, you know, the Indian place – I hope everyone likes Indian food.'

'You should have a nose jewel,' said Michael, admiring Rose's sari.

'I've always wanted one, but I'm too scared to have my nostril pierced.'

'Put some different music on, something lively, and come and dance with me.'

'I can only do graceful dancing in this.'

'Well, unless you want to take it off, we'll do graceful dancing.'

'I don't want to dance,' said Rose, 'I want to mope about and be a skeleton at my feast.'

'Oh, all right then,' said Michael.

Leo and Maisie were sitting on the settee, and Michael and Rose sat on the floor at their feet. Rose put her head on Leo's knee, and he stroked her hair.

'What did Daddy give you?' asked Maisie.

Rose pointed to a picture on her previously bare wall. It was a nineteenth-century painting of gipsies telling the fortune of two young ladies.

'I wondered where it had come from,' said Maisie. 'It's very charming. It does something for this room. Makes it come alive.'

She went over to look at it more closely. The two young gipsics, a man and a woman, were leaning against the cottage wall. The woman, a baby in her arms, was reading the palm of one of the ladies. The pastoral background and the details of the clothes and flowers were painted with an unpretentious skill and fidelity. The whole thing romantic but not cloying. It wasn't the sort of picture Rose would have chosen for herself, but its giver made it immediately precious to her.

Standing there, hearing the buzz of conversation, and looking at the picture, Maisie remembered that she was pregnant, that her life was veering out of control. Almost simultaneously she experienced one of those flashed moments which happen outside of time. It was just seeing the picture of the gipsies, the bright colours of their clothes, the baby's fingers on its mother's tambourine, and knowing, for sure, that she, Maisie Shergold, was pregnant and wasn't going to do anything to alter that. For a split second her spatial sense shifted, and she was looking down on everyone in the room, frozen in time and was also acutely aware of her mother, in another room, resting on a bed. She became aware, too, that Glantz was watching her, and she moved towards him. He was still half-listening to Irene.

'We are discussing the life force,' he said, as Maisie joined them. It turned out that Irene was talking about the life force and Glantz was talking about how far a neurosis could be said to be genetic.

'The past can sap the life force,' said Maisie.

'You must keep the past in its proper proportion, though we are part of everyone and everything we have ever known,' said Glantz. 'A tangled web. We must spin new living threads.'

'But the old threads,' said Michael, joining them with a fresh drink in his hand, 'will always be there. You cannot just cut out the past – like surgery. Things that happen become like imprints on the soul. We are our past as much as our present.'

Glantz smiled. 'I think I would have great difficulty with you, Michael. You are a Celt, they never let go of their past.'

'No,' said Michael, 'no matter how much we try to run, it's there. Have you never had fears that your work might affect you, drive you mad, in fact? Draw you into the maelstrom?'

'It is a danger,' said Glantz. 'I always keep a careful eye on that. I keep an eye on myself, though Freud said a degree of neurosis is of great value as a drive, especially to a psychologist.'

Michael felt warm to him, and sorry for him. 'Let me get you a drink,' he said. 'You've been clutching an empty glass too long.' He brought him a drink and, even more helpfully, introduced him properly to Imre Thèk.

The two men fell on each other and were soon deep in talk, finding their minds akin, Europeans bred in the bone. Usually they had to contend with the uniquely detached English mind, but in each other they had met another who understood the meaning of politics, the possibility of anarchy and revolution, death and the end of civilization.

Irene still sat there, between them, with her orange juice, looking like a ripe juicy fruit herself, a manifestation of the life force.

Then Leo was calling out like a schoolmaster, 'Those who want to drive there come with me, those who want to walk, go with Maisie, and someone go and see if Evelyn is ready.'

He managed to herd everyone to the 'End of Empire' in time. A table for eight was laid for them. The atmosphere was serene and ordered, colourful and sensual. White napkins folded into water-lilies, naïve exuberant peacocks, dancers, warriors and lotus flowers enlivened the walls, over all poured a seductive, restful pink light from the table lamps. The waiters were grave and silently, soothingly attentive, without excessive fuss. There was a wonderful delicate aroma of Eastern spices.

Rose, in her sari, sat between Leo and her grandmother.

They settled down, Glantz dropping his menu on the floor; Indian music flowed like a fountain, plashing the air gently, quietly, just enough.

Maisie looked round the table at the faces, at these people all entwined in her life. Leo and Rose, their heads together over the menu. Irene, flirting with Michael over the chapattis, Michael looking withdrawn, unattainable. Glantz trying not to look so often at Rose in her beautiful green and gold sari, her earrings catching the lamplight. Her mother and Imre Thèk enjoying their day in London.

Later they sang 'Happy Birthday' to Rose, who scowled at them all and told them to shut up, the waiters looking on grinning, showing a gold tooth here and there.

And then they lingered over almondy Indian ice cream and many coffees before they all found their way back to the house in twos and threes. Maisie walked back with Michael and Glantz.

'I must go soon,' said Glantz, 'I am going back to my own flat tonight. Rose needs the room.' He was very glum, and Maisie felt sorry for him, and she and Michael tried to cheer him up. Rose was a silly, immature girl, they said, he could do much better. It was supposed to be a temporary arrangement, leaving the swan room, said Glantz, but he knew really it was more than that, a chance to get rid of him, make a break.

When they got back Glantz went round everyone saying his farewells as if they were last goodbyes. He left Rose until last, but Leo cut it short by offering him a lift to his flat.

When they had gone, Rose, to everyone's relief, began to cheer up at last. She liked having her grandmother there, and she was going to share a bed with her. Thèk was in the swan room.

The party was breaking up. Irene had gone with Leo, Michael and Maisie said goodnight, and Rose, happy now, made some lapsang tea and took it to bed.

'How do you stay so all right, Grandma, so happy?'

'I don't stay happy. I have good days and bad days, like everyone.'

'No, basically you're happy.'

'Well, I suppose I've accepted the fact that life is a gift-horse, and you don't look it in the mouth.'

'I've broken off with Bernard.'

'That's good, dear, you'll find someone more suitable one of these days.'

'Bernard was very intelligent, Grandma.'

'Yes, I know, Rose, but he was a bit stale, wasn't he?'

'What do you mean? Mouldy?' Rose began to laugh, with a nice little feeling of relief.

'Yes, a bit mouldy, quite an interesting mould on him, I expect, but you don't want that sort of thing, not at twenty years old. Goodnight, dear.'

Imre Thèk lay in bed, looking at the stained-glass swan, and thought, as he did every night of his life now, of the nights he had spent in his cell, the iron sound of the slammed door, the stain on the ceiling which was his only mental stimulus, apart from his own thoughts and memories and fears. He switched on the bedside radio, and found a late-night concert. He wished Evelyn would come to say good-night, and was glad when she did.

Michael and Maisie got ready for bed, and talked about what they were going to do. 'The most sensible thing,' said Michael, 'is to follow our hearts. That is the only guide – the other things are false guides.' He touched the smudgy bruise on Maisie's neck. 'It'll be gone soon.'

'I don't know what to do,' said Maisie.

'I'll tell you what to do,' said Michael. 'You must do what I say. Come to Ireland.'

'But I'm not the sort of person who can go about just letting life wash over me, just bumping into things.'

'Now you're with me,' said Michael, 'you have to be like that.'

'Why?' The idea of not being autonomous was startling, and strangely seductive.

'Because I'm like that. Give yourself up to me, let me lead you.'

'Lead me where?'

'Oh, just round and about and up and down in this world. First to Ireland.'

'My work. What about that for a start?'

'Leave it, girl.'

And so, in her heart, she changed. She said goodbye to everything without regret. It was easy.

She slept in Michael's arms, her mind settled and made up to leave her life behind and go with him to Ireland and up and down the world and see where he led her.

# PART FOUR

*Ireland and London*

# I

IRELAND had been waiting, quietly, to change Maisie. Michael had led her to a different country, a foreign place, somewhere where things were not as she had expected and, in their newness, startled and surprised her. But in all this, part of Maisie was left behind. And, in all this, the balance of power between her and Michael had shifted. It had shifted to Michael.

Even while they were crossing over, waves and wind howling and hungering round the boat, it had started then. Maisie had not realized until now to what extent she had, in fact, held that balance of power. But now, among his own people – even on the boat he met those who knew him, called out to him, calling him Mick, and a group on deck playing the spoons drew him into their circle. He was going home. She was setting out in an unknown country. She was his girlfriend, his woman.

And with the rough weather, and the early stages of pregnancy, she was feeling slightly queasy. She said nothing at first and tried to ignore it, but later had to go and lie down in the cabin, covered over with her big travelling-coat. She lay there with closed eyes and wondered who this Irishman, this Mick Curran, was to her. And how it was she had become Mick Curran's woman. He no longer dressed with the slightly eccentric dash he had assumed in London. Now he wore his native clothes, a becomingly rough old coat, loose sweaters and soft corduroy. He was going back home.

The crossing over, they spent their first night in a large, turn-of-the-century hotel. It had once been a fine establishment, but now it was run down, its tennis courts and exotic gardens all grown over into a tangled mess of vegetation, strangled in briars. The food was good, only Maisie still felt a slight nausea which would not quite leave her. Michael ate steak and drank whisky. He said he was going to hire a car and show her a bit of the country. She could see he secretly thought Ireland was something special, his treasure.

And so they drove about his place, his country, mile after mile, and sat by streams and lakes, walked by the sea on firm hard sand, wandered over springy hills of short tufted grass. They ate in little cafés and in castle dining-rooms and drank in dozens of pubs. In these pubs they listened to endless talk – talk about the Irish government, the English government, the drug-smuggling that was said to go on in the coves round the coast, talk about life and death and have you heard this one, now listen, then. Sometimes the old men played on fiddles, listening as they played, carried into some other region, lost in it, their faces concentrated, a gap-toothed grin of self-forgetful joy. Maisie would watch her lover as he sat in these dim little pubs, a jar of Guinness in front of him, his dark head against the wooden settle. At home in his native land. At night they put up all over the place, in cottages, pubs and hotels. Once or twice they stayed with people Michael knew. They never stayed more than one night anywhere.

Gradually Maisie's sickness left her. She noticed that her breasts were getting heavier, but that was the only outward sign. She reckoned the child had been conceived the day of the visit to the catacombs.

The shift in the balance of power had made them hunger more for each other sexually, made them new to each other.

But they spoke less intimately to one another, their verbal intercourse became less probing, more concerned mostly with day-to-day things.

Although they spoke less to each other, they were unusually inseparable, touching each other often, living side by side through the days and nights. Physically, sexually, they were at the height of their passion for each other. Mentally there was not so much a rift as a lull, as if they had got to know as much as they wanted of each other. There was no more questioning, they rested in what they knew, knowing there was a divide between them. Unbridgeable. This fed their sexual craving – as if sex might take them across this divide. But it never did.

One morning, they made love out of doors. It was late March now and the sun had some warmth in it, though the air was cold. The night before they had stayed with one of Michael's musician friends and his girlfriend and had shared a bedroom with the couple's six-year-old child – it had precluded even the most furtive love-making.

So in the morning they stopped near a copse of beech trees, growing in a scooped-out valley. Here they found a soft place to lie in the moss and last year's leaves. Michael folded his coat under Maisie's head, and they made love there without undressing, finding their way to the warm flesh through layers of clothes.

Afterwards Michael lay for a while, heavily on her. She did not mind. She lay still, with the man's heavy weight on her. The hollow where she lay cradled her body, and she thought when she died how she would like to be buried in this place. Unvisited, unmourned. Birth and death clung together like two halves belonging to each other, part of each other, one thing. She felt Michael's heartbeat which throbbed from the very centre of the earth, and the sap of the trees and every living thing ran in her veins. They made their way back to the car, leaving the copse to busy crows building their ramshackle nests in the top branches.

Wherever they went Maisie's eyes drank in new sights. Unexpected things gave her a deep pleasure – there were more animals and birds; for the first time in her life she saw kingfishers, and otters. Used to surroundings teeming with the human species, it was healing to know a more balanced world.

The people they met seemed classless.

One day they met a young woman walking in the middle of nowhere. She was carrying a baby in a sling made of her jacket. It was such an unusual sight – to see this woman, so far from any village or town, she seemed so independent, unafraid. She spoke to them briefly, politely, saying there was a wind getting up. Maisie caught a glimpse of the baby's curled-up fist.

They also met, from time to time, couples and bands of people who were dressed in an exotic but practical way, in flowered skirts and cotton and leather cummerbunds and feathered hats; these people were usually accompanied by wild-looking lurcher dogs. They spoke with accents from Bristol and London – they were English hippies.

Sometimes they drove through villages of the utmost melancholy and desolation – a huddle of ill-built houses, made of slabs of concrete. A garage, a pub. The only sign of life the graffiti.

One evening, just as it was getting dark, they picked up a little family on the road. The man was young, very correct and stable-looking, the woman slight and pretty; they were carrying what looked like all their worldly goods, slung about them. Their little girl was carrying a cat in a cage. They were moving house, they said calmly, inconsequentially. They spoke Gaelic to each other. This family was dressed in layers of clothes, perhaps wearing as many as they could to lighten their burdens. They wanted to be dropped at a crossroads. Here there were no houses in sight, or anything else, but they seemed sure about what they were doing.

They also saw the same tinker several times in different places. Always, when they saw him, he was reading a book, sitting peacefully by the roadside, his horse tied up nearby. Maisie wanted to know what he was reading.

She did not know where they were going – just let Michael lead her where he liked. She did not know, half the time, whether they were north, south, east or west.

Then one day they pulled up outside a farm, a farm like many others they had seen. Michael sat silent for a while. Then he said, 'Well, Maisie. Let's go in.'

He opened the car door for her, and she followed him through the cross-bar gate, which he closed behind them, across a path of planks laid on the mud, into a farmyard. Two sheepdogs rushed out barking, scattering hens, then quietening suddenly.

They passed a milking shed where a man was working. Scarcely looking their way, he answered Michael's greeting. There were three cars in the yard, one partly dismantled.

The farmhouse door stood open, muddy sacking on the doorstep. Several cats crouched about on the window-sills. A pile of mud-caked wellingtons was heaped just inside the door.

It was dark inside and smelled of bread baking. After a while, Maisie made out a room that seemed entirely comfortless except for one easy-chair by the stove. There were piles of newspapers in the corner, a stuffed horsehair sofa which was broken, a flitch of bacon hung up among the cobwebs, a flagged stone floor, a television set. There was a glass-fronted bookcase full of books. On the walls there was a calendar from the *Irish Farmer and Stockbreeder* and a picture of the Pope before last.

In the darkest corner of all, a small boy was playing with a basket of kittens. He had a rabbit's paw on a string and was teasing them with it.

'Hallo, Mick,' said the child.

173

'Hallo, Declan,' said Michael. 'Where's your grandmother?'

'She's not here,' said the little boy, 'perhaps she's in the field. I've called this kitten Mouse.'

Michael went over to the boy, who let him pick him up without a struggle, but without much collaboration.

'That's a funny name for a cat,' said Michael.

'It's a kitten.'

'It's a nice name for a kitten,' said Michael.

'Who's that lady?' asked the boy, not looking at Maisie.

'This is my lady – she's got a funny name too. She's called Fig.' He put the boy down.

'I'll call the tabby one that,' said the little boy, picking up another kitten. He shot Maisie a small quick smile, full of humour.

Maisie smiled back and followed Michael through to the kitchen. The mother cat jumped off the table where it had been helping itself to the newly baked soda bread laid out to cool on racks.

'Wait here,' said Michael, 'I'll go over to the field and find her.'

Maisie waited. She looked around the kitchen. A pot of something was cooking on the stained Aga. More piles of newspapers in the corner. A stack of washing-up waited to be done in the sink and overflowed on to the floor. The long trestle-table was laid with a crumpled white cloth, clean apart from the cat's muddy paw-marks, and good cutlery. A bowl of primroses was set in the middle of the table beside the bread. Then she watched Michael from the window. He had put on wellingtons and was walking across the field; she watched as he walked away from her, his shoulders moving slightly as he walked, in that way he had.

Then she noticed a woman bending, cutting cabbage. The woman stood up and Maisie saw her give Michael what she had cut and stoop for more.

After a while Michael and his mother began walking

back to the house, stopping now and then to talk. As she came nearer, Maisie saw that the mother was tall, as tall as her son, and had thick, iron-grey hair. Even at this distance the tense, almost angry manner was apparent in her walk and her demeanour.

She seemed neither pleased nor displeased to see Maisie, but perhaps to regard her as another pair of hands. 'Will you do the potatoes?' she asked by way of a greeting. Michael she seemed to regard in something of the same light – someone come to help with the continuous work of the farm and the house.

'You'll be needed to finish the milking,' she told him. 'The tractor's broken down since yesterday, and your brother has his work cut out what with that and everything else. There's never anything but work,' she told Maisie with grim, bitter, satisfied anger in her voice.

Her anger was there too in the way she clattered the plates as she washed them, handing them steaming-hot to Maisie to dry – there was nowhere to put them down. The two women worked, clearing the pile of dirty dishes, scrubbing the potatoes clean, preparing the cabbage. When the food was ready, Mrs Curran thumped the browned potato pie on the table.

'Go and ring the bell, Missus,' she said to Maisie. 'It's by the door.'

Maisie found the rusty old school bell under a bush by the door.

They sat round the table, Michael, his younger brother Liam, a heavy, full-lipped, ruddy-faced man who looked nothing at all like Michael (Maisie had not even known of the brother's existence until now), Liam's wife Annie (a thin wispish, beautiful woman, flat-chested in a flowered pina-fore) and their son, Declan – and Mrs Curran.

Maisie realized that not only was she now Michael's woman, she was part of a tribe; through Michael, she was being drawn into this matriarchal tribe as a camp-follower.

With each mouthful she became more and more uneasy, even slightly panicky. She wanted to get out of this place.

The seat of power was Mrs Curran. Everything emanated from her, she worked ceaselessly. Even when she sat after the meal, in her chair for a while, she knew what was going on in every part of the farm and would not give the reins over to anyone else for a moment. And she knew exactly what she was doing, she thought everything out, through to the bitter end.

Maisie thought that as soon as possible she and Michael would leave the farm.

But that night, tired out, they slept well on the makeshift bed he had made them on the parlour floor surrounded by silver-framed photographs of a proud, handsome woman carrying a drooping bouquet of lilies, and a man so very like Michael in looks. The mattress was rammed between a roll-top desk spilling bills for cattle-feed, and a piano.

When Maisie woke next day, Michael was already up working outside. There was a knock on the door. It was a young woman with bright tawny hair tied back from a freckled face, and a full figure, voluptuous, supple and strong.

'I've brought you a cup of tea,' she said.

'Oh – thanks. I'm Maisie.'

'Oh, yes, I know,' said the girl. 'I'm Kate. Is there anything else you'll want now? I could make you a bit of toast. Breakfast's gone.'

Nobody had said anything to her, but Maisie's intuition was so sharp where Michael was concerned that she knew without being told that the girl and Michael had a sexual link. She thought, 'I must be imagining this – it can't be so – and yet it is.'

'Thank you. I'm not hungry,' she said. 'I'll get up now.'

'Oh, don't hurry yourself,' said Kate, 'you rest there.'

'Are you Michael's sister?' she asked desperately, clinging to straws, knowing the answer. She was pale with fear, and the cup and saucer trembled in her hand.

The girl smiled and shook her head. 'There's no sister,' she said as she went.

Maisie got up and dressed with quick, shaky hands, at the mercy of her instincts and passions. All her old life might as well have belonged to someone else. Here was Michael's woman, pregnant, jealous, trapped like some poor bloody animal.

'Will you hang the washing, Missus?' said Mrs Curran, in the kitchen. Christ, thought Maisie, if she goes on calling me Missus I'll kill her.

She would ask Michael about Kate that night, when they were in bed – the only time they were alone together. But for several nights she could not bring herself to ask, afraid of the answer, though she hedged round the subject.

'I've known her all my life,' said Michael. 'She's part of things here.'

'Part of you?'

'I suppose you could say that.'

Further than that Maisie would not press him, she knew she might not be able to bear the truth. And she even fancied his love-making was more casual. And yet surely if Michael was anything to this woman, she would not have treated Maisie herself with such equanimity. She wondered too how the family regarded her relationship. They seemed remarkably cool about it.

'Does it matter that we share a bed?' she asked.

'No. It doesn't matter a damn.'

She must pull herself together. It all came from giving over her power to Michael, giving up her autonomy. She was in his power.

'Why doesn't it matter? Is it because sons may do as they like – bring home any loose woman they please?'

She had no way of knowing what anyone here thought

of her, and her relationship with Michael. No one said anything. Somehow it made things more dangerous. Michael's mother, Maisie realized, frightened her. There was an unnerving silence behind her brief words, behind her actions. Michael had said his mother had a sense of humour, and Maisie had looked for it in the deeply lined face in vain. Perhaps it had left her one day – perhaps after days of rain had turned the fields to mud and the tractor had broken down again. And she had then changed into a witch.

Maisie turned away on to her side and raised herself up on one elbow. Michael reached out and pulled her roughly, gently, towards him, pushing her under him.

'That's it,' he said. 'Anyone can see you're a loose woman.'

Covering her body with his, he entered her without preamble. They came together then, easily, quickly, their bodies mated, knowing what to do; part of the earth's weal. Afterwards he fell asleep on top of her and she had to heave him off.

Anyway, there was a sort of joy in it, this brief, blunt kind of mating. But if the mated feeling enriched and satisfied some part of her, she knew she was in danger of losing something else, perhaps had already lost it – a kind of integrity, a singleness and uniqueness. She felt it seeping away from her, seeping out on to the floor of the hovel where she lay next to this man already deep in a heavy sleep.

Although partly this was to do with living under the tribal roof. On this bloody farm, she thought. Sleepless, she decided she would begin once more to reclaim some of what she had lost. She would take things into her own hands. She would find them somewhere to live where they could be alone. She would look for a cottage to rent.

For she wanted to stay in Ireland. The country itself refreshed and strengthened her like sweet, pure water. She imagined her child born here, brought up in the soft air and open vistas, and the rough, true, classless way of things here, the fields ploughed and open into furrows under the sky.

# 2

T HE first night in the cottage that Maisie found for them, the fire smoked and a gale rattled at the windows. There was no electricity, and the oil lamp they took up to the draughty bedroom smoked too.

'Put the bloody thing out,' said Michael.

In darkness so absolute, it made the sense of sight quite useless, they lay naked against each other. The bed was old and had a dip in the middle, where they lay together.

'Are your eyes open?' she asked Michael.

'No, are yours?'

'Yes, but I can only see blackness.'

'Don't try to see. Forget about seeing. Feel. Feel my hand.' His hand, roughened with work now, roamed about her soft body.

'There's not a glimmer of light anywhere,' she said. 'We're in total darkness.'

'Yes, it's wonderful. Don't mind it.' He was stroking her gently, firmly. Her heart was beating heavily, she did not know if she minded the dark, or if she was afraid of it; if she was afraid, there was nothing to do about it.

'I want you to like this darkness,' he said. 'Give yourself up to it, give yourself up to me.'

He shifted her carefully on top of him, facing upwards –

there was hardly room in the dip of the bed for them to lie comfortably side by side. With one hand he held her pinioned to him, with the other he caressed her.

Deprived of sight, the other senses reared up in the dark. She heard the sound of the gale rocking the house; her lover's breath; her own breath. And she breathed in the smell of his flesh, his hair; her own flesh, warm, sweet, moist; the slightly musty bedroom unused all winter; the rough, clean linen. The taste of each other, like apples. And touch.

She lay helplessly cradled into his body, held there by his arm, she could not have moved if she had wanted to. She cried out, in the dark little house, rocked by the wind, herself rocked in the man's arms, she cried out that love had veered at the last moment away from its object, how it had been scattered at the last, the very last moment, to the winds. How wishing to bring her lover closer had only parted them.

After they had made love, they stayed in that position, she lying on him, and talked softly.

'You're glad to be away from the farm,' he said.

'Yes,' said Maisie, 'I want you to myself.'

He said nothing for a while, but lay stroking her belly.

'I shall have to see a doctor, I suppose,' she said, 'before long.'

'You're not worried. No hurry is there?' said Michael.

'Well, no – but I'm getting a bit, well, in medical terms I am an "aged primate".'

'That sounds terrible.'

Maisie laughed quietly. 'What shall we do tomorrow?' she asked.

'I must go over to the farm in the day.'

'Oh, why?'

'They need another hand there. The tractor's still broken. It'll take a while to mend it. It holds the work up, everything takes longer. I'll use the farm car, if I can keep it going.'

Maisie was silent.

'Will you be all right here?'

'Yes, I suppose I will. I'll get some work done – the Dublin paper needs a conclusion.'

'What's it about?'

'The treatment of scours in cattle.'

He gave her thigh a painful little pinch. 'What's it about?'

'The golden age of the medieval ikon,' she said, rubbing the place. 'I'll have to rewrite it so that I can read it – and write a conclusion. I'll do it while you are stirring the silage or whatever you do.'

'A farm is a lot of hard work. Unremitting. Sometimes I feel guilty to have escaped.'

'What made you leave?'

'One of us had to go – Liam or me. We couldn't both come into the farm, and split, it would be nothing. Anyway, I was restless and only interested in music. There was an idea afoot that I should go in for the priesthood – I was a bit of a favourite with the priests at school, I'll never know why – and I fled from the prospect. I've done what I wanted and left my mother to the same old grinding work. When I do come home I have to help.'

'You're like the prodigal son – in reverse.'

'Well, I didn't notice any fatted calf.'

'You're the one who has prospered,' said Maisie. 'Your mother is – quite formidable. She affects them all, all of you, you are all marked by her. I would have been if I had stayed.'

'I'm glad you didn't get drawn in.'

'Is Kate drawn in?'

'Inextricably.'

'She's not one of the family?'

'As near as dammit.'

'I think she loves you.'

After a while Michael said, 'Don't worry about her.' He slipped her off his body and tucked her in beside him and went to sleep.

How love spoils everything in life, all other pleasures,

thought Maisie. A curse. A sickness. And how jealousy spoils love itself.

Next morning she woke up nearly falling out of bed. The wind had gone and sun shone on the window-sill.

It was nearly midday before Michael could start the car, he had practically to take it apart and put it together again. Maisie hoped he would not be able to start it, but at last she heard the engine running smoothly and Michael, his face smeared in oil, was off to the Currans' farm.

When he had gone Maisie felt emptied. The pain of being separated from him made time on her own, instead of being rich and significant as in her past life, a time of barren waiting for his return.

She got out her papers and shuffled them about, staring without comprehension at footnotes she had made. She made herself a cup of coffee and ate a biscuit, then, thinking she should eat more sensibly, took a piece of cheese and an apple. She sat on the doorstep in the sun. She ate her apple, noticing how the overgrown garden was sprinkled with celandines. After a while she looked round for sticks to light the fire; perhaps it would burn better today. She found a stiff brush and swept the bits of carpet. She made the bed and opened the bedroom window. Then she started making a thick broth with vegetables and barley. Peasant food. Tomorrow she would have to go to the village for supplies. She put the iron pot of broth in the oven beside the fire and hoped it would cook there.

Then she got on with her writing.

Michael came in just before dark, she heard his car coming down the lane. She saw as he passed by the window that he looked tired, in need of a wash, like any man at the end of the day, and she loved him more for the ordinariness. He came through the door. He kissed her.

'What have you been doing?'

'Making broth for my beloved,' she said. 'And you?'

'Tinkering with the tractor, washing out cowsheds. Oh, good. The fire's not smoking.'

They sat down and ate their meal, and afterwards Maisie washed up and tidied the little kitchen.

'Could you live like this always?' Michael asked her.

'I might like it.'

'You'd soon miss the libraries, theatres.'

'Well, Dublin's not far away. How is your mother?'

'As ever.'

'Annie and Declan?'

'Oh, Declan sent you this.' He searched in his pocket and found a scrap of paper with a drawing of something that could be anything. 'What is it supposed to be?' asked Maisie, smiling.

'It's you,' said Michael, putting on his glasses. 'He's fallen in love with you. Look, those are your eyes, I hadn't noticed before that one is bigger than the other, let me look.'

He turned Maisie's face to him and stared at her critically. 'Yes, I believe he's right.'

Maisie laughed and put the picture in with her Dublin notes. 'And Kate?' she asked, watching his face.

'She wasn't there today.'

'Where is she?'

'I don't know. Probably her grandmother is ill – she lives with her grandmother, who is ninety years old and losing her marbles.'

'It's a wonder Kate isn't married, such a pretty girl, and strong-looking, just right for a farmer's wife, I should have thought.'

'She won't marry until her grandmother dies,' said Michael.

'Oh,' said Maisie, 'would you like some pudding? I forgot – I made a bread-and-butter pudding.' She took it out of the oven, it smelled of oranges and nutmeg.

'It looks delicious,' said Michael. 'I love puddings.'

'We're getting short of food,' she said. 'I'll have to go to the shop tomorrow.'

The next day Michael dropped her off at the village on his way to the farm. She intended walking back, a matter of three miles or so, it would help to pass the day.

Mrs Maloney in the general shop was friendly and inquisitive. 'You're in Murphy's old cottage,' she said, 'that's nice. The cauliflower are the best buy and there's some lovely apples.'

Maisie bought more than she meant to. 'You'll not be carrying it all back yourself,' said the woman. 'Oh, no, not at all. I'll not hear of it, Maloney'll bring it for you in time for lunch.'

So Maisie enjoyed her walk back unencumbered, stopping to pick a few early primroses on the way. However, the groceries did not turn up until just before Michael came home, and he had to wait for his cauliflower cheese.

And so the days passed. Maisie borrowed a bicycle from Mrs Maloney and began cycling to and from the village. She felt very well physically; her mind began to slow down.

One afternoon Michael drove out unexpectedly from the farm. He had brought Declan with him and they had tea and made smoky toast over the fire.

'Come back to the farm with us now,' said Michael, 'I have to take Declan home.'

'I'll stay and keep the fire going,' said Maisie. When he came back, they sat by the fire and talked.

'Will you come to Dublin with me?' she asked, sure that he would.

'Oh, I want to, I want to show you Dublin, all my haunts.'

'The Book of Kells.'

'But I must stay – there's so much work – I can't leave yet.'

'I hadn't thought of going without you.'

'You'll soon be back. Only one night away. I'll finish off

in the top field. I will soon have served my sentence and be free again.'

'You have so much guilt about the farm. It's your mother – she's a guilt-inducer.'

'She's had a hard life, my father was a weak man.'

'What happened to him?'

'He went to England and we lost touch with him. He started to come home less and less, until he didn't come at all. We sort of forgot about him. He's probably living in London somewhere – if he's still alive.'

'You look like him – in the photograph.'

He started raking out the hot embers of the fire, making it safe for the night. 'Let's go to bed,' he said, 'I'm going to miss you tomorrow night. I hope the car gets you there all right, I've done my best with it.'

'At least you'll have a comfortable night without me,' said Maisie as they both rolled into the dip in the bed.

'Oh, I'll probably stay on the farm and work late, it's easier and means I haven't commandeered all the farm cars. You can ring me at the farm. Now let's stop talking.'

Next day Maisie drove the rackety car to the farm and dropped Michael off there. 'Be careful,' he said, 'the clutch is still slipping a bit.' She kissed him and did not watch as he went through the gate. She reversed into an opening in the hedge and set off down the lane towards the main road to Dublin.

Once she had said goodbye to her lover, she started in a determined way to recall her lost self. She would have enjoyed the drive if she had been in a better car – she several times heard alarming noises from it and expected it to fall to bits – but it got her there.

She parked it in the college car park, which she found by means of a little map the university had sent her. Among the other cars it looked muddy, disreputable, an interloper. Still, she gave it a little pat.

The first person she saw when she walked into the

college was Philomena O'Grady, who came towards her as if expecting her, as if she had been waiting for her. 'I came especially,' she said, 'when I saw your name on the programme.'

They had lunch together in the students' canteen. 'Now I've caught up with you, you'll not escape,' sad Philomena. They had spent the afternoon wandering about Dublin, with Maisie wishing it were Michael who was with her. It was a Michael sort of place – elegant and casual, human and fallible. Music spilled from every pub door, there were buskers and beggars in every doorway. They walked down Grafton Street looking at the clothes, window-shopping.

After Maisie had given her paper, Philomena said, 'You must stay with me.'

'I have a room in the college,' said Maisie. But Philomena had a ruthlessness that Maisie felt too tired to stand against.

'Tomorrow.we shall see more of Dublin,' she said. 'It would be stupid to go back without seeing the sights of this fine city.'

Really, she was right.

Maisie telephoned the farm, but, unable to get hold of Michael, left a message that she would be home at the weekend. Later that night, Philomena began to reveal her past and probe Maisie about hers. The Irishwoman was taking combs out of her hair, loosening it from its chignon. 'When I saw you at the conference,' she said, 'I wondered what you were doing with the likes of a Michael Curran. Brandy?'

'No. No, thanks. I thought you got on rather well together there, at the luncheon.'

'Well, we understand each other – fellow-countrymen. We recognize the cut of each other's jib, you might say. We came out of the same nesting box. Do you like my metaphors?'

Maisie said nothing, absent-mindedly accepting a brandy. She was trying to distance herself from Philomena's words, trying not to listen too closely, as the Irishwoman went on, 'I can understand what he sees in you. Not what you see in him, though. He is not what you think. He is a bird of a different feather. He is storm-tossed – his boat has a ragged sail.'

Maisie was beginning to feel angry at Philomena's persistent probing. She left the brandy undrunk and said she was very tired and would like to go to bed.

'Don't you know by now,' said Philomena, 'that men do not want love? Do not know what to do with it. They prefer their toys, their subterfuges, their mothers, their tarts, anything, anything.'

'I don't know that,' said Maisie quietly. 'Where am I sleeping?' She gathered up her things and Philomena showed her to a plain little attic room.

'Sleep well, Maisie,' she said, and closed the door behind her.

Tired-out as she was, Maisie lay awake, heavy-limbed in the narrow bed. The little attic room seemed to be like a ship's cabin, adrift, the black sky above her and the sound of a gale getting up.

She placed her hands over her belly. Her baby, growing there in its own dark world. She stroked her belly gently, as if soothing the baby to sleep, and fell asleep herself.

She woke next morning to Philomena standing by the bed with a cup of tea. 'It's raining,' she was saying, 'but it will be clear by lunchtime. Breakfast is nearly ready.'

She had made a wonderful breakfast of bacon and eggs, toast and honey. They sat opposite each other; between them was a bowl of fruit, dull, smoky-red apples and a bunch of dark grapes. Philomena poured coffee.

'We'll do the galleries and museums,' she said, 'and we'll have a pub lunch.'

All morning, she never stopped talking wittily, quite brilliantly. But Maisie was quiet, as she followed Philomena up and down museum steps, in and out of great doors, stood with her in front of ornately framed pictures; sat with her and tried to decipher the handwritten menu in a pub, where a beautiful greyhound sat delicately shivering by the empty stone fireplace.

Someone Philomena knew joined them briefly in the pub and was introduced: 'Annie Dillon, Celtic Studies' – a white-faced young woman dressed like an Edwardian widow in black weeds. Maisie took the girl's thin white hand which was smudged with black – perhaps newsprint – and the fingers heavy with many rings. Everyone was talking and swearing and calling out the names of friends. There was a smell of fish and malt and wood – and Philomena's soft, velvety perfume.

'I'll have just bread and cheese,' said Maisie. 'I'm not really hungry.'

'I can't eat all that,' she protested when it came, a half loaf of home-made bread and a huge wedge of cheese. She offered some to Annie, who put a piece of the cheese into her black beaded bag for her supper.

'She only pretends to eat,' said Philomena, when she had gone. 'She's anorexic, poor girl.'

When they left the pub at last, it had stopped raining and the sun had come out. There was more to see. A room full of Irish gold treasures. The Book of Kells. It was while they were looking at the opened Book of Kells, that suddenly Maisie could bear it no longer. 'I'm going back,' she said.

Then again she said fiercely, 'I'm going back.'

Philomena knew there was no point this time trying to keep her. She shrugged and walked off, as if she had been jilted.

With a sense of release, Maisie made her way from the university to the car, abandoning things she had left at Philomena's house, including her notes and a book that she was attached to. In a very short time now she would be back with him. She would see him again, touch his arm, hear his voice.

As she was driving out of Dublin the sky was glorified by a sunset such as she had never seen. The heart of the sunset was molten-gold, a bright, streaming, living gold that brought to Maisie's mind the gold room in the museum with its treasures of gold cups, reliquaries, croziers, vases and necklaces, but it was the gold of a thousand million such treasures melted down and flung against the sky, and even then its glorious brightness could only have been spilled from the sun, the most powerful source of brilliant light in the universe. The clouds were tinged with all shades of yellow, ochre to citrus, and then to green and to a deep purple, and the outer clouds were dark purple and even darker, nearly black – night's harbingers.

Maisie parked the car and wound down the window, making the colours leap more brightly in the air. It was such a sight as should have made the people come out of their houses to see. If it had been a display put on by the city council, perhaps they would have done so.

She wondered if Michael was watching it. She wanted to keep it to show to Michael. Look, Michael, at this beautiful sunset I have found for you. But you couldn't do that, take these things to give to your loved person, they weren't even yours, they could not be had. They spoke not of having, but of not having. Rather, they spoke of relinquishing. And as she watched, imperceptibly the dark shades of night, the purple and grey increased as the gold gradually lessened, giving itself up to oncoming night in a slow renunciation. Maisie wound up the window and sped on her journey. She was so glad to leave Dublin which did not hold her lover, and travel out into the hills which did.

On the way back the fan belt went and she was held up trying to find a garage to fix it. At last she drove up the lane to the little white, low-lying house nestling in the rain. There was thin smoke coming from the chimney and the other farm car was parked outside. He was at home. Maisie felt a quick rush of joy at the thought of seeing him, without having to wait.

She went in.

He looked awful. He was crying and kept saying, 'Oh, Maisie. Oh, Fig.'

At first Maisie thought he was ill. And then it dawned on her, with a great sickening flood of feeling, that there was someone upstairs and at once she knew it was Kate.

She took this information in without being told. She knew it, but fed it to herself as little by little as she could to protect herself from shock, but still she felt as if she had been hit by something heavy, as if a car had knocked her over. She did not know what to say, words had become redundant.

Then Kate came downstairs, her blouse unbuttoned and done up hastily with a brooch, her skirt twisted, her feet bare. She looked calm, though, as if nothing was amiss. She'll offer me a cup of tea in a minute, thought Maisie. And that is what she did.

Maisie stared at her and then at Michael, and then she gathered up her books and one or two things – anything that was upstairs she left, she would not go up there. Michael stood like a man just woken from a dream.

She threw the things in the back of the car and without looking back she drove away.

# 3

S HE did not remember how she got back to the house in London. One or two things stood out in her mind: she remembered leaving the car in some back street, where there was a crowd of children playing, because the car park was full. By now the children had probably vandalized it, which did not matter one way or the other. She remembered sitting in a café for a long time, or maybe it was not a long time, where there was one of those noisy, hissing coffee-machines. Somewhere she had glimpsed, in a busy shopping street as she passed by, a beautiful hippie couple sitting on the pavement with their dog. The couple were kissing each other with spontaneous, graceful movements, oblivious of passers-by. The girl had long hair like a Rossetti painting.

Then she had a flashed picture of Philomena in a blue nightshirt, standing in the bedroom doorway, and she sup-posed she must have stayed the night there. That was about all. She did not recall a journey, except being in a taxi. She had been in one place, and now she was in another.

She did not remember coming into the house, picking up the mail, climbing the stairs of the silent house. She was scarcely aware of taking off her coat, putting on the kettle.

Perhaps it was the jet of steam filling the kitchen that clicked her mind into the present, and the wave of physical nausea that helped to drag her into her real situation and surroundings. After she had vomited into the bathroom basin, emptied herself as it were, she began to be aware of herself as sentient – and the real pain started. She washed her face and made herself a cup of instant coffee, which she did not drink. She drank a glass of water.

There was the rest of her life to get through. There was the next hour to get through.

She dragged the duvet off the bed and wrapped herself in it. She lay on the floor and reached out to sleep, her only refuge, it lifted her in its arms and carried her down muffled corridors.

It deserted her just before dawn. Opening her eyes suddenly, she wondered what dreadful thing had happened.

Then the pain began again.

There was the rest of her life to get through. This dark hour before the day began, to get through.

She crawled out of the duvet and went into the kitchen. She found a bottle of wine with some left in it and washed down two aspirin tablets with the horrible vinegary stuff. The flat was stone-cold, the central heating had been turned off while she had been away. She sat in an upright chair, wrapped again in the duvet, and waited for the dawn.

When it came, bleakly beautiful, the pencilled sky over the chimney-pots, she dressed and went out into the empty streets and made her way to Kensington Gardens. The paths were strewn with magnolia petals. She sat beside the Round Pond and tried to turn herself into a statue, her warm flesh into marble or stone. She wanted not to be. To disintegrate. To become water, or stone. Or any dead thing. To fracture into pure matter, no longer to be herself, Maisie Shergold, who looked away from the sharp green new leaves, the flowers and these shiny, bright-feathered ducks, as if it all hurt her eyes, hurt something inside her. But she couldn't manage to disappear, or leave this too solid world; there she still was, living, breathing, getting cold sitting there, even beginning to want a cup of tea. And for the first time since she got back to London she wondered where Rose was. There had been no sign of her last night, the house had been empty. She remembered she had gone back with her mother and Thèk and supposed she must have stayed on in Brighton.

She started walking slowly back to the house, though she did not go straight back in a determined way, but wandered up and down other streets, taking a longer, more circuitous route.

'Empty,' she thought. 'That is what I am. A hollow woman. Never to be solid flesh again.'

She noticed, without emotion, a tramp asleep, or dead, among the gravestones of St Mary Abbot's churchyard, his head resting on a black plastic bag for a pillow, full of his worldly goods.

She came upon her own house as if by accident. Her key in the door, she heard the telephone ringing somewhere inside the house. As she went upstairs it stopped. Rose's door was locked.

As Maisie opened the door of her own room, the telephone began ringing again. She picked it up, her hand shaking.

It was Rose, she sounded odd.

'Mummy. Oh, thank God you're back. Something dreadful has happened. I've been trying to get in touch with you. Oh, Mummy. Please get down here – oh, why didn't you ring from Ireland? Nobody knew where you were.'

'Rose, where are you? What's happened? What's the matter?'

'Please come down. I'm in Brighton.' She was crying.

'Yes, yes, of course. What's happened? Please say.'

'Oh, Mummy. Grandma's dead,' said Rose, her voice breaking.

'No,' said Maisie. 'No. She can't be dead, Rose.'

'Yes. She died the day before yesterday. It's so awful, it's so *awful*. Daddy's here – he came this morning. Imre's in a terrible state – like a sleepwalker. Daddy is seeing to everything – he's doing everything.'

'She wasn't ill,' said Maisie sharply.

'She had a stroke,' whispered Rose. 'Imre found her on the kitchen floor. She'd probably been there for three or four hours, the doctor said.'

Oh, God, thought Maisie, it can't have happened. Not like this, without warning. Maisie felt angry with her mother that she had not been able to warn them, prepare them. What was she thinking about? Being so heartless.

'I'll come straight down,' she said.

'Oh, yes, Mummy. I'm so glad you're back. You didn't leave a phone number in Ireland and I didn't know how to find you. We were going to get in touch with the police this morning – to find you.'

'I was going to telephone you and I didn't do it. I'm sorry, Rose. But I never thought anything like this would happen.'

'You just forgot about her,' said Rose, sobbing. 'You should have looked after her.'

'Yes,' said Maisie.

She put the telephone down. She went out of the room and sat on the stairs, looking down the spiral to the well of the staircase.

Strange sounds came from her, long moans and dry, orphaned howls, the empty house echoed with them. Maisie could hear these strange sounds winding and curling their way up the staircase and down it, the sound falling down into the well and then rising like smoke. After a while the sounds stopped, but she sat there for a long, long time.

Then she got up and went back into her room. She checked the bag she had brought from Ireland – it was still packed, and most of the things so hastily flung in she would need.

As she had a wash and looked round the room before

194

leaving, she felt as if she was being watched by someone. This eerie feeling persisted right up to the moment Rose answered the door of the Brighton flat. Maisie put her arms round her daughter, and they clung together in an embrace. Well, it's taken something like this, thought Maisie, finding some solace and relief in finding the barriers between them genuinely down at last. 'Daddy is out, seeing to things,' said Rose.

Imre Thèk looked shocked and haggard. He was in the kitchen washing out tea-towels and keeping himself occupied. But the look in his dark eyes was hard to take and Maisie held him and kissed his unshaven cheek.

'I'll make some coffee,' he said.

They sat round the kitchen table drinking coffee, surrounded by everything that reminded them of the dead woman. The cups and saucers with the gold band she used often . . . Maisie remembered her mother's thin fingers, her wedding ring and another ring with an amethyst and the exact way her hands moved, lifting a cup to her lips. The coffee pot with its pattern of little golden bees among flowers, little golden bees, whose wings seemed to buzz, they were so marvellously painted. Golden bees more alive now than the woman who had made her breakfast coffee every morning.

And as Maisie got milk from the refrigerator she saw it was packed with food in her mother's neat way. Her mother's kitchen. Still a kind of home up till now. At least a home if she had wanted one. Now no longer. For she no longer had a mother, she was motherless.

She had lost Michael and now she had lost her mother. In this new motherless, loverless world Maisie would have felt incorporeal if it had not been for her pregnancy, which she now remembered as if she had retrieved it just in time. It comforted her. She began to feel glad, really for the first time, that she was pregnant, and somewhere right at the back of everything, she was relieved that she would not need to tell her mother about it, and felt free in some respect which she did not yet examine.

Neither did she examine the way she knew she was using the pain of her mother's death to assuage that of her lover's betrayal, cauterizing the first wound with more pain.

Though she kept forgetting that her mother was dead, resting as it were between bouts of pain. There they were, drinking coffee round the table, waiting for her to come in; except she would never come in now. Where had she gone? Where was she? She must be somewhere, Maisie thought. The calendar on the wall had reminders written in Mrs Sharpe's writing under certain days, and tomorrow there was the Amnesty coffee morning, that was probably what the cheesecake in the fridge was meant for.

Scenes from the past kept relaying themselves, like snatches from an old film – a picnic on the sand dunes, her mother pouring milk from a silver thermos flask. Being measured for a new dress as she stood on the table, the tape-measure sliding through her mother's hands. Running across the daisied grass to her mother who sat in a deckchair slicing up runner beans.

Rose kept going into the bedroom to lie on the bed and sob. Imre looked stricken, almost frightened, as if he did not know quite what he was doing or where he was.

'Would anyone like a slice of cheesecake?' asked Maisie. Thèk shook his head and Rose did not bother to reply. It lightened things a little when Leo came back, laden with carrier-bags full of food and drink.

'I thought we might need it,' he said, giving Maisie a hug.

'You're wonderful,' said Maisie. She remembered her mother saying of him, 'So sociable and knowledgeable about things that interest me.' And almost simultaneously she had a picture of her pouring whisky for Michael, looking at him with detached, cool interest. They would never have been friends, they had little in common. Both gone now, she reminded herself.

Evelyn Sharpe's funeral was to be not in Brighton, but in the village about twenty miles away where she had been married and lived with her husband for the first years of their marriage and where her husband, Maisie's father, was buried. Imre Thèk drove them there, Maisie sitting beside him. Leo and Rose sat in the back of the car.

It was a lovely day and Maisie reflected sorrowfully that now her mother's eyes were closed for ever against the beauty of the world. They had driven through a golden tunnel of laburnum. It had reminded Maisie of one of the illustrations in her Russian fairy-story book – the trees with showering leaves of gold, shining coins in a story similar to the Twelve Dancing Princesses. She had felt no pleasure in the flowery tunnel, she too was cut off from the beauty of the world, or rather, it now inflicted pain, not pleasure. And then Maisie cried tears at last for her mother. She died too soon, no one had time to say anything, finish anything.

'Behold, I shew you a mystery.' The thin voice of the young vicar, just out of clergy school by the look of him. Maisie had asked for the Book of Common Prayer – the 1662 version: her mother would have wanted it. The unsurpassed, noble and unflinching words bore them all up. Such is the power of words. It was like being given plain, sustaining food to give them strength to get to the graveside.

Then they sang Evelyn Sharpe's favourite hymn. It sounded brisk and sensible – 'who so beset him round, with dismal stories, do but themselves confound'. She was still watching them. At the graveside Leo led Rose to sprinkle earth into the new grave. Maisie stood by herself and wished Michael was with her. Whatever he had done, at that moment she wanted him there, to touch his warm living flesh, to have his living presence there in that place. She remembered the night in the Kiev hotel when he had said, 'Bones – decay – all part of the same creation', and as she stepped forward and looked down into the deep grave, she heard him saying it in his Irish voice.

Perhaps it was being slightly in shock that made her at first mistake the grave-digger, as he rested with his spade over his shoulder, for the hitch-hiker who was going to Swaffham. He did look a little like him, that ambiguous, half-baked look. He did not look altogether on the side of his clients, as if he knew something and wasn't going to say what it was.

They shook the cold hand of the vicar and left the place, looking back at the grave-digger, now hard at work. Sobbing against her father's chest, Rose sat in the back of the car again.

'Shall I drive?' Maisie asked. Thèk looked drawn and tired, as if he had given up in some inward way.

'Thank you,' he said.

Back at the Brighton flat, a weird sort of hilarity set in, as drinks were poured. But there was a guest they were all so aware of. They were aware of it. All of them.

Leo read the will, and it turned out the flat had been left to Thèk. Evelyn's money went mostly to Maisie, with a useful amount to Rose. She had also left sums of money to various charities and odd small amounts to obscure, probably hard-pressed acquaintants. It was typical of her that there was an up-to-date will, and no mess or confusion about anything.

'May I take the copy of *Alice*?' Maisie asked, as they left.

'Of course, yes,' said Thèk. He did not know what to do or which way to turn.

'Will you live here now?' Rose asked him, her face blotchy.

'I don't know. I have a home,' said Thèk. Maisie knew it was two rooms over a bookshop.

'Will you be all right?' she said.

'Yes, thank you.'

'What can we do?'

'Nothing,' he said. 'Thank you.'

Maisie hugged him a little. 'God bless you,' she said.

He smiled at this, thinly, 'Oh – God,' he said, as if to say, all that means nothing to me, nothing.

As they drove back to London with Leo, Maisie said, 'We must keep in touch with Thèk.'

'They were so good together – it's such a waste,' said Leo.

'I hope he stays in Grandma's flat, I hope he doesn't sell it,' said Rose.

When they got back Rose asked her father to stay the night. Leo hesitated. 'All right, I'll phone Irene,' he said.

'She'll be all right?' Maisie looked doubtful.

'Just one night,' said Leo. 'She won't mind. She has friends nearby.'

'I'll go and make up a bed,' said Rose.

'Well, I'm quite tired, and it's still a drive to Hampstead, it would be nice to stay.'

Rose went off to find clean sheets for the swan room.

'It will help her,' said Maisie.

'What about you?'

'And me. Nothing stays the same. Life offers everything and then it is snatched away. I keep thinking of my mother, on her own like that.'

'She wouldn't have known very much – most likely.'

'We can't tell. She might have been saved if someone had been there.'

'Well, you could not possibly have spent your life with her in case she had a sudden stroke. She wouldn't have wanted that, you would have been in the way. She had her own life – a pretty good life.'

'Well, she lost a husband and had a daughter who only went to see her when it suited.'

'She was interested in life, she had friends, a lover – and a very nice daughter and granddaughter.' Leo took out a handkerchief and blotted her tears.

'I have broken with Michael,' said Maisie. It was an effort to actually say the words, making it a reality. Her own words cut her to pieces.

'Well, there's plenty more fish in the sea,' said Leo. 'He wasn't really your sort, anyway, Maisie – you must have been aware of that.' Maisie wished she had not said anything, and turned away, but Leo went on, 'He was a bit of a surprise to me – self-centred sort of chap. What happened?'

'Oh, I don't know – there was another side to him . . .' She trailed off, she didn't want to think about it, talk about it.

'You're feeling low,' said Leo. 'Why don't you come and stay with us for a bit?'

'Oh, Leo, you are funny.' Maisie pressed her hands to her eyes.

'I never wanted to let you go. I really wanted us three to live together, Irene, you and me – and Rose if she wanted to. The whole trouble was – it wasn't that I didn't want you, it wasn't ever that. I just wanted more than one life. That was it.'

Rose came back and said should she make coffee.

'It's cold,' she said, switching on the fire. 'Bring your chairs round the fire.'

The three of them drew nearer to the heat.

'Do you think Grandma can see us?'

'Who knows?' said Leo.

'It does feel like it,' said Maisie. They fell silent, watching the bright filaments of the fire.

'I may as well tell you both,' Maisie said at last. 'I'm pregnant.'

Leo looked at her. 'I thought so,' he said. 'I remembered what you were like last time. It makes you more beautiful.'

'What a mess you have got yourself in,' said Rose. 'Why isn't he here? I bet he's turned out to be married or something.'

'Something like that,' said Maisie. She wanted to get

away from them both. She felt as if something was crushing the breath from her, as if she was shut up in a box.

'Well, we'll help to sort things out,' said Rose. 'Won't we?' She put her hand on her father's knee.

For a moment Maisie remembered why she had let another woman take away her husband. Everything is about power, she thought wearily.

'I'm tired,' she said. 'I'm going to bed.'

She slept soundly that night and did not wake until she saw Leo standing there with a morning cup of coffee for her.

'I must be off,' he said. 'I'll ring very soon.'

'Thanks for everything,' she said.

'If you need anything . . .'

'Thanks.'

'I've said goodbye to Rose. She's crying again. You'd better go and see her.'

'It's better to cry.'

'Yes, I know. Goodbye, Maisie.' He kissed her cheek, and then her mouth. 'If you fancy a ménage à trois, just give me a ring.'

'Oh, Leo, you bloody idiot.'

'It would be fun.'

'Oh, yes, marvellous fun.'

'I brought your letters up.'

Among them was one from Professor Werner. And a grand-looking invitation to some sort of White Russian fund-raising shindig. And there was a letter from Ireland.

# 4

MAISIE looked at the letter from Ireland lying in the fold of the duvet. She picked it up again. It had a Dublin postmark. Michael's fast, free-flowing handwriting. She thought about tearing it up unopened. She thought about just putting it away inside a book and trying to forget it. She thought about returning it. She opened it. She read through a mist of something like terror.

*Dearest Maisie,*

*Maisie, listen – I have to try to wheedle my way back to you. Listen, Maisie, all I want to do is follow you, and make you come back to me. What stops me – something – I don't know. Perhaps I am afraid of you, I think you will destroy something that must not be destroyed. I'm going to try to make you understand about Kate. No, don't go away, Maisie, please listen. Because I love you and you love me.*

*It's hard for me to talk about Kate to you. It must be hard for you to listen – if you are.*

*This is it, how it is – the truth of the whole damned thing. She sort of rescued me when I was about fifteen – made sure I'd end up heterosexual. I'm grateful* to her and I do love her in a way, Maisie. We've had this sexual thing going since I can't remember – it's always been there. How could I just turn her away? I couldn't.

I'm sorry, Maisie. But it's a background, ordinary thing that's always been there. It's nothing like the way I feel about you. How am I going to get you back? I know you will be full of damned principles and arguments, all the while I know we want each other. Are you going to batter our love to death? I suppose you'll say I did that. I was taken by surprise, Maisie – I had not thought she would expect everything to be the same. I reckoned bringing you to Ireland would end it naturally. But she thought things would be the same, and I couldn't hurt her. She seemed to take you into the arrangement – that's what took me by surprise. It was not intended on my part. I couldn't just chuck her out. To be honest, Maisie, I never could do that ever. I'm not saying it's over with her – it's one of those things that's never over. I realize that now. I would change it if I could. I can't bear to lose you through it.

Can you understand and tell me what to do?

I suppose in some way I have always been in the hands of women, and expect them to sort things out. Sort it out for me, Maisie.

And I suppose I was always expected eventually to marry Kate when her grandmother died. She is close to my mother – something like a daughter, someone for my mother to have as an ally against the men – drunken useless lot that we are. Somehow Liam's wife never fitted into the daughter slot – it was always Kate.

I don't love her in the same desperate way that I love you, Maisie. She is not my sister, but in one way that is what she is. Can I keep her and have you too, Maisie? No? I suppose not.

I made a mistake taking you to Ireland. I wanted to

*bring my life together, the different parts of it, it didn't*
*work at all – why did I think it might?*

*This letter is reaching out for you, don't let me go.*
*Why did we meet and fall in love if it is going to end like*
*this? We still love each other. I thought we had something*
*we would never throw away. Don't throw it away,*
*Maisie. I know you want me still. One thing I have*
*learned – true human passion, like ours, is quite rare. Did*
*you know that? I must see you, Maisie. Don't throw it*
*away – it is a gift.*

*Michael*


Maisie put the letter back in the envelope, and went over
to her bookshelf, taking a book at random and hiding the
letter from herself between its leaves, replacing the book,
not noticing which one it was. She chose her clothes for the
day, smoothing out the brown woollen skirt and laying it
on the bed, finding a blouse to go with it, and a long casual
jacket.

The second ménage à trois she had been offered in
twenty-four hours, she thought bitterly. She thought this
with the civilized part of her brain. There was another part
that knew he was speaking only the truth, this part was
telling her to write back at once saying she still loved him,
asking him to come to her on the next boat – or the next
flight, whichever would be quicker.

She stood under the shower, shocking her flesh by
turning the temperature up very hot and then very cold –
she emerged gasping for breath. She dressed and rubbed her
hair half-dry, and fastened a pearl necklace under the collar
of her blouse. She slipped the letter from Germany and the
invitation to the monarchists' ball into her jacket pocket.
Last of all she put on a little eye shadow and, using her
finger, a trace of lipstick. With these rituals of daily life she

was attempting to hold on to herself, that self that was called Maisie Shergold. For she was beginning to feel as if split into two people, two Maisies. These two Maisies argued with each other, pulled different ways, and her comings and goings now began to be accompanied by this internal dispute. Sometimes one or the other of these Maisies won for a while, and she felt on firmer ground, but it never lasted. All the time everyday life had to go on, outwardly undisturbed by the racket in her head.

She went down to Rose's, tapping on the door with one hand and opening it with the other. 'Come up and have some breakfast, Rose,' she said. Rose's face was swollen with crying.

'Come on,' said Maisie, 'we have to keep going. I'll pop out and get some croissants. You get some coffee on.'

'I'll come with you,' said Rose.

'Yes, come with me.'

When they got out, passing a coffee-shop Maisie suggested they had breakfast there. They sat in the cheerful little place feeling wan and ghostly. 'I hate the world,' said Rose, tearing her roll up into pieces. 'And most of all I hate places like this – bright, cheery places – it's all so false. A veneer over the dreadfulness of life. And look at that woman – how can she bear to get up in the morning and put all that stuff on her face, curl her hair – she's taken ages over it – put pearls round her neck? It's all such a waste of time.' She was looking savagely not at her mother but at a pretty woman behind the counter, dispensing cream puffs and éclairs with an indulgent air.

'It's pathetic. People are pathetic,' said Rose.

'Eat,' said Maisie.

'What is the use of life?'

'It is a gift,' said Maisie. 'Don't throw it away.'

But she did not feel it as such – she spoke in this way because she felt she had a duty to help her daughter, her own flesh and blood, survive this. The survival of her genes, she thought. And she loved and pitied Rose with her bleak look, her eyes which looked so drained of light.

'Just when Grandma was so happy,' said Rose. 'What is the sense in that? Nothing good ever seems to happen.'

'It's not what happens.' Maisie raked about in the rag-bag of her mind. 'It's what you do with it.'

'But death – Grandma was happy and she just died. What is death?'

'It's a bridge,' said Maisie. 'It's part of a journey.'

'Do you really believe that?'

Maisie hesitated. 'I really believe I haven't seen the last of Grandma.'

'A life after death?'

'I don't know about that – but I don't think life just stops. Perhaps I think life and death happen simultaneously – I mean, when we are in life we are in death and vice versa. Two sides of the same coin.'

Rose wasn't listening. She was asking the woman at the counter for more coffee.

'Thèk is an existentialist,' she said. 'I think that is what I shall be. It is what I am.'

Maisie was thinking about Michael's letter and his words were at the back of her mind all the time. What he had said in the letter ran parallel to her own thoughts and silently counterpointed her conversation.

'Yes, it's the best thing to be.' She felt in her pocket for the other letters she remembered putting there.

'I was talking to Thèk before you came down,' said Rose. 'We sat up most of the night – you know, when it happened. At least, he was doing most of the talking. About everything – it was later he went so quiet. You're not listening, Mummy.'

'Yes, I am, you were saying you were going to be an existentialist.'

'Saying I *am* an existentialist.'

'I think it is a very intelligent viewpoint – an impregnable position.' She gave Rose a small smile and said slowly, opening Werner's letter, 'All life is flux, once you have accepted that, perhaps you can start to live in the present. The difficulty is keeping it in mind.'

She began reading the letter in an abstracted way as she drank her coffee, but soon became absorbed.

*Dear Dr Shergold,*

*We met at the Kiev conference, and sat next to each other at the luncheon. At once I liked you. Now I have summoned my great courage to write this letter.*

*I have lately been oppressed by guilt. Perhaps this is due to my age, I do not know. Everything that one has done in life rises up to confront one – there is no escape. It seems after all that there is a strange pattern to one's life, things come together in an inexorable way. But this thing which I would put away and put out of my mind will not depart.*

*Dr Shergold, this concerns the Ikon of the Steppes, in which you have some interest.*

*I did not tell you all I knew. There is a part of its history which only I know of.*

*Now I will tell you.*

Rose took the roll from her mother's plate. 'Aren't you going to eat this?'

Maisie shook her head. 'No, you go ahead. The jam looks delicious.'

'Loganberry,' said Rose, spooning some on to her plate. She gave her mother a piece. 'Eat,' she said. Maisie put a piece into her mouth, noticing the sharply sweet, subtle taste of loganberries. She returned to her letter, which had acquired a magnetic pull, the words leaping out to her in Werner's small, finicky writing.

*It goes back to my father, a colonel in the German army. During the bombardment of Kiev he acquired as booty, either looted or more likely taken as a bribe, or by way of hostage, the work of art known as the Ikon of the Mother of God of the Steppes. Exactly how he came by it is unclear to me, or how much the monk who restored the Ikon was involved in some deal, my father told the story differently at different times, but I grew up with this Ikon as a familiar part of my life – it hung in the dining hall.*

*I hated my father, and I feared him, and as I grew up I had not the courage to stand against his tyranny. I grew up with that – and with the Ikon.*

*One day as we sat at our food my father began to choke on a piece of meat. I sat and watched him choke and did not try to help or summon help. I wished his death. The only witness to this was the Ikon.*

*I got rid of that witness. I sold the Ikon for a small sum to a dealer in such things.*

*Why do I tell you all of these events? I have chosen to confess to you now that this burden weighs so heavily on me, because of your interest and research into this Ikon. If you should discover its whereabouts, I should like to see it once again.*

*Do you believe, as some do, Dr Shergold, that this Ikon is an instrument of salvation?'*

*Conrad Werner*


'Anything interesting?' Rose asked her.

'How would you like to come to a rather grand ball?' Maisie gave Rose the invitation.

'Why is it in Bath? You'd think the Royal Pavilion in Brighton would be the place – Brighton is where your monarchists hang out, isn't it?'

'I don't know why. A trip to Bath might be a good thing.' She could not think why this should be so.

'Well, isn't it a bit soon? After Grandma?'

'Grandma wouldn't mind at all.'

'No, I know. But I don't feel like going.'

'All right, we won't go. I don't feel like it either.'

But Rose was looking better. Maisie was glad to be with her at this time. She felt useful and less despairing. In a way her mother's death had released something in her and she felt able to draw closer to her daughter, closing the gap that had been left by death. She would be able to help Rose, perhaps.

She was feeling stronger too in that she had rejected within herself both Leo's and Michael's flawed offer. Her role now was to protect her unborn child and Rose, her adult child. It was a momentary rush of brave optimism. The clamour inside her head stilled for the time.

'Let's go and open your shop,' she said. 'Let's go and play shops. We have to do something.'

Rose hesitated, and Maisie drew back. 'Only if you want,' she added.

But they ended up there. It was only the second time Maisie had ever been inside the tiny shop, she felt as if everything might fall on top of her, all the boxes and pictures and old vases, and stifle her.

'We need not stay long,' she said.

'Look at this,' said Rose.

It was a wooden egg, a Russian Easter egg painted deep vermilion with a picture of Grandfather Frost on it. Maisie stared at it, passing it from one hand to the other. It was probably the same period as her Russian fairy-story book.

'A nice thing,' she said as she handed it back. 'I'm going to do some shopping and then I'll call back for you.'

She managed to find a delicatessen among the boutiques and antique shops. Thus, thought Maisie as she bought pasta and olive oil, they would get through the days; living, breathing, eating, working, they would traverse this portion of time. But she was experiencing some form of spiritual vertigo as she picked her way.

# 5

H E APPEARED in dreams. Before she slept Maisie bequeathed her bitter griefs to the soft darkness which subdued her pain for a while. She now loved the blackness of night in which she could lie, broken-hearted, without any pain, it was something like death. Sleep brought dreams which filled up her emptiness with brilliant consoling images.

He came to her in dreams. The flute-player, the wanderer who chanced by her empty house, her prison-house, and played sweetly. When she woke, these bright dreams left trails like the tail of a comet, left a silence like that after birdsong. And for a short while she was happy and still free from pain, but the fragile aftermath of such consoling dreams did not last.

Then one morning she woke up to a bed soaked in blood. She had felt nothing, the haemorrhage had started silently, painlessly, in her sleep. For a moment she lay bleeding, scarcely awake, wondering what to do, or whether to do anything. She flung back the duvet and watched the dark blood coursing down her legs, trickling down to her feet and running between her toes. The fine hairs on her legs were sticky with it. She stared, fascinated, and watched the dark dribble of blood for several minutes, waiting for it to stop, but it did not stop. She telephoned Quentin Freeman at his home. While she waited for Quentin, Rose knocked at the door – she had got into the way of coming up to have a cup of coffee with her mother before she left for work.

'It's all right,' said Maisie. 'But stay with me until Quentin gets here.' She was shaking a little from shock, and asked Rose to make her a cup of sweet tea.

'I can't find any sugar,' said Rose, frantically looking through the cupboard.

'Give me a spoonful of honey, then,' said Maisie, 'and please don't look so worried.'

Rose spooned honey into her mother's mouth, and put pillows under her feet. 'I'll come with you to the clinic,' she said.

'No need,' said Maisie, 'call in after you have shut up shop and see if I'm still there.'

'I'm not going to work,' said Rose.

'Please go,' said her mother. 'Let's try to keep things as normal as we can. Go to work.' Everything was breaking down around her.

When Quentin arrived and made reassuring noises, Rose calmed down and went off to work. After that everything for Maisie started to go from bad to worse. It wasn't going to be very straightforward. She would lose the baby, and it ended up being a general-anaesthetic job. Under the anaesthetic Maisie, floating somewhere near the door, saw Quentin put the baby aside, as if it were something of no account. She tried to get to it to help its struggle for life. But she saw it taken off to be disposed of. She felt rage and helpless panic, seeing its toes and fingers perfectly formed. When she had fought her way out of the anaesthetic she questioned the nurse frantically about its fate, but knew it was already sealed.

Quentin came and soothed her with his common sense and matter-of-fact professional manner. 'It'll all be forgotten with time,' he said. Maisie knew there was no point in saying anything, or trying to explain why she would not forget it. It was something he could not be expected to understand, something outside his world picture, which had hard boundaries.

A nurse brought her a cup of weak tea and a tranquillizer and she slept until the late afternoon, waking to find Rose and Leo sitting by her bed with a bunch of anemones.

Leo took her hand. 'We can take you home,' he said. 'You're fine.'

'Oh, yes, I'm fine,' said Maisie.

'It's so extraordinary,' said Leo. 'Irene is in here too. She has had her baby.'

Maisie closed her eyes and lay back on the pillow.

'I'm really quite tired,' she said.

'I've called it Clare,' said Leo, 'it's a rather nice baby as babies go. I think it smiled at me. It's got all its fingers and toes, anyway.' He looked rather smug. For the first time in her life Rose saw him objectively, with new eyes. She was appalled by his tactlessness. She was surprised that she was able to feel this anger towards her father.

'You had better go and be with Irene,' said Maisie, her eyes still closed against this place where such things had happened to her, all beyond her control.

'Oh, it's all right,' said Leo, 'she's got the coven with her. Her coven of women friends – you know – they all wanted to be with her at the birth, a sort of communal effort. Quentin got really icy, he managed to chuck them out, but they're back now, all suggesting the most ridiculous names for my child. Rainbow and such-like. I've called the baby Clare – after my favourite aunt.'

Maisie could not help laughing a little at this, though she wept as she laughed. She sat up, and Leo made the pillows comfortable. 'To tell you the truth,' he said, 'I feel a little bit out of it. I'd rather sit here with you.' He placed the flowers on the bed.

'They're lovely,' said Maisie.

'It's perhaps turned out for the best,' said Rose.

'Has it?' said Maisie, but managed a little smile. Rose had been through a lot too. She looked older. Poor Rose, her father with a fresh little new daughter; her grandmother who had seemed indestructible gone; her mother in a physical and emotional accident.

'I'm glad you brought me something to read,' Maisie told her.

'There's an article about women artists you may be interested in,' said Rose.

Maisie made up her mind that when she got home she would try to be different with Rose. There was something about her daughter that worried her, something different around the eyes – they had lost some brave, foolhardy, ingenuous quality.

When she did get home the next day things got off on the wrong foot. Rose had altered her mother's room, she had taken down the bed-curtains and sent them to the laundry, and cleared the table of everything. The wicker chair stood by an open window and the cold air blew across the room – the weather had turned almost wintry, threatening snow even though it was nearly May. The room looked as if it had been fumigated, it looked cold and tidy and empty.

'I tidied up for you,' said Rose.

Maisie went across to close the windows, feeling on the verge of weak tears.

'And I made you a quiche – asparagus quiche. There's some new potatoes, they're all ready.' Rose went into the kitchen to put the potatoes on.

'It's nice of you to do all this,' said Maisie, touched at the thought of Rose making pastry, wishing she felt hungry, wishing she did not feel like putting her head down on the table and wailing. She looked around the room, finding no consolation anywhere.

'Where is the letter rack?' she asked.

'Letter rack?'

'Yes, you know, the bronze letter rack, it's always on the table. With everything else.'

'Oh, I'll find it for you, just a minute.' Rose came out of the kitchen and found the letter rack in a cupboard Maisie used for storing files.

'Why did you hide it in there?'

'I was just tidying up. I wasn't hiding it.'

There were two letters from Ireland amongst the batch of mail, but Maisie seemed not to see them, only turning a little whiter.

'Where's the typewriter?' she asked.

'I'll put everything back as it was,' said Rose in a loud, definite voice.

Please, we must not quarrel, thought Maisie, I'm being a bitch.

'There's no hurry,' she said, 'let's have our meal first. Open a bottle of wine – there's a bottle of something in the fridge.' They gave each other small, relieved smiles. Rose put the quiche on the table. 'Let's watch the film,' she said, 'while we eat.'

Rose was in fact being exceptionally sweet, thought Maisie. She even seemed happy as she organized the plates, the salad, sprinkled parsley on the potatoes. She switched on the television.

'It's one of those old black and white films,' she said, 'they're brilliant.'

It was *Odd Man Out*, with James Mason. There was a definite likeness there, only Michael's eyes were light-coloured and his jaw not so heavy. But there was something, a dark, charismatic quality. The film had started, it was the bit in the air-raid shelter, the hero, Johnny was injured and hunted. The black and white images more desperately real and true than colour could ever be.

'Why do black and white films have so much more emotional impact?' Rose wondered.

With one part of her mind Maisie was watching Johnny, only it was Michael, his dark head leaning back against the wall, speaking with that slightly accented Irish voice. In this case it was an actor's Irish, but it was very like Michael's voice.

With another part of her brain she answered Rose. 'There's less to distract the eye, it's more dreamlike in a way, less like reality, but more like it in that it's more poetic.'

'They seemed to use lighting so much better,' said Rose, 'to create mood.'

'That's right,' said Maisie.

Running, limping brokenly now from one place to another, finding no safe place, the hero inhabited Maisie's imagination. There was something about him. Rose took her plate.

'Would you like some more quiche?'

'No, thanks – it was very good, though.'

'Have you seen this film before?'

'Years ago.'

'He looks like Michael,' said Rose.

'Do you think so?'

'Yes, a bit.' Rose got up to refill her glass. 'He persists in writing to you. You'll have to tell him about losing the baby.'

'I don't have to tell him anything at all,' said Maisie. 'Switch this off, please, Rose, I want to rest.'

'Shall I put your clutter back on the table now?'

'Yes, please, and the anemones.'

Rose put the typewriter, books and flowers back on the table. It's not that Rose just likes to be in charge, thought Maisie, that is making her happier. She does love me, as I love her.

'When I'm feeling better,' she said, 'we'll do something nice. Have a holiday, perhaps. What about this monarchist ball thing, when is that – shall we go to that?' She looked through the letter rack to find the invitation. 'It's on Friday – I'll be all right by then. We'll go to it, shall we?'

'What larks!' said Rose sarcastically.

'Oh, stop being so world-weary, Rose, it will probably be splendid, interesting.'

'All right. If you're well we'll go. I'll dress up as Elizabeth the First. What will you be? Don't we all have to go as monarchs? All wearing our crowns?'

Maisie laughed. It was lovely to laugh, it just came out. A proper laugh.

'Let me have a rest now,' she said.

When Rose had gone, Maisie took Michael's letters to bed with her.

She looked at the date stamps. One stamp was very faint, the other black and smeary. Both letters had been posted in Dublin, one the day before the other. Which letter should she open first? Perhaps it would be for the best not to open either. Never know what he said, for nothing that he said now could ever make it right, take them back to before it had happened, undo it. His words, any words he could possibly come by were like snowflakes falling in a fire.

She was very tired and his writing was hard to read, a little chaotic.


*Dearest Maisie,*

*I am in Dublin. This address will find me.*

*I am afraid to telephone you though I attempt it several times a day. Do you know, Maisie, my hand shakes – I think, I'll do it in an hour, later in the evening, tomorrow. Did you think I could be such a coward? I wonder if you read my letters.*

*I met Philomena. She said you stayed the night with her. How did I ever think her beautiful?*

*She is a poisonous woman. One of those intellectual women who use their brains as a weapon chiefly – a very*

*potent weapon. Men don't do this on the whole, they use*
*their brains for things not to do with relationships. In*
*relationships they are stupid. Like me.*

*It all goes round and round in my head. Could we*
*live abroad, Maisie — the two of us? Siberia, perhaps —*
*it's beautiful there, Sergei told me about it. Some place*
*where nature is huge and important and we little beings*
*shrink to our proper size. I would return to Ireland only*
*as an old man, when all the fires have burned out — you*
*see, I do have to come back eventually, that is my*
*predicament.*

*Will I ever see you again, my dear, dear woman?*
*Sweet Fig, I am falling to pieces.*

*Michael*

She cried a little at this, but she knew that he spoke the
truth, that his bonds with Kate were unbreakable. What kept
him from telephoning was that he could not say the only
thing that might reclaim her, that it was over with Kate for
ever. Maisie suspected that he was spending most of his time
in Dublin in the congenial company of his drinking and
musician friends, and that he was falling to pieces only
intermittently, when alone.

Yet the image of Johnny, walking wounded, did not
leave her . . . walking wounded. They were both that now.

Then again she thought what fools women are. And then
again, no, it is the same for him.

She was too tired to read any more and fell asleep briefly,
the opened letter in one hand, the unopened in the other
hand. When she woke she opened the second letter.

*Dearest Maisie,*

*I'm writing this and I'm not exactly sober. I'm imagining*
*what you might be doing. I'm remembering the way you*
*walk, you have a lovely walk, drifting along like some*

*bloody angel, I always thought. And now more beautiful
than ever being with child, my child, Maisie.*

*Maisie, if I telephone, will you talk to me? If I come
to London, would you see me? Coward that I am – it's
easier to send these missives.*

*I love you, Maisie – don't throw it away.*

*Michael*

*P.S. Did you ever read Hopkins? The Brothers were
very keen on him.*

*'I wake and feel the fell of dark, not day.'*

*Michael*

Maisie put the two letters back in their envelopes.
Whenever she thought of Michael she had only one picture
of him. His sick, stricken face when she had come back to
the cottage in Ireland, that look that had changed everything.

'I wake and feel the fell of dark, not day.'

His letters had not made the reasons for his betrayal any
clearer to her. It was to her an act beyond comprehension.
His argument about Kate, his explanation of his relationship
with Kate she could not follow. She could not, would not
understand it. It meant nothing to her.

She would not read Michael's letters over again. Everything that he said she remembered. She put the letters
between the leaves of random books on her shelf – she might
forget about them.

When Leo called on her the next day, he asked, 'Do you
still love him? Will you see him again?'

'He appears to me in dreams,' said Maisie. 'Apart from
that I have nothing to do with him.'

# 6

IN THE end, Rose would not go with her mother to Bath. She had withdrawn scornfully into herself.

'What are you going for?' she asked. 'It's pointless. It's not as if you have any interest in restoring the Russian monarchy. I certainly hope not, anyway.'

There was truth in this, thought Maisie, all her days had become pointless, and she floundered in them. She did not try to explain that her life was hard to live, and uneventful days nearly killed her. She would have liked to have been living through wars and earthquakes, catastrophes of all kinds, anything to fill the heavy hours. 'I have something to pass on,' she said, 'some new information about their ikon. It's more satisfactory to do it personally.'

Maisie noticed that Rose's temporary closeness had not lasted. She regretted that. But absorbed in her own life struggle, she telephoned Thèk and asked if he would accompany her. She made it into a favour so he could hardly refuse. They arranged that he would drive up to town and pick her up. Maisie told herself it would do Thèk good.

She did not wear a crown. She felt hardly recovered from her miscarriage, but careless of her own well-being.

They arrived early after an unexpectedly quick drive

down the M4, listening to Mahler on tape, talking a little. Only a handful of people so far had gathered in the elegant Pump Room. They were greeted by the tall Russian Maisie had met at Walsingham. He drew her over to the window where a few early comers were drinking and watching several swimmers in the Royal Bath, their pale flesh rising and dipping in the steamy sludgy water. With a small shock of surprise, Maisie noticed they were swimming naked – it looked surreal, the wisps of steam rising from the heavy, greenish-brown water, the pink limbs of these swimming human creatures.

She told him quietly something of what Werner had said in his letter, though she was discreet about the German professor's personal revelations. Her host thanked her, kissing her hands, his face alive with emotion. How is it, thought Maisie, that they feel so deeply? It's like being in love. In love with an idea, an image. 'The last piece of the puzzle is in place,' he said.

He asked her then about Michael – where Michael was – how sorry he was not to see him, he had expected him. Maisie could not quite decide whether this was simply courteous interest, or a sort of checking up. He also asked about Thèk, and seemed interested in Maisie's brief potted history: Hungarian . . . mathematician . . . her late mother's dear friend.

More guests were arriving. The room began rapidly filling with people. Maisie looked round at the exotic company, the epaulettes of the Tsarist uniforms which several men sported, the bright poppy splash of a woman's dress, the flash of crystal on the long table.

'I feel like a traitor here,' said Thèk as she rejoined him. 'Or a spy.'

He had said it quietly, for Maisie's ears only, but it was overheard by an old man with blue eyes, sharp as the cutting edge of a skater's blade, who spoke in good, only slightly broken English. It was Menshikov, whom Maisie had last seen in Brighton, at Denisov's house. She introduced him to Thèk.

'My friend, you do not believe our people wish the return of a monarchy – a Tsar once more?'

Thèk laughed incredulously, and spoke with some passion. 'No. You Russians see reality through a mist of fables, untruths and dreams. You have no sense, no real sense of history. Or even space and time. Your view of these things is disjointed and bizarre. Dangerous. And as for a return to monarchy, you have lived too long under a system based on collectivism.'

Maisie was beginning to wonder whether it had been wise to bring the Hungarian into this particular milieu. But Menshikov seemed unperturbed by Thèk's outburst.

'For myself,' he said, 'I have never lived in Russia, though I hope to end my life there. But my dear, what you say about ah . . . collectivism . . . our position is not so far away in psychological terms, both communism and monarchism require the submergence of the individual to something higher, an ordering power. The great advantage of monarchy is that ultimately the higher power is God, the monarch only his representative. God Himself,' he reiterated, sparks leaping from his bright old eyes.

'Ah, God,' said Thèk in despair. 'Always God. It is history trying to fly backwards. It is not possible.'

Angrily he waved away a waiter bearing a tray of drinks, and the waiter had to duck before offering it to Maisie and Menshikov.

But Menshikov persisted seriously, calmly. 'No, no,' he said, 'the restoration of the monarchy is a culmination of history. The old order had to break up, be cut down, nearly annihilated before it could grow back, more strong, more true.'

'You speak of it as a natural living organism, something that should be, in nature as it were.' Maisie tasted the champagne, it was very fine indeed.

'Yes, the monarchy is like a tree. Like a tree, it has shape and harmony.'

'A gallows,' spat Thèk violently, 'for the free human spirit.'

'You do not believe in structures?'

'Not hierarchical structures,' said Thèk, 'they are built on fear and dread.'

'My dear, hierarchy is intrinsic to systems of order.' Menshikov spoke lightly, but Thèk was still angry and impatient.

'Life is worthless if it is not free,' he said, 'and also very boring. Full of ennui. Stale. The stability of your hierarchies is stifling and stagnant. Like stagnant water. Revolution will eventually always break through. Revolution is excitement – fresh, fast-flowing water – the human spirit freeing itself, purifying itself. Down with the monarchy. It shackles and chains us all.'

'You speak the words of Satan himself,' said Menshikov, but he was laughing, sure of his own faith, very slightly sozzled by the effect of vintage champagne on his old body.

For some reason Maisie thought of Irene and her cyclical view of life, her creative wheel structure. Systems of order, patterns could be cyclical, they need not even be static. They could be ever-changing.

'I used to love kaleidoscopes,' she said, and as the two men looked uncomprehending at this irrelevance, she said, 'You know – how the pattern is always changing with just the smallest flick of the wrist, all the pieces in the pattern rearrange themselves into another, different but equally beautiful and symmetrical pattern. The feeling is of constant movement within an ordered universe.'

Thèk and Menshikov did not pursue this line of thought, though they looked momentarily thoughtful.

Perhaps Irene had something in her ideas, thought Maisie, something Leo was too sure of himself to understand. He hadn't married her for her ideas.

Maisie was beginning to be tired standing. The champagne was making her giddy. All around her she heard the mix of languages, Russian, French, English, twining and weaving in each other. It all sounded like gibberish.

The conversation now was about the French Revolution, how it had speeded up history, speeded up how time fled by.

Falling in love is like that, thought Maisie. It is an overturning of things. It sings through creation. It speeds up time and simultaneously makes it stand still. It is like standing on top of the highest pinnacle on earth and being able to see a long way. Seeing everything breathtakingly laid out below, and you are breathing thin, life-giving air. But paradoxically, it blinds and narrows the view, certain things are no longer visible to you. Some things are supercharged with energy and beauty, other things fade away as if their existence no longer mattered, love being a cipher which selects differently.

Thèk was offering her a chair. She thanked him and sat down. And she thought how often love was ultimately, like most revolutions, destructive. How it tears things apart. She thought how her careful life had been torn down – the painfully built structure – how it lay about her now like a ravaged city, and there was nothing to hold on to. She saw the time since she had met Michael, the speeded-up time, go by, flick, flick, flick like an old film.

One of the reasons she had not wanted to come on her own, and had dragged Thèk there with her, was that she was feeling unsure of the very ground she walked on. It was as if it could open and swallow her. Outwardly she remained the same, and partook of life's comings and goings as everyone did outside madhouses, but inwardly she could hear the weird, ghostly wind blowing across the bomb-site of her spirit, and it made her afraid. Life, in one way, seemed somehow over for her, like so much rubble. Except she still moved and talked and had her being. Sometimes she wished for Leo to be with her. In a sense he had always been more

223

real to her than Michael, more bodily real. But Michael was the one who burned fiercely in her imagination and had cut open her heart so easily, so exactly.

Thèk drew her over to the buffet, set out in splendour along one side of the room. 'Would you like something to eat?' he asked her, piling piroshkis on to a plate and plunging a silver spoon into an elaborate trifle, spoiling the pattern of crystallized rose petals. 'Really, Maisie, you do not have sympathy for this crowd, do you?'

'Oh, yes – I can understand very well the glamour of kingship, of a royal line. I see the advantage of being born by chance to power, rather than scrabbling for it for all sorts of possibly unworthy motives. And I suppose it is a structure which, generation after generation, can stand the strain of events.'

'You can talk like that because you do not know what a tyrannical society is like. Even in this country you had to chop off a tyrant's head.'

'Charles the First? Yes, but they sewed his head back on before they buried him.'

Thèk gave a small grim smile at this.

'Yes, well – the Russians would never have done that, no half-measures with them. No compromises. It is always an extreme position. This lot will be no different in the unlikely event of them having power.' Thèk looked at her seriously. 'You should beware of glamour,' he said.

Glamour, 'the supposed influence of charm on the eyes'. Thèk was right to warn her. Maisie remembered how Rose had described Michael, as if it was a term almost of contempt, as glamorous. It was his glamour now that she could not forget, it was why she could not let go of him, his magic, his glamour. The trouble is it moves one, it is not nothing.

Where was Michael now? What was he doing? He should have been here with her, glamorous in this exotic place, although his sort of glamour he took with him everywhere.

She had dreamed the night before that she could not decipher his letters. She had tried to read them but they were just marks on the page. And she had also dreamed that she was trying to telephone her mother and could not get through.

'Shall we go?' she asked Thèk. 'Do you mind?'

'We will leave them to it,' he said, abandoning his trifle.

They left quietly as the first experimental fireworks puffed into the air and fell in pink smoke over the thick, slabby water of the baths. As they drove back to London, Maisie felt disturbed by the evening. 'They are too sure,' she said. 'Their view is so narrowed. I fear for them, and I pity them. I am somehow glad that Denisov did not live to see what might happen.'

'Maisie, they are a lot of deluded idiots. I don't want to think about it.'

'I should not have dragged you there,' said Maisie.

'I was glad to take you. I'm not really doing anything that matters. Well – I've started writing, but it's not going very well.'

'Mathematics?'

'No – poetry. People always write poetry when everything else fails.'

'Have you settled in the flat?' She probed him but it was a silly question. Maisie had a picture of him seated at her mother's desk, writing poetry, the light falling across his bent head.

'I'm thinking of going back to Hungary,' said Thèk. 'It is possible for me now. I think I want to go back. I have a sister there.'

'I shall miss you,' said Maisie, 'if you do.' She was surprised by the pain it gave her; she really liked Thèk and regarded him as a friend. Everyone was going, leaving, dying.

Thèk settled back in the driver's seat as they turned on to the motorway. 'Well, perhaps you will visit me. It is a beautiful country.' He slipped the Mahler tape into the player. 'You don't mind hearing it again, do you?' he asked.

Changing into top gear, he said, 'May I give you some advice?'

'Please.'

'You are a sensible and beautiful and clever woman. But you let strange things happen to you. Some people are like that. I think perhaps I am the same myself. You could choose otherwise.'

'You mean I go about bumping into things?'

'Yes. Perhaps you should stop doing that. You have the possibility of so much. Perhaps you go up strange, unlikely paths.'

'It used not to be like that,' said Maisie.

'Was it better before? Or now?'

Maisie hesitated, and said slowly, 'In spite of everything, it is better now.' She meant that. Now her feelings were ripped bare, and she was more alive even though she was in pain.

Thèk gave her a sweet smile and said nothing. He dropped her at the house but would not come in, and carried straight on with his journey.

A note had been pushed under her door. It was from Rose, telling her that her telephone had kept ringing so she'd answered it, it was Michael and she had told him to go to blazes. That was the right thing to do, wasn't it?

# 7

THE world had suddenly gone quiet for Maisie. In spite of her underlying exhaustion, she still craved the excitement of change to ease her pain. But nothing happened. Michael did not telephone again and Maisie wondered exactly what Rose had said to him. 'I just told him to sod off, that's all,' said Rose, adding darkly that Irene had instructed her that men take away all your gifts if you insist on being besotted by them. Maisie wondered if Michael had mentioned the baby. But she would not ask. A short note from him did arrive – it contained no more pleas to see her, only telling her that he was in England for a three-day university tour. That he had been home and both he and Declan sent their love.

Well, she would be out of the country soon. She planned to take Rose, who had never been to Russia, to St Petersburg.

The choice of that city had not been entirely at random. After all her involvement with the ikon she would not miss its restoration to an Orthodox church. It was to find its home in the Church of the Apparition of the Virgin, where the monarchists were to gather for a special service. St Petersburg, then, of all cities – it had never been Leningrad to the monarchists – was to be the venue for this event. The

European press was getting interested; this Russian business had stirred up many hives. The situation looked a little dangerous and volatile, and the monarchists were treading softly, keeping their activities to themselves. But Maisie had been invited to attend the ceremony.

Apart from her interest in seeing the ikon restored to a Russian church, Maisie was not really looking forward to her trip to St Petersburg. She had a general wish, though, to be on the move, and she felt she must go for Rose's sake. Rose needed a complete change of scene, she thought, after this sad spring.

They would be staying with the Abrahamovs, a pair of very old academics Maisie had known for some years. They were an extraordinary old couple, and Maisie loved them, but she would not want them to know of her sadness. They both disapproved of unhappiness. It was something indulged in by those with no inner resources. They themselves had lived through many tribulations, including the death of children. The old man was now practically blind, and his wife suffered from severe arthritis, but that did not prevent them from living full intellectual lives and travelling. Maisie had no qualms about Rose staying with such old people – they were both now in their eighties, but had far more energy and life than she. If anyone could chivvy Rose up it would be them.

In preparation for the trip Maisie had been clearing up a backlog of work. She was compiling a book (one for a series of art books) about the Russian ikon. It was to be a basic sort of book, but the illustrations had to be chosen carefully and the text had to be clear and interesting. The thing had been hanging about too long. Sometimes she sat half-way through the night working before she fell into bed.

She had never put the lace curtains back round her bed. She had changed the whole room round, pushing the table where she worked up against the window, and she had bought a nineteenth-century American patchwork quilt for the bed. It altered the character of the room with its rich, darkish colours, lending it a sort of heavy stability. She had started to pack. Pictures of Michael at the farm flew in and out of her mind. She saw him running across the field with Kate, like two figures in a landscape, Kate's bright hair loose and flowing out behind her. She saw Declan playing with the kittens and Kate stooping down to give him a kiss, and his quick, charming smile, Michael standing silently watching them. She saw the three of them off in one of the ramshackle cars, happy and carefree. She glimpsed them naked in the bed on the floor, where she had slept with Michael, under the indulgent eye of Michael's father and the cool stare of his mother over the drooping lilies. Maisie despised these imaginings. She worked steadfastly, stoically, she ate and slept enough to keep herself going, and when she woke she felt the fell of dark, not day.

# PART FIVE

## St Petersburg

# I

THE Abrahamovs met Maisie and Rose at the airport and took them straight out to a restaurant, insisting on buying them a good meal to welcome them to St Petersburg. 'We live only on scraps these days,' said Elena Abrahamova, 'we are too old to bother much about food. But you young people must eat.'

Maisie remembered them as being frugal and careful with money when it came to things like food and clothes – Elena was now wearing a rather strange hat which she might well have made herself out of an ancient piece of bric-à-brac found at the bottom of a drawer somewhere. However, they spent lavishly on things that interested them, their home stuffed with fabulous spoils from extensive travels. They had travelled in Arabia, China, India, Finland and Iceland as well as much of Russia, always living on a shoestring, parking themselves on people they hardly knew but who were overcome by their erudite charm, and felt honoured to have them as guests for as long as they wanted to stay. Which made it all the stranger that Maisie and Rose were being treated to this expensive meal.

Maisie admired the wily old pair. Elena Abrahamova certainly looked as if she had lived her eighty years and more to the full, the intimation of experience showing in the lines and creases of a face that would be beautiful until her dying day.

The thing you noticed about Vasily Abrahamov was the gaze from his large, dark brown eyes when speaking (most people had to look away). Maisie had seen no one else, ever, do this in the same way; the gaze was unfaltering, fixed, yet in some peculiar way unseeing – this was not connected to his blindness. It was something he had always done, and it was as if now his blindness had caught up with that disconcertingly frank, unseeing stare. There was an innocence in it, the look of a young child who first looks at new things in the world with unadulterated self-forgetful interest. As if the eye was a receiver only. It was impossible to believe that those brown eyes could not see, and Maisie wondered seriously whether his blindness was not something he had invented for some reason.

Just as Maisie had predicted, Rose's cynical façade did not stand a chance in the face of these formidable old people. She smiled openly and politely, even warmly, when they took her hands and said, 'Is this really Rosa?' She was just Rose, herself, with them, a young woman Maisie had not seen for a while. She did not flinch when they patted her hands, when Elena inspected her earrings with a magnifying glass she kept in her battered purse. ('Sweet,' she said of the starry clusters Rose had had for her birthday.) And Maisie's dryness of spirit, her inner sadness, seemed nearer to self-pity in the face of their stoicism, which was both innate and habitual. In a way Maisie wanted to be left alone with her sadness. It was all that she had left of her love affair and she did not want to lose it. It kept her company, the sadness, like a friend stricken with a fatal illness, but whose last days you want to share.

She wondered how Elena and Vasily Abrahamov would fare the one without the other, they were so intertwined, every gesture and thought. If their bond was severed by death, she thought, the stoicism would still be there, even in the face of that. Perhaps they would meet their end together – done to death by brigands in the Khyber Pass, or some such fitting thing.

'We were sorry to hear about your mother,' they said. 'Such sad news.' But that sort of grief, it was implied in the tone of voice, was to be taken as a matter of course, it was the way of things.

Vasily had been a professor at the university, teaching literature – his special interest had been the Icelandic Sagas – but now he had a new, very different enthusiasm. It was Walt Whitman, whom he was translating into Russian. And he was researching a young unknown Russian poet who had died of starvation during the siege of Leningrad; 'Such a loss to us.' Elena had been a travel writer and still wrote the occasional piece, gave talks and slide lectures; she was in great demand.

They could not have done half of what they did if they had not lived in this particular Russian city. 'There has always been a certain freedom here,' said Elena. 'It is because of the quality of the light, you know. It affects everything.'

Maisie thought it probably had more to do with the Abrahamovs' patrician inability to be anything other than intellectually free. They seemed to have led charmed lives in some ways, moving about apparently freely and never seeming to watch what they said or wrote. But Maisie reckoned they always knew what they were up to, neither was a fool.

They lived in a yellow-washed eighteenth-century house overlooking the sparkling water of the Neva. The drawing-room was dappled in moving reflected light from the water, which played over the mirrors and tapestries and rich carpets which hung on the walls. Everywhere in the big room were souvenirs of their travels, made of silver and jade, copper and mother-of-pearl, and many beautifully carved wooden pieces. Maisie especially admired a silver dish with enamelled tulips. The long sofa was piled deep with richly coloured and embroidered cushions. At one end of the room was an opened grand piano.

'We have a little entertainment for you this evening,' said Elena. There was no concession to the fact that her guests had had a long journey.

'I think I'm too tired,' Rose was murmuring. 'I won't keep awake much longer.'

'You must not miss this,' she was told, 'the most wonderful lieder singer in Russia – perhaps the world. Oh, no – you must stay awake. Once he sings you will not feel tired.'

Friends of the old couple turned up in ones and twos and sat about the room, chatting, waiting for the famous baritone to arrive.

Suddenly he was there. A man in his late thirties, with magnificent, almost impossibly romantic good looks, in the splendour and prime of life. He was to sing Schubert – the *Winterreise*.

In spite of his wonderful beauty and magnetic personality, Rose fell asleep, leaning against her mother. Maisie herself was drawn into the music, she was tired and the music flooded her.

Kiev. The pathos of the snowy statues in the garden, shut out from the feast. The crunch of snow under Michael's boots as he held her: 'You are my prisoner.' The way he looked sometimes, as if he wanted something out of reach. She had wanted it to be her, it had been her. She had lost it, thrown it away, denied it. The one thing.

There was a tenacity in the music, in the voice of the Russian singing Schubert. Something brave and tenacious. After all, she closed her eyes, after all, the man's voice, in its beauty, was drawing something out of her, drawing out poison, leaving her weak and well.

Maisie went to bed that night with a new feeling, fresh, childlike. As if cleansed, she slept through the light St Petersburg night as after a fever has left the body. She slept fitfully, waking to find it half-light, sleeping again, and waking to more light.

Next morning she left Rose to sleep and, feeling hungry, went in search of some breakfast. It seemed there wasn't any. Having given them such a welcome, their hosts went to the other extreme and told Maisie they must now fend for themselves as they, the Abrahamovs, led such abstemious lives, they were sure Maisie and Rose would not want to share their frugality. If they wanted to make themselves coffee that was quite all right, but coffee was such a price these days, they wouldn't mind providing their own? Smiling charmingly, Elena produced an empty enamelled tin for the purpose.

They really were getting slightly cranky after all, Maisie thought, dryly remembering how she and Leo had entertained them for several weeks on full board, even paying for theatre tickets. Oh, well. There were shortages in the city. She smiled back. She went up to warn Rose that there was no breakfast to be had and that she must take enough roubles when she went out to feed herself for the day.

'What do you want to do today, anyway?' she asked Rose, who looked very tired still and said she was going to go back to sleep and then she'd go and wander about for a while.

'Please don't drag me off doing cultural things,' she said. 'I don't want to look at museums or art galleries, I just want to drift about by myself.'

'You don't want to come to the auction with me?'

'What bloody auction? I thought we were on holiday.'

'We are on holiday. I thought you liked auctions. Anyway, I have to go. When Daddy knew I was coming to St Petersburg, he made a point of asking me to bid for something for a client of his. Actually this is quite something and should be interesting. Lately, you know, all the stuff has been shipped out for auction – the flood-gates are opening – but now the Russians are catching on and they're hanging on to things to auction themselves. I expect there will be a lot of foreign buyers there.'

'What have they asked you to bid for?'

'A fifteenth-century Dormition of the Virgin. Exciting?'

'Riveting, but you're not going to persuade me to come.'

'Well – enjoy your day, then. I'll see you this evening.'

'Yes . . . oh, I suppose I'd better get up.'

Maisie smiled at her daughter. She checked on the address she had in her handbag of the venue for the auction. 'Go and find some breakfast,' she said to Rose.

Maisie's feeling of lightness and peace had stayed with her. It had been a long time since she had walked down a street with such a mood of calm and optimism. She noticed the other people in the world, fleshed out again in a real sense. She smiled at the citizens of St Petersburg. She shared the world with them: 'We are all alive at the same time,' she thought in wonder. The same century, the same day, a sunny day in St Petersburg. Love, no longer trapped, fixated, flooded out over the created world. She felt celibate and free.

Her pleasant, quiet mood persisted even as she looked through the dusty stacked canvases in the auction room. There were so many and the place was in such a muddle. A lot of the stuff was worthless, abstract landscapes of a certain sort, State-orientated pictures of the thirties and many nine-teenth-century ikons. Seen like this, out of its religious context, Maisie reflected that the ikon was a strange, stiff, awkward sort of thing – it wasn't like a painting in the usual sense. Thrown about the place like this, what did they mean? People were buying them as they might buy decorative wallpaper. Perhaps they would still work their purpose out in the households of the godless.

Dealers were sitting about on the magnificent curving staircase. They shifted to let her go upstairs. Here, laid out in some sort of order was the cream of the collection. There were one or two Symbolist paintings – Russian Rossettis –

several paintings from the Moscow avant-garde group that were expected to achieve high prices, and a huge, dynamic early-twentieth-century work by a painter who was beginning to interest the art world. There had obviously been an underground art market all through the post-Revolutionary years which had now thrown up paintings such as these.

There were only two ikons, the Dormition that Maisie had come to see and an eighteenth-century Our Lady of Kazan, valuable mainly because of the silver and gold casing which was set with precious stones. Maisie examined the Dormition carefully. There was no doubt in her mind that it was genuine, unmistakably late-fifteenth-century and from a Novgorod painter.

'Must we keep meeting like this, Mrs Shergold?' The sweet, chirping voice was familiar, but she could not remember the name of the tall pale Englishman, from one of the London sale rooms. 'I expect you're after the Dormition,' he went on, 'it's going to run up beyond its value.'

'It wouldn't surprise me,' said Maisie, trying to recall the man's name. The mild, dreamy look was deceptive – she guessed he was interested in the naïve painting of a family having a meal. He laughed and chirruped, 'You're quite right.'

Nightingale, that was it – Simon Nightingale.

'Come for a drink,' he said, 'it doesn't start for a couple of hours. You know old Pearson, don't you?' Another tall Englishman leered jokily at her. She had never seen him in her life. But they all ended up eating salad and pancakes stuffed with caviare and drinking a peppery vodka.

Old Pearson squeezed lemon over his pancake. 'They tell me the auctioneer is more used to dealing in horses – it should be an interesting afternoon. You're after the Dormition, Nightingale tells me.'

'That's right,' said Maisie.

'It's an odd way of doing things, I must say. There's so

239

much stuff, half of it hasn't been properly categorized – everything chucked in together. If you get your ikon, have you got a licence to get it out?'

'That part is nothing to do with me,' said Maisie, 'thank goodness.' She knew she should stay and talk shop, that way she might glean a few hints as to who she might be up against in the bidding. But she really did not feel like being with Nightingale and Pearson after their second vodkas. She was not doing her duty, but for once she didn't care and made an excuse to leave.

'See you there,' she said.

'Expect we'll manage to stagger back, won't we, Pearson?' Nightingale cheeped happily.

Maisie went out into the sunny street and walked about for a bit. Then, on the spur of the moment, she ran up the steps to the Russian Museum – she'd not been there for ages, and there it was lying in her path. Inside it was pleasantly cool and ordered. A few soft-footed people wandered about, almost on tiptoe, as people do in museums. The place was not at all crowded. She thought she would have a look round, then go and get a coffee, perhaps read a newspaper, until it was time to go back to the auction.

She was in the Marine Gallery, she discovered, which housed the paintings of the great Russian painter Aivazovsky, Russia's Turner. Leo had once, years ago, had one of his early landscapes through his hands. A huge painting dominated the room she was in. She was looking at . . . the sea. Sparkling, frothing, wet. You could have jumped into it. A great wave threw itself up, with a great shattering force, a violent crack. Deep underneath there, deep in the deepest depths, there was a force, a single power which held together the chaos, the seeming chaos, of the surface waves, which tossed about so furiously, so madly. And quite by the way, a ship was tossed, broken, sinking; small humans, unimportant, soon to be obliterated, were hanging on to the broken mast. It hardly seemed to matter whether they survived, one knew they would not survive this sea. Against its power their little lives were inconspicuous, of no consequence at all. The rending sound of the mast was swallowed up in the roaring mouth of the sea.

The painting was about abandonment. The sea itself was abandoned to its own power, given up to it. And the little figures were abandoned in another sense – abandoned by everything, like a fistful of warm little toys thrown into the foam. There was no sign anywhere of Divine providence, only of an overwhelming creative power and energy. It was called *The Wave*; Maisie called it *Abandonment*.

She turned away from the great picture. The place was emptying.

She saw him first.

He was putting on his glasses to look at his catalogue. At first she thought she had seen him, not in reality, but in some inward way. As it was so impossible that he should be here, some part of her brain denied it, told her it was not so.

Only when he turned and recognized her, came over quickly to her, seized her by the hands, his face bright . . . only feeling him, the warmth and touch of his hands, hearing him say, 'Maisie, Maisie'. . . only then did she think it really might be him.

'Hallo, Michael,' she whispered. 'Is it you?'

He wiped his glasses, then, folding them with one hand, he put them in his pocket. His every small movement, the expressions which came and went around the mouth and eyes, seemed to her incredible and unique, and engaged her shaking heart. His eyes looked very green, greener than she remembered them, with a light like the light that flickers over the sea.

He was holding her wrists then, delicately between finger and thumb. 'Your little wrists,' he said. The words were jagged, painful.

Maisie was so overwhelmed by this meeting, it was as if they had never left and lost one another. Amazed that they had ever parted, she had forgotten how it had happened. They did not embrace each other then, or kiss. Only touched each other delicately, lightly, with feathery touches.

'Why are you here?' she said. 'In Russia?'

Michael laughed at the incredible fact of his being there, meeting her, and stroked her fingers. He ran his fingers lightly over the contours of her face.

'Let's go and find somewhere to sit down,' he said, 'before we fall down.'

He led her out of the building, down the stairs.

Somewhere a table and two chairs appeared on the pavement outside a restaurant. A little boy came and asked them what they wanted to drink.

'Coffee,' said Maisie. Her legs were still shaking. 'Coffee, please.'

But Michael said he needed something stronger and had a vodka. 'I'm beginning to like the stuff,' he said, raising his glass. 'To us, Fig,' he said. He drained the glass.

'Why are you in Russia?' she asked. 'Here in St Petersburg?'

'It must have been to find you,' he said.

She thought she had never been so wildly happy.

She drank some coffee. He ordered another vodka. 'Would you like something to eat?'

She shook her head and laughed at such a strange idea.

'No, but what are you doing here?' she said again. 'I can't take it in – that it's you, Michael.' She was looking at him, the features she had not been able to recall, the way his dark hair grew, the bitter edge to that flashing, open smile. Her happiness was such a relief, all considerations thrown recklessly, thankfully to the winds.

'I'm with Sergei and his lot,' said Michael. 'This is where it's all happening – the music scene, I mean. I've been here all week, working hard – Sergei fixed up the whole thing. It's been very exciting.'

'Sergei here?'

'Yes, it's work. I was just taking a few hours off, the recording is all done now. I've been really strung up – when I saw you I thought I'd finally gone crazy. Where are you staying, Maisie?'

'With friends. Rose is with me. Where are you staying?'

'In some dive with Sergei and the boys. Everyone sleeps on the floor. Six blokes sharing a washbasin, it's pretty basic – well, bordering on the sordid, really.'

I can't take her back there, thought Michael, and Maisie thought, I can't possibly take him to the Abrahamovs.

(So the gods, it seemed, had set up this meeting, in the face of every other likely eventuality, every other path that might have been taken – and then lost interest in their predicament.)

'Do you have to be back?' she asked. The thought of letting him out of her sight threw her into a panic. He would disappear, she would lose him in this big city . . . she saw herself running down the Nevsky Prospekt frantically searching for him.

'No, I'm a free man now the recording's done.'

'I have to go back to an auction,' she said, 'I'm bidding for a client. Oh, God, I have to go back.'

'I'll come with you,' said Michael.

They held hands as they hurried to the auction rooms. When they got there it was all something of a blur to Maisie. The horse-trading auctioneer, who turned out to be nothing of the kind, Nightingale and Pearson suddenly sober and all as sharp as splintered glass.

Maisie lost the ikon to a private Russian collector – some said the wife of someone in the government. She was glad anyway that it was to stay in Russia. She said so to Michael. He put his arms round her and kissed her then.

'You and your ikons,' he said.

# 2

UNABLE to say goodbye to each other, they ended up collecting Rose from the Abrahamovs' house, where she was reading Tom Wolfe in the bedroom, and all three going round to the sleazy lodgings to meet Sergei. By this time Rose had had enough of her own company to be sociable. She took Michael's appearance with a certain resignation, as if she knew it was bound to happen sooner or later, and as if her mother had purposely gone out and found him.

As they climbed the dismal tenement steps to the fourth floor, Michael said that everyone was supposed to be going out on the town to celebrate that night, as they had finished their recording. 'It won't be a drunken orgy or anything,' he said, 'at least I don't think so. Prepare yourselves for a bit of squalor now, though,' he added, as he opened the door for them.

The room was smoky and very warm, it smelled of spicy cooking and hashish. Michael made his way across the room between musical equipment and lounging bodies, and opened the window, letting in the noise of heavy traffic. Everyone looked very surprised, and sat up and said how wonderful to see these unexpected guests. They kissed Maisie solemnly and shook hands with Rose, greeting her with warm, flowing eloquence, speaking in Russian.

The girl violinist, Lila, was washing a cooking-pot at the sink. She turned and smiled at Maisie and Rose, wiping her hands on the edge of the ragged chenille tablecloth. She greeted them sweetly. 'I will make coffee,' she said. Michael helped her find a collection of wooden bowls and enamel mugs under chairs, and wash them.

Maisie could see that Rose was fascinated by them all, by their sangfroid and carelessness. She was especially enchanted by Sergei, whose witty, exuberant broken English she drank in like an elixir.

Lila covered the chenille tablecloth with a piece of oilcloth ringed with stains, and set the bowls and mugs round with instinctive ceremony, managing to invest what she was doing with a pleasant human ritual. Everyone thanked her.

'You must come with us,' said Sergei, 'we are going to make the town red. Will you come with us, Rose?' He turned towards her, he was irresistible.

'You go,' said Maisie. 'See the other St Petersburg.'

'Maisie and I won't come, Sergei,' said Michael. 'We've got a lot to talk about. They'll take care of Rose,' he said to Maisie. He looked at her hesitantly, anxiously, thinking she looked sad. 'Are you all right?' he asked her.

'Yes, I'm fine,' she said. She was beginning to find the presence of so many people, when all she wanted was to be alone with Michael, hard to bear.

At last they were all ready to go. It was arranged that they would bring Rose back to the Abrahamovs. Then they were gone, clattering down the steps, laughing and shouting.

Michael and Maisie stood by the window, looking down at the concrete yard with a few silvery birch trees shivering in the sun, and the stream of traffic. Michael closed the window, and the silence settled round them. Neither of them knew what to say, they groped towards speech.

'You haven't changed,' he said. 'You're still the same.'

'I've changed,' said Maisie.

He touched her waist, putting his hands around it in a deliberate possessive gesture. She kept still, looking at the birch trees, then at last at him, a little curiously, for, feeling his hands around her waist, she realized he must have simply forgotten about her pregnancy, about the baby she was to have had, his baby. She was astonished that he had forgotten, but she did not want to talk about it. How could she really know anything about this man, she thought, how his mind worked, what was in his mind, if that had been so forgettable, so unimportant in his scale of things?

'Well, it's been decided for us, hasn't it?' he said. 'If we turn away from each other now, we are flying in the face of . . . flying in the face of . . . something.' He said it as if he believed cosmic forces had brought them together. Perhaps that was true.

'All the million different ways we could have taken. Yet step by step we were brought together,' he kissed her hair, 'to the same country, the same city, the same room – on the same day, at the same hour. Maisie.' His hands tightened round her waist, his thumbs stroking towards her groin. He made it sound as if there was no turning back now. In a way she knew she had gone along with that by coming here at all. Michael's closeness, his close physical presence, the fact that he wanted her so much sexually – if she had not wanted this, she should not have come, for she had known it would be like this.

He led her to the bedroom, where there were several unmade beds – mattresses and half-clean sheets and rough army blankets lying everywhere. Piles of clothes spilled out of unzipped bags and there was a litter of empty cans and bottles.

'I'm sorry about the mess,' said Michael. He tried to tidy one of the beds, but could do nothing about the dirty-looking sheets and ancient pillows with no pillow-cases.

'Not here, Michael,' said Maisie. She suddenly felt drained and depressed. There was a little silence.

'No – not here,' said Michael. 'Come on, let's go out somewhere. What about your place?'

'That's impossible – the people I'm staying with – it's impossible.'

'We'll have to find a hotel room,' said Michael.

'Let's just go out for a walk. Have a drink somewhere.'

'Yes, all right, Maisie,' said Michael. 'I'm sorry to have brought you here.'

'Don't be sorry.'

As they went down the staircase, Maisie felt further depressed by the deadening smell of urban poverty, set in concrete; of old people living on cabbage and young people living on drink. The infinitely dismal wailing of a baby came from behind closed doors.

'Christ, how can you live here?' said Maisie.

'We only sleep here,' said Michael. 'It's just a doss, we don't notice it. I'm sorry to bring you here, Maisie,' he said again.

'Rose didn't seem to notice it either,' admitted Maisie, as if questioning her own sensibility. But she could never have gone to bed with Michael in this place, lain with him in those unsavoury sheets. It did not occur to her to wonder if she would have felt differently at the beginning of their affair when even the litter in the streets seemed glorified.

They went to a place Michael knew, near the river, and sat with their drinks in a little courtyard. There was a flower-stall there; a toothless woman, dressed in a heavy winter coat in spite of the warm weather, shuffled her bunches of gladioli.

They sat opposite each other.

'Do you want to talk about Ireland?' Michael drank quickly. She thought he looked impatient, even angry.

'There's nothing to say,' replied Maisie. 'I got your letters,' she added.

'You never answered, though.'

'No.'

247

'I was waiting for a word from you, Maisie. Waiting every day for a word. Were you punishing me?'

'No.'

Maisie was watching the flower-seller fumbling with the flowers. As someone bought a bunch of them, the old woman took the money, stowing it in her leather bag, in that peculiar way peasants have of touching money, as if it is a commodity, like eggs or grain. She felt Maisie watching her and gave her a toothless grin. Maisie smiled back.

'What are you laughing at?' Michael got up, draining his glass quickly. 'Would you like another drink?'

'I haven't finished this one,' said Maisie. He went to buy himself more vodka, coming back with a whole bottle, which he put on the table. The look in his eyes was wild, incoherent, almost puzzled.

'Did you have to get rid of the baby as well as me?' he said. He sounded aggressive.

'You've got a fucking nerve,' she said slowly. She was angry now. She wept a little.

He put his hand on hers. 'Don't be angry,' he said. He looked confused, unhappy.

She saw this human, fallible, faithless man, this slightly drunk, bewildered, angry man, who did not know which way to turn. This man who still loved her. Whom she still loved.

She told him then about losing the baby, the brief facts. And she told him about her mother, that she was dead.

He listened, his eyes down, to all this and then he told her he was sorry. Everything was his fault. He just went round messing up people's lives. He heaped coals of fire on his own head – her mother's death was probably caused through her worry over Maisie, and their relationship.

'That really is nonsense,' said Maisie. Then, changing the subject, she began talking about how she had come to be in St Petersburg. 'Rose needed a change and anyway I wanted to attend the mass for the ikon's return to Russia.'

'You mean our ikon?'

Maisie smiled. 'Yes – our ikon. A church in St Petersburg was chosen – probably safer than Moscow for the monarchists, and a better rallying place.'

'Safer? Haven't you heard what has happened in the city?' Maisie shook her head.

'One of the monarchists has been murdered in the street. In the Kirovsky Prospekt – he had been addressing an open-air meeting in the park.'

'Oh, God, how dreadful – what a foolhardy thing to have done.'

'Yes, he must have thought he was in Hyde Park – well, he wasn't. He found that out.'

'It's dreadful, dreadful. Who did it?' she asked. She had tears in her eyes.

'I don't expect we shall ever know. There are plenty of theories.'

'When did it happen?'

'It happened at lunchtime – just before we met in the museum, in fact.'

'You never said anything.'

'It was such a shock seeing you, I had forgotten about it – until now. Do you think they will be warned off, your monarchists?'

'No, I don't think so.'

'I don't think so either.'

'Do you care – how it all ends for them?'

'Maisie, I've told you before, if you've got any sense you don't get mixed up in this sort of thing. They're all as bad as each other. I hate politics, it stinks. Music is where I live, I'm just not interested in all the rest.'

'Yes, that's why you're here in Russia . . . it's got nothing to do with some cosmic plan – with meeting me.'

'Yes, it has. We're being given another chance. Let's start again, from the beginning, as if we were strangers. As if we had just met now – here. I saw you and I came over and asked if you wanted a drink. I'd never met you before. Like that.'

'Things don't work like that. You can't wipe it clean and start again – we're not children's chalk drawings on a slate. We're flesh and blood.'

'Let's try.'

'It's no good.'

'Let's try – just do what I say. Just trust me, let me lead you.'

'You said that once before.' And then she remembered the time, with a shock that it had ever happened, when he had put his hands on her throat. It seemed incredible to her now that it had not angered her more deeply at the time. She had been in a dream.

'This time I'll lead you more carefully,' Michael was saying. 'I'll be careful.'

'Perhaps I would be better at it – leading, I mean.'

'No.'

'Why not?'

He shrugged. 'This time I'll be more careful,' he said again.

Maisie sighed.

'Let's walk,' she said. She felt restless. The news about the murder saddened her.

As they left the courtyard Michael bought a bunch of white gladioli and put them in her arms. 'Now you look like a Quaker bride, in that grey thing you're wearing.'

'Now I've got to carry these about St Petersburg.'

'I'll carry them,' he said, taking the flowers. He smiled at her, that smile that was like no one else's. She kissed him then. He put his arm round her, looking happy.

'Let's be happy,' he said. 'To hell with everyone.'

'I'd like to see where it happened – the assassination,' Maisie said quietly.

'That's not being happy.' He hesitated. 'Come on, then,' he said.

She knew she was falling in love all over again, only this time there was more pain in it, and more knowledge. How could she help loving him? Everything he said, every inflection, every movement.

He took her to see the place where the Russian had been gunned down in the street. The blood-stained pavement had been covered in flowers. Who were the people, wondered Maisie, who came and laid their wreaths of red, blue and white flowers – the Tsarist colours – weren't they afraid to be seen? Apparently not. It was not just old people who came, there were all types and ages, even children. The spot was heaped with carnations and cornflowers, peonies and lilies.

Maisie took one of the white gladioli from Michael, and laid it on the place. 'This is one good way,' said Michael, 'to make sure their cause will live on.'

Maisie felt very shaken. She wondered suddenly if Rose was all right. Abruptly she said, 'Goodbye, Michael – I must get back,' and she started to run for a tram she had seen which would take her in the right direction for the Abrahamovs' house. Michael ran after her.

'Don't come with me,' she gasped as she jumped on the tram, which had begun to move. Michael thrust the flowers in her arms. 'I'll come tomorrow,' he shouted.

She sat down, getting her breath, she held up a hand to wave. He was standing there now, looking very young. It was something she usually forgot about him – he was so young. Neither of us has mentioned Kate, she thought, as the tram rattled along.

When she got back to the Abrahamovs, Elena greeted her. 'How sweet,' she said, taking the flowers from Maisie, 'sweet of you.' She asked Maisie to fill a Chinese vase with water. She placed the vase of flowers on an ivory and mother-of-pearl inlaid table. They looked exotic and rare in that setting.

'Have you heard the news?' asked Maisie.

'Yes, that is the way of the world now. Vasily is very angry, he has gone to bed. Goodnight, my dear.'

In her room, Maisie prepared for bed, but she would not sleep, she was not sure if Rose had a key. She sat up in bed reading, hoping that Rose would not be too late. She felt slightly uneasy about her, and was relieved when she arrived at last, her eyes bright, full of unaccustomed animation, not at all tired now.

'Sergei will be going home soon,' she said. 'He has invited us all to a picnic, the Abrahamovs as well, all of us. Will you come to the picnic?' Rose was still wide awake.

'Yes, of course. I don't know if Elena and Vasily will come. In spite of everything, they are getting too old for picnics, perhaps.'

'We have to take a train to the place, I can't remember the name – Sergei knows it. I hope the weather stays fine.'

'Go to sleep, then.'

'I'm glad I came to Russia,' said Rose. 'Are you, Mummy?'

Maisie pretended she was already asleep.

# 3

THEY woke to a sun like solid gold, burning against a periwinkle sky. It was going to be a very hot day.

Elena and Vasily were enchanted with the idea of a picnic. Elena found a battered straw hat and tied a piece of net round it. Wearing this, she made some lemonade to take.

'A picnic will do Vasily so much good – he is depressed today,' she said.

'Sergei said we are all to meet at the railway station,' said Rose. 'He will bring Michael and anyone else who wants to come.'

Rose put her drawing materials in a large canvas shoulder-bag. 'I'm going to sketch,' she said. Maisie was surprised and pleased; Rose had done little of the kind since leaving university. There was a new tone in her daughter's voice, eager and lively. Maisie put on a white linen suit and tied a white silk scarf round her head.

When they got to the station, Sergei and Michael had just arrived with the drummer in the group (an older man, who seldom spoke) and a boy with an undernourished look and a merry smile, and Lila. They had brought a big cardboard box full of rye loaves, hard goat's cheese and strawberries. Michael had brought his flute and flagons of wine, and looked to Maisie more attractive than she had ever seen him, he had taken to wearing his dark hair a little longer, and she liked it.

'You look ravishing,' he said to her, touching her face.

'So do you,' she said.

'All of us are ravishing,' said Sergei, not knowing what the word meant but liking the sound of it. He helped the old people on to the train, making a great fuss of them.

The train was a stopping country train, and had wooden carriages. It pulled out with a great jerk. Michael and Maisie stayed in the corridor together, Michael holding the back of her neck with one hand, and steadying them both with the other hand on the sash of the open window. As they left St Petersburg and its suburbs and made for open countryside, the smell of grass came through the window and, in the heat, the fields of rye seemed to shimmer and move like water. There was a burst of laughter from the carriage, where everyone seemed happy and convivial.

Michael whispered in her ear. 'I want to make love to you,' and then, in the other ear, as if they were two separate secrets, 'I love you.'

But in spite of her happiness, Maisie tried to name her feelings and objectify her desire for this man, in a brave, high-spirited attempt to refuse herself permission to be overcome by love, as she had been and as she knew she could be once more. Michael, knowing intuitively what was going on, tried in subtle ways to break through her fragile defences, but she remained light and hung on to her precarious gaiety. It was a tightrope she was walking. If she fell, she might never again be restored to herself. The vertiginous feeling was like being drunk. She was in some sort of ecstasy, which had some connection with grief.

The sights and sounds around her impinged on her with unusual intensity. Michael was an integral part of it all, but he was not the centre of it, not the focal point. There was no centre, no focal point, everything she saw and experienced was interrelated, everything part of everything else.

'Are you happy?' He probed her feelings.

'Brilliantly happy,' she said, smiling and kissing him. But he was perplexed by something. The first feeling he had ever had about her, that she could slip away from him, came back to him strongly. He stroked her hair, arranging the strands that escaped her scarf to his liking.

They were speeding past great rolling expanses of rye grass and buttercups. Then they stopped at a tiny wooden station with a Pepsi Cola sign on the platform as if it was the name of the place, none other being visible. A man with a long-handled axe got on.

Rose left the others and came out to join them while the train was stopped. She leaned out of the open window. 'Isn't it all beautiful?' she said.

There was the feeling of the train being a temporary home. Everyone seemed to settle down quite naturally and do the sort of things they would do at home. People were playing cards and having meals, not in the way English people do, with a packet of egg and cress sandwiches, surreptitiously, but laying everything out, producing a cloth, bringing out bottles of pickles, everything. Someone was even shaving into a bowl of water held by his little boy. The boy cursed as the train started again, spilling soapy water. Rose went back into the carriage with the others.

Michael shifted Maisie in front of him and stood holding her from behind. She felt his warm breath on the back of her neck, she breathed in the sweet warm country air.

Underneath her undoubted very real passion for him, there was this insistent voice which questioned everything, reminded her of what had happened in Ireland. Yet love was not a bargain – I'll only love you if you'll love me only. Only me, for ever and ever. Once she had been drawn to his look of freedom, his non-attachment, she had wanted it for herself.

He wanted to reclaim her, she knew, by making love to her. From this she held back. She wanted the choice to be hers, not his. She would not be consumed by him. There was no doubt that she loved him, but she would not claim him. How often does he think of Kate? she wondered. Every day? She was surprised that the thought gave her no pain at all.

Something was different now. She had retrieved her self. Because of this, her love spilled out towards the world in a way it had not done when it had been trapped, narrowed to those things that were to do with her lover . . . the station where she had met him, everything he came in contact with she had loved as if it was part of him, his environment and aura. Now her love and her interest spilled over to Sergei and Rose and their friends, to the Abrahamovs in the railway carriage, laughing and making a noise. To the old couple with their pickled herrings, and the man shaving and his serious little boy holding the bowl as steady as he could in the rocking train. It spread out to the fields of rye and the buttercups reflecting the bright gold of the sun, to the very breeze which Maisie drew in with her nostrils.

Other people had been shadows to her, now they were infinitely human and real. Yet it was all precarious. Michael's hold over her emotions was still alive, still potent. The look of loneliness in his eyes struck at her heart, but she hid that from him.

The train stopped at a halt in open country, and Sergei started to bundle them out. 'Follow me,' he said, leading the way across the track.

They walked single-file through the long grass threaded with poppies and many other wild flowers. It felt high above sea-level here, the air was thin and dry and hot.

Sergei led his little tribe to the shade of a clump of heavily foliaged trees. In this oasis, they sat and rested in the lovely black shade, and spread out their picnic.

'It's good to be out of the city,' said Vasily, 'where such terrible things happen.'

The drummer produced some small hard-boiled eggs like gull's eggs from his pockets, and silently offered them round. He ate his, shell and all, to general fascination.

Rose made sketches of the old people, Elena in her hat, Vasily with his strange gaze. And she made several sketches of Sergei. She told him she would like to paint his portrait. He was very pleased.

Michael played for them on his flute for a while, obligingly playing what was asked for. Then he and Maisie wandered off. They found a small stream and sat down by it. It was very hot, and Maisie took off her scarf and soaked it in the water, and wiped her face, and Michael's face.

'It's too hot to be out of the shade,' she said.

'I want to be alone with you,' he answered. He kissed her, the sun scorching down on them.

'We must go back,' she said. 'The sun is too hot to bear.'

'Do you love me?' he asked. 'Do you still love me?'

'Yes,' she said.

They walked back to the shady trees and sat with the others, drinking Elena's lemonade, watching a hawk hovering in the blue sky.

'How cruel nature is,' said Rose. She said it in a lively, curious way, as if it had just struck her.

'It gives an edge to life,' said Elena. 'What a soft, cosy, boring world it would be without cruelty.' She meant it.

'Yet you are upset and depressed by things that happen in the world – by the murder in the Kirovsky Prospekt, for instance,' said Maisie.

'No, it is not me who is depressed by it,' said Elena, 'it is Vasily. He is an idealist and believes society is perfectible. Vasily believes everything should be achieved by education and dialogue. I do not share this belief.'

Vasily's eyes were closed, but he was not asleep. 'In my last life,' he said, 'I was living in classical Greece. It was preferable. I preferred it.'

Sergei was standing by one of the trees, eating strawberries, his face in profile for Rose to draw. He was pointing to the horizon. 'Look,' he said.

They all looked in surprise. A dark storm-cloud was rolling in. It was an incredible sight, it looked more like smoke from a great explosion or fire than anything else, but it was a dark rain-cloud unrolling like a black carpet across the sky, still in the distance.

When they got back to the halt where they would pick up their train, it had become quite dark. But it still did not rain. On the way back Maisie sat in the carriage with Michael's arm round her.

At the next stop some gipsies got on. They sat apart, aware of their apartness but proud and swaggering, not in a boastful way – the swaggering was natural to them. One of the women had a baby dressed in rich, princely gear.

Maisie closed her eyes. Sergei began singing, and they all sang Russian songs in the gloom. Like people being taken across the Styx.

# 4

ALTHOUGH the lovely weather had broken, and it was
heavy and sultry, still it did not rain. Everyone was
waiting for it, wishing it would. The metallic sky seemed to
rest on the golden domes and rooftops.

Sergei had invited Rose to go back with him to Kiev and
meet Annya, and paint his portrait. So it was arranged that
Rose should do this, and that she and her mother would
meet up in Moscow for a look at the capital before they
returned to London.

Maisie would not go with them to Kiev. Nothing would
have made her miss the Eucharist when the ikon was to find
a Russian home. And she could not, in any case, have
brought herself to leave Michael, who had one more engage-
ment in St Petersburg: he was to give a whole day workshop
of his own songs at the School of Music. The Russians loved
him and took his work more seriously than anyone else had
ever done.

Maisie asked him if he would go with her to the
Eucharist. 'I am going everywhere with you,' he said.

When it came to it, they had some difficulty in finding
the church. A taxi dropped them off at what turned out to
be the wrong place, and they walked about for some time
before they found it, the Church of the Apparition of the

Virgin. It was already jammed with people. It was doubtful whether two more people could be squeezed in, but they found a space to breathe, stepping up on to a stone ridge at the back of the church. Here they leaned back, against scooped-out recesses, which made Maisie feel as if she and Michael were living frescoes. They had a perfect view over the heads of the mass of people, and they were not too near the heat from the thousands of candles.

They had entered another world, although this church did not have the same ancient and mysterious feeling that had belonged to the one in Kiev they had visited. It was lighter, its atmosphere more joyful and optimistic. There were pillars covered in lapis lazuli, beautiful ironwork, banks of white geraniums whose scent freshened the heavy air and mixed with the smell of incense, angelic statues with gold-tipped wings leaning in towards the centre from the domed ceiling.

The iconostasis was one of the most exquisitely harmonious that Maisie had ever seen, each ikon enriching and balancing every other. She longed to see it more closely. She was surprised that this church had been hitherto unregarded by her, and was not marked on the tourist map. It was obviously used and loved. 'Look,' she whispered to Michael. 'The ikon.'

People were waiting in line to kiss with reverent fervour the famous Ikon of the Steppes, which was placed apart in front of the iconostasis. All the while, through the long service, that peculiarly Russian sound of the choir, that low, warm, rich, reverberating sound, with a thrilling harsh edge, rose and fell, rose and fell. Maisie thought of Denisov, and wished he was here, thought perhaps he was. She thought too of the murdered Russian, no doubt now a martyr to the monarchist cause.

A huge basket of crumbled bread was blessed. A priest removed the red napkin from a gold cup of wine. Then a line of people patiently formed a queue, like a bread queue; priests and acolytes moved amongst the press of people who kissed their robes.

Maisie, absorbed in the scene, was becoming dimly aware of something unconnected to what she was watching – sudden bright stabs which spotlighted the gold-tipped angels, a different, whiter, more eerie light than the warm glow from the racks of candles. And again, underneath the sonorous music of the choir, a sound like gunfire or thunder. Then another sound, a sudden noise which she could not identify. She looked at Michael.

'Rain,' he whispered, 'it's a storm.'

At the end of the service, the doors were opened to a sheet of water falling from the sky. As they prepared to go, hesitantly because of the inevitability of getting drenched, Michael spoke to her quietly. 'Don't go that way,' he said softly, quickly. Maisie caught a glimpse of what he had seen. Waiting out in the pouring rain were half a dozen armed soldiers.

Maisie felt faint. 'We must warn them,' she said.

But Michael seized her hand and, holding it in a tight grip, pulled her sharply towards a small door on the opposite side. 'Shut up,' he said.

When they were outside he said, 'Don't be a bloody fool, Maisie. Let's just get out of here. I'm not going to end up in a police cell. Anyway,' he said, 'we're all going to be drowned.' The streets were deserted and running with water.

A lone tram loomed into sight, lit up like a ship, and moving slowly. Michael hauled Maisie on board and they collapsed on to a seat, soaked to the skin.

'Where is it going?' Maisie wiped the water from her eyes.

'Away from whatever is going on in there,' said Michael. 'I'm glad I was with you,' he added.

'You sensed all along there would be trouble,' she said.

'Yes, I've been brought up with a nose for it, I suppose.'

'I'm glad you got me out, Michael, but we deserted them.'

'There's nothing either of us could do. It's all a foregone thing. We are onlookers, bystanders. Anyway, perhaps it's not God's plan – the monarchy, I mean – perhaps God has got something different and even more mysterious in mind.'

Looking at Maisie's distressed, anxious face he said, 'I expect they will just pick up a few people for questioning and then release them. Some of them may be kicked out of the country. They haven't actually done anything – they can't be that much of a threat, there's no army as far as we know.'

'The interest of the people makes them a threat,' said Maisie.

'Yes, well, that's not our problem. Our problem is where the hell are we?'

The tram had stopped because of the depth of water they were in. They were near the river, and the whole wide street was completely flooded. Further down, the river was in full flood, a yellowish-brown, fast-flowing torrent of water. Someone was paddling a boat along the drowned street, shouting something. No one else was about.

'Jesus,' said Michael.

'The Abrahamovs' house must be flooded.' Maisie felt a stab of alarm.

Holding on to each other for safety, they began to make their slow way through the water, which at times was up to Maisie's knees. It took them nearly an hour to reach the Abrahamovs' house, it was so difficult making a way through the flood-water. Sometimes someone in an upper window called to them to be careful.

When they got to the house, they found the water up to the ground-floor window-sills. Michael climbed on to a sill and managed to open a window, and he pulled Maisie into the house after him. A weird and desolate sight met their eyes. The Abrahamovs' treasures from all over the world were floating, bobbing about in the dirty water.

Michael fished out a goblet and a bronze Chinese opium pipe. Maisie started to laugh. She had no idea why, the laughter just seized her. Michael gave her a sudden grin, and kissed her.

They found Elena and Vasily Abrahamov sitting up in bed fully clothed. Elena was reading to her husband from *Leaves of Grass*. She motioned them to be quiet, ignoring their weary and dishevelled appearance. They sank quietly to the floor and listened as they were told 'Of the terrible doubt of appearances . . . of the uncertainty after all, that we may be deluded.' Vasily nodded his head as Elena read, translating the words in his mind into his native tongue.

Elena silently pointed to the samovar, inviting Michael and Maisie to help themselves. Beside the samovar were glasses in beautiful silver holders. They helped themselves gratefully to tea. Vasily, hearing them, greeted them, telling them to listen. 'Go on,' he said impatiently to his wife.

'Maybe the things I perceive, the animals, plants, men, hills, shining and flowing waters . . . the skies of day and night, colours, densities, forms, maybe these are (doubtless they are) only apparitions, and the real something to be known.'

This time the lightning and the thunder came together, rattling the glasses on the table. Sitting there on the floor, wet through, listening to the words of the poem punctuated by thunderclaps, Maisie was overwhelmed with loneliness, and she reached out for Michael's hand. 'Come on,' she said, 'we can't sit about here drenched.' But they finished their tea, telling the Abrahamovs what had happened.

'The police do not know all the secrets of this city,' said Vasily. 'The crypt of the Church of the Apparition gives off to underground tunnels. I doubt very much if the soldiers got their hands on the ringleaders. Not the ones they wanted, anyway – they've probably picked up a few entirely useless suspects.'

'Yes,' said Michael, 'it could easily have been us.'

'You must go and get all those wet things off,' said Elena. 'It is very foolish of you to sit about like that.'

But before they did, they brought up as many of the Abrahamovs' treasures as they could find. Then Maisie led Michael to the room she had been sharing with Rose. She had left the window wide open and the rain had come in and soaked Rose's bed by the window.

They took off all their clothes. They were both grimy from the flood-water they had waded through, and they wiped each other dry. They were shaking with cold. Maisie got into her bed.

'Come into bed,' she said. They held each other until they had stopped shivering. Michael kissed her cold mouth.

It would have been all right if she had died that afternoon. The world was this room, this man, this particular afternoon which had no beginning and no end in existence. This room – the white damask curtains, heavily fringed, the elegant chair, prints of troikas in the snow on the walls. A decorous room. The brass bed they lay in was high and narrow, with stylized flowers on the enamelled panels at head and foot. The world was this room, the world was here and now.

Michael lay in Maisie's arms in the narrow bed, and grew warmer. She bent over and kissed him. 'We are both covered in mud still. Do you mind?' he said. She shook her head.

Huddled together under the duvet, their legs twined and wrapped in each other, their bodies remembered each other. The storm had passed over, and they could hear it only intermittently in the distance; it left a sort of peace in its trail. They made love like old friends, like a long-married couple. It was better than it had ever been between them, because they were asking each other no questions. Both of them had decided that things were as they were, that it was so and that was it, what happened afterwards . . . well, there was no afterwards.

It had been such a long time since Maisie had held him close like this. Naked, he was a different creature, as she was different, stripped of more than clothes. 'How different we are without clothes,' she said.

Michael laughed. 'Tell me,' he said.

'Quite different creatures. Don't you feel different naked?'

'You feel different to me naked, Maisie. Different to me. Much, much better. You feel incredibly better. I can't describe what you feel like – like nothing else in the entire universe.' But she meant that in taking off their clothes, they had been changed.

No one had ever felt like this to Maisie. No one ever would. 'Our bodies are so hard to tear apart.'

'They are thanking each other,' said Michael strangely. Maisie wondered if they were saying goodbye. She did not know, they led a life hidden in part from her.

'I'll run a bath,' she said.

'I haven't any clothes to put on,' said Michael.

'Good. I shall keep you here. Now you are my prisoner.'

She took his clothes into the bathroom and laid them on the hot tank to dry, and found him a towelling robe. The bathroom was a large room, converted from one of the original bedrooms. Maisie ran the water. They both got into the huge, old-fashioned bath.

'Did you lock the door?' she said.

'Yes, of course.'

'I don't think our hosts would approve.'

'After all we did for them. Retrieving their opium pipes.' Michael began methodically soaping and washing Maisie's back.

'How lovely water is,' she said, 'how lovely to be made clean by it.'

'Shall I wash your hair?'

'Have you ever had a bath with Kate?' asked Maisie.

'Shut up about Kate,' said Michael.

'Did you wash her hair? She has lovely hair.'

'I can't stand this,' said Michael. He got out of the bath and began drying himself.

'It's not going to work, is it?' he said.

'I don't expect so.' Her voice sounded odd, thin, far away, someone else's voice. 'Did you make love to Philomena?' The same voice asked it. She hadn't known she was going to say this and the idea had not occurred to her before, it was preposterous.

'Yes,' he said. He put on the dressing-gown. He did not look at her.

She nodded her head slowly. 'Why?' And why did she ask? Did it matter why?

'Because you weren't there. Because she was getting her own back on you for not having an affair with her. Because I was drunk and miserable. Oh – I don't know why. Christ!'

'I thought you did not like her.'

'I don't like her.'

'I remember you said women seem to decide things for you. Any woman you come across does what she likes with you, as if you had no say in any of it. It must be really inconvenient and awful for you. I suppose it was the same with me.' (She thought of him saying 'Because you loved me first,' and how it had moved her.)

'Have you finished being sarcastic?'

'You seem to have made love to practically everyone.'

'Practically everyone,' agreed Michael. He unlocked the door and went out, slamming it.

Then he came back. 'Look,' he said, 'I may be a weak and stupid bloody man, but as it happens I love you. I don't love Kate – not as I love you. Certainly I don't love Philomena. I love you – very, very much. I should get out – the water's cold.'

Maisie got out and dried herself carefully and put on her

Russian kimono. She was staggered by what he had told her, completely taken aback, even though she had suggested it might be so. 'I never knew you,' she said, 'I never knew anything about you.'

'I'm tired,' he said. He looked tired. 'Let's go to bed.'

They went back to the bedroom and climbed into the high, narrow bed. They slept in each other's arms because if they had not they would have fallen out of the bed. It was a dead sort of sleep.

# 5

M AISIE woke early the next day. She unwrapped herself from Michael's arms and slid gently out of bed. Looking out of the window, she saw the river still in flood, but less turbulent. She went into the bathroom and washed, and cleaned her teeth. She took Michael's clothes from the hot-water tank and shook them out. Back in the bedroom, she put them beside him on the chair. He had settled comfortably in the middle of the bed and was sound asleep, lying on his stomach. Moving about quietly, she dressed and sat down on the window-seat. She sat there for a long while, very still, watching Michael's soft, steady breathing, looking at the tidy pile of creased, stained clothes beside him, a pair of socks on top. She noticed, straining to see each detail, as if she must take everything in, that the socks weren't actually a pair. One was a dark blue, the other a lighter colour. It must have been because of the chaos at Sergei's lodging. She hadn't noticed it when they were wet. She knew it would be something she would remember.

After she had written the few words she could manage to think of – there isn't any other way to say goodbye than to say it – she left the note on top of the socks, and left without waking him.

Downstairs the water had been pumped out and the

floors were now being dried by huge, noisy vacuums, wielded like toys by two strong-looking women. Out in the streets the sun was drawing steam from the wet pavements, from which the flood-water had retreated.

This time Maisie found her way to the Church of the Apparition more easily. It had escaped the floods because of its elevated position, and was busy with old women, dressed in black, who were scraping candle-grease from the floor. One or two people, the first pilgrims to the ikon, were kneeling in prayer.

Maisie went up close to the iconostasis. The Ikon of the Mother of God of the Steppes stood on a low lectern. A thousand candles burned in front of it. What did it mean to her? she wondered. Why did it move her? That serene, wakeful gaze of the Mother, that lively, beginning-of-the-world feeling about the Child. What was its unfathomable purpose? What drew her to it? There were no answers to her questions.

Standing there, she felt emptied. On the edge of the world, her toe feeling its blue rim, her foot slipping, sliding. She felt very afraid. Then, as if she had been given an antidote, something to save her, she felt strongly that she was not going to slip, that she was part of the world, really and truly a living part of it. As she stood underneath the roof of the church, as underneath the roof of the world, she felt everything to be invested with livingness. Even the stones of the building that was now arched over her were living stones. They were living as she was living, stone and flesh the same, the same living stuff.

And so, having opened herself to creation, somehow she could let him go. Because he was truly and always part of her, so she could let him go and took him to herself in one delicate movement, hardly detectable, infinitely sweet and bright.

And it was true that his glamour had not been nothing. For this glamour was in the livingness of things, an integral part of the creative exuberance. A shining forth. And she knew that everything, even death, which allowed its renewal, was part of it.

One of the old women in black was replenishing the burnt-down candles. Maisie took a fresh one from the box. She lit it and placed it in front of the ikon.

As she was making her way out of the church, someone touched her on the elbow from behind. It was Werner. 'Dr Shergold,' he said. She remembered that she had written to him and told him that the ikon, which had such a strange place in his life, was to find a home in this St Petersburg church.

They began to go down the steps to the street.

'It was kind of you to write.'

'Were you here yesterday?' asked Maisie, wondering if he could tell her anything of what had happened after she had left with Michael.

'No,' said Werner, 'I arrived too late for that, but . . . I feel this is my own pilgrimage. And I have made it.'

He looked more ordinary than she had remembered him, more balanced and humble. She smiled at him and they shook hands.

'I have to go,' she said, 'I am leaving St Petersburg today and I must pack.'

They went their separate ways, but she did not go back to the Abrahamovs' house. She would not go back until she was sure Michael would be at his workshop at the Music School. She knew he would not miss it. But she also felt that he would not let her end their affair, he would continue it on his own terms to the clap of doom. He never left his women of his own accord. His mother. Kate. He would never leave her of his own accord. And he would put it all down to the fates.

Holding her life carefully in her own hands, she went back to the little open-air coffee-house by the river where she had sat talking to Michael. She had not finished saying goodbye to him, to it all. She sat with her coffee, saying goodbye. The flower-seller was there. The sun shone and the air was clear and sparkling after the storm. She bought a newspaper. There was nothing in it about Nikitich's murder, nothing about any arrests. There was a long piece about the Ikon of the Steppes, and its return to Russia, and the controversy of where it should be. It was a disgrace that it should be in an obscure church, it should be in Moscow, in the city's art gallery, said the newspaper, a movement was afoot to prise it from the church. But in a climate where crucifixes were the latest fashion, the article sounded merely peevish.

She could have passed the afternoon looking at the Picassos in the Hermitage, she could have spent the time in a second-hand bookshop, looking for books that might be useful to her. She just sat in the sun, watching people come and go, making her last farewells to the lover who had touched something in her that would never be touched again.

In her mind she lit another candle to the ikon, and let him go again. And again, she let him go.

The flower-seller was talking to an old man who had bought some flowers. Maisie listened. They were talking about the old Tsar.

'It's all the same,' said the old man. 'Red or white Tsars – it makes no difference to us. They're all Tsars.' The old woman laughed uproariously, as if it was a very good joke. The old man laughed with her, a high-pitched, infectious laugh. They looked across at Maisie and invited her to join their laughter. Maisie folded her paper and drained her coffee and laughed too, until there were tears in her eyes.

At last she made her way back to the Abrahamovs. The house had been put to rights by the minions the Abrahamovs had managed to summon. The place smelled odd, like a river instead of a house, but apart from that things were in order.

Maisie told them she was going to catch the night train

to Moscow to meet Rose, and asked if it would be all right to telephone Kiev. Then she remembered Sergei was not on the telephone, and wondered what on earth to do. She was determined to leave that night, she had to go at once.

She went up to her room and began packing. Rose had left half her things and there were quite a lot of them. All the time Maisie was wondering what she would do. Perhaps she could leave a message for Rose and hope she would telephone. Perhaps she could write to her and give her a Moscow number where she could get in touch. It crossed her mind that it would be easier to stay until Rose did telephone, as had been previously arranged. But Maisie knew she must go before Michael finished at the Music School.

She tidied the room. Then she cleaned the bath. She telephoned the railway station to find the time of the train and reserved a sleeper. As she put the receiver down, it rang. It was Rose.

'Hallo, Mummy. I just thought it was time I rang.'

'I'm leaving for Moscow tonight,' said Maisie. 'I shall travel overnight and I shall be staying at the Gorky, it's near the embassies, it's easy to find. I'll wait for you there.'

'Is everything all right, Mummy? I heard about the floods. I heard on the news about the ikon, there are pilgrims setting out from everywhere. I saw it on the television. Has the monarchy taken over yet?' She laughed.

'I think it's more likely that if anyone takes over it will be the army,' said Maisie. 'The Tsarists have gone to earth.'

'Oh,' said Rose. 'Anyway, Sergei says it's always the same people who are really in power behind everything, holding the strings. That it's all done to fool the people. I've painted Sergei's portrait and I am painting the family now, having a meal. I think it might be good, Mummy. I want you to see what I've done.' She sounded fresh and bright and eager.

'That's wonderful,' said Maisie.

'Yes. I spoke to Daddy on the phone and he said I'd be

an idiot to give up the business and what I should be doing is beginning to collect all the stuff from the Revolution onwards – all the stuff that everyone thinks is rubbish, you know, the pictures of the Workers and the Party and Lenin and everything. Art that followed the Party line. He said it'll be worth its weight in gold in twenty years or less.'

'I expect he's right.'

'I don't want to do that,' said Rose. 'I want to go to art school.'

'What, painting, you mean?'

'Yes, serious art school. The Slade. I'm going to do it. I'm going to sell the business and I'm going to paint.'

'I'll see you soon, anyway,' said Maisie.

'Is Michael coming with you?'

'No – I'll be alone.'

'We'll do Moscow on our own, then.'

Maisie zipped up the bags. She would have to go to the station and wait there if she was really to avoid Michael. After the Music School he would come looking for her at the Abrahamovs. She hoped he would not come to the railway station to find her.

Oh, God, and yet she hoped so desperately that he would. That he would follow her. Take her back. Capture her. Make her his prisoner.

She rang for a taxi and went to thank the Abrahamovs and make her farewells. When she got to the railway station, her train was in, but it was over an hour before it was due to go. She bought a book and went to find a place to settle on the practically empty train.

Her book was the sort of thing she scarcely ever read. Never read, in fact. The hero was called Sasha, and the heroine Valentina. There was a picture of them on the cover. Valentina was young and beautiful, spirited and in love. She said things like: 'Sasha, you are the only man I shall ever love.' Sasha was a handsome soldier, strong-willed but modest. He said things like: 'Valentina, you are my heart's desire.' Sasha also asked, 'Why do you love me? Me? I am not worth it, Valentina.'

As to loving Michael for his qualities, well . . . she hardly knew him. There's no getting to the bottom of a person. So you might just as well love the colour of someone's eyes, the grace of their movements, their flash, quirky smile, or whatever. Valentina loved Sasha's full brown eyes and white, even teeth. Sasha said, 'I can feel your heart beating next to mine, Valentina. I love you.' And Valentina said, 'Oh, Sasha, when you kiss me I nearly faint with love for you.'

A woman with a little girl got into the carriage. Maisie looked up briefly and returned her eyes to the page.

Sasha said, 'It is a cruel fate that takes me away. I have to go with the army. I have to go this very evening.' And Valentina could not speak for tears.

The little girl took two sweets out of her pocket and offered one to Maisie. Maisie smiled at her and said, 'No, thank you,' and the little girl looked pleased she would not lose one of her sweets.

Maisie turned to the end of the book and found the lovers reunited. Sasha said, 'I always knew I would come back to you. Always.' And Valentina said, 'I love you, Sasha.'

Maisie wondered whether if she looked out of the train she would see Michael on the platform desperately searching the crowds for her. She looked out of the window, and could not tear her eyes from the always-changing tapestry of faces which fluttered and ribboned the platform. Perhaps she would see him, something in her would rush out to him, rush out to join him, and be reunited with him. But if she did see him, perhaps she would just sit there. Just like this, still, and pretend it was not him looking this way and that, frantically searching for her.

There is never any whistle before a Russian train leaves

the platform. It just starts up all of a sudden. With a jolt it started to move out of the station.

The woman and the little girl waved to someone on the platform. And Maisie closed her book.

The woman with the little girl asked if they could have the window shut.

'Yes, of course,' said Maisie. She got up and shut it.

Elizabeth Buchan
**Perfect Love**  £14.99

From the author of *Consider the Lily*, winner of the 1993 Romantic Novel of the Year Award, comes a stunning new novel of passion and bravery of family and children, and of the extraordinary, heart-stretching agony and joy that is adultery . . .

Prue Valour believes in the survival of marriage – from the moment, two decades earlier, when she decided, in spite of a twenty-year age gap, to cherish Max with all the fervour and burning conviction of a modern Joan of Arc.

But life has a way of throwing in the unexpected, and contented, busy Prue finds herself precipitated into a passionate affair that shakes her to the core. As she is caught between two worlds, between innocence and new knowledge, between the gluttony and surrender of desire and the stark realities that ensue, the novel pinpoints the extraordinary bargains and accommodations struck between people who love one another.

Elizabeth Buchan
**Consider the Lily**   £5.99

'An excellent story . . . strong imaginative power . . . wonderful sense of atmosphere' JOANNA TROLLOPE

*Consider the Lily* . . . waxen, exotic, doomed to bloom for its short, sweet season. Consider the rose . . . tenderly beautiful yet resilient, twining its way into the English garden . . .

Winner of the 1994 Romantic Novelist's Association Novel of the Year Award, *Consider the Lily* is a glorious fusion of love and gardening, of family life and coming to terms with loss. A haunting, passionate story played out between three people, it is also a poignant and beautiful novel of England between the wars that propels the reader into its own rich and nostalgic world.

'Wonderfully stylish and absolutely compulsive reading' PENNY VINCENZI

Alison McLeay
**The Dream Maker**   £4.99

It is 1819, and although the Napoleonic Wars are now only a memory, they have brought nothing but misery in their wake for Flora St Serf. Her father's court martial has led the family to disgrace and social ruin, cut off from inheritance and with the powerful Elder's Bank calling in all their loans.

Confined to shabby lodgings, sixteen-year-old Flora makes secret friends – with beautiful, wayward Lydia, and with Dedalon, the French automaton-maker and evolutionist who insists that love and the human soul are illusions.

Certainly Flora finds precious little love in George IV's dissolute London, until she falls inexplicably for the very man she believes responsible for her family's downfall – Darius Elder himself . . .

From London to the frozen shores of Canada's Hudson Bay, their fates will spiral together in a dangerous and forbidden dream that could eventually destroy them both.

All Pan Books are available at your local bookshop or newsagent, or can be ordered direct from the publisher. Indicate the number of copies required and fill in the form below.

Send to:      Pan C. S. Dept
              Macmillan Distribution Ltd
              Houndmills Basingstoke RG21 2XS

or phone:     0256 29242, quoting title, author and Credit Card number.

Please enclose a remittance* to the value of the cover price plus £1.00 for the first book plus 50p per copy for each additional book ordered.

*Payment may be made in sterling by UK personal cheque, postal order, sterling draft or international money order, made payable to Pan Books Ltd.

Alternatively by Barclaycard/Access/Amex/Diners

Card No.

Expiry Date

_____
Signature

Applicable only in the UK and BFPO addresses.

While every effort is made to keep prices low, it is sometimes necessary to increase prices at short notice. Pan Books reserve the right to show on covers and charge new retail prices which may differ from those advertised in the text or elsewhere.

NAME AND ADDRESS IN BLOCK LETTERS PLEASE

. . . . . . . . . . . . . . . . . . . . . . . . . . . . . . . . . . . . . . . . . . . . . . .

Name _____

Address _____

_____

_____

6/92

# READ MORE IN PENGUIN

In every corner of the world, on every subject under the sun, Penguin represents quality and variety – the very best in publishing today.

For complete information about books available from Penguin – including Puffins, Penguin Classics and Arkana – and how to order them, write to us at the appropriate address below. Please note that for copyright reasons the selection of books varies from country to country.

**In the United Kingdom**: Please write to *Dept. EP, Penguin Books Ltd, Bath Road, Harmondsworth, West Drayton, Middlesex UB7 ODA*

**In the United States**: Please write to *Consumer Sales, Penguin USA, P.O. Box 999, Dept. 17109, Bergenfield, New Jersey 07621-0120.* VISA and MasterCard holders call 1-800-253-6476 to order Penguin titles

**In Canada**: Please write to *Penguin Books Canada Ltd, 10 Alcorn Avenue, Suite 300, Toronto, Ontario M4V 3B2*

**In Australia**: Please write to *Penguin Books Australia Ltd, P.O. Box 257, Ringwood, Victoria 3134*

**In New Zealand**: Please write to *Penguin Books (NZ) Ltd, Private Bag 102902, North Shore Mail Centre, Auckland 10*

**In India**: Please write to *Penguin Books India Pvt Ltd, 706 Eros Apartments, 56 Nehru Place, New Delhi 110 019*

**In the Netherlands**: Please write to *Penguin Books Netherlands bv, Postbus 3507, NL-1001 AH Amsterdam*

**In Germany**: Please write to *Penguin Books Deutschland GmbH, Metzlerstrasse 26, 60594 Frankfurt am Main*

**In Spain**: Please write to *Penguin Books S. A., Bravo Murillo 19, 1° B, 28015 Madrid*

**In Italy**: Please write to *Penguin Italia s.r.l., Via Felice Casati 20, I–20124 Milano*

**In France**: Please write to *Penguin France S. A., 17 rue Lejeune, F–31000 Toulouse*

**In Japan**: Please write to *Penguin Books Japan, Ishikiribashi Building, 2–5–4, Suido, Bunkyo-ku, Tokyo 112*

**In Greece**: Please write to *Penguin Hellas Ltd, Dimocritou 3, GR–106 71 Athens*

**In South Africa**: Please write to *Longman Penguin Southern Africa (Pty) Ltd, Private Bag X08, Bertsham 2013*

# READ MORE IN PENGUIN

## BUSINESS AND ECONOMICS

### North and South  David Smith

'This authoritative study ... gives a very effective account of the incredible centralization of decision-making in London, not just in government and administration, but in the press, communications and the management of every major company' – *New Statesman & Society*

### I am Right – You are Wrong  Edward de Bono

Edward de Bono expects his ideas to outrage conventional thinkers, yet time has been on his side, and the ideas that he first put forward twenty years ago are now accepted mainstream thinking. Here, in this brilliantly argued assault on outmoded thought patterns, he calls for nothing less than a New Renaissance.

### Lloyds Bank Small Business Guide  Sara Williams

This long-running guide to making a success of your small business deals with real issues in a practical way. 'As comprehensive an introduction to setting up a business as anyone could need' – *Daily Telegraph*

### The *Economist* Economics  Rupert Pennant-Rea and Clive Crook

Based on a series of 'briefs' published in the *Economist* , this is a clear and accessible guide to the key issues of today's economics for the general reader.

### The Rise and Fall of Monetarism  David Smith

Now that even Conservatives have consigned monetarism to the scrap heap of history, David Smith draws out the unhappy lessons of a fundamentally flawed economic experiment, driven by a doctrine that for years had been regarded as outmoded and irrelevant.

### Understanding Organizations  Charles B. Handy

Of practical as well as theoretical interest, this book shows how general concepts can help solve specific organizational problems.

# READ MORE IN PENGUIN

## BUSINESS AND ECONOMICS

**The Affluent Society**   John Kenneth Galbraith

Classical economics was born in a harsh world of mass poverty, and it has left us with a set of preoccupations hard to adapt to the realities of our own richer age. Our unfamiliar problems need a new approach, and the reception given to this famous book has shown the value of its fresh, lively ideas.

**Lloyds Bank Tax Guide**   Sara Williams and John Willman

An average employee tax bill is over £4,000 a year. But how much time do you spend checking it? Four out of ten never check the bill – and most spend less than an hour. Mistakes happen. This guide can save YOU money. 'An unstuffy read, packed with sound information' – *Observer*

**Trouble Shooter II**   John Harvey-Jones

The former chairman of ICI and Britain's best-known businessman resumes his role as consultant to six British companies facing a variety of problems – and sharing a new one: the recession.

**Managing on the Edge**   Richard Pascale

Nothing fails like success: companies flourish, then lose their edge through a process that is both relentless and largely invisible. 'Pascale's analysis and prescription for "managing on the edge" are unusually subtle for such a readable business book' – *Financial Times*

**The Money Machine: How the City Works**   Philip Coggan

How are the big deals made? Which are the institutions that really matter? What causes the pound to rise or interest rates to fall? This book provides clear and concise answers to a huge variety of money-related questions.

# READ MORE IN PENGUIN

*Cosmopolitan Career Guides*: a series of lively and practical handbooks produced by *Cosmopolitan* writers on a wide range of subjects.

**Cosmopolitan Guide to Working in Journalism and Publishing**
Suzanne King

Careers in journalism and publishing are seen as highly desirable, but what exactly do they involve? Suzanne King describes the work undertaken by those in all sections of the industries, from newspaper reporter to magazine editor, TV researcher to radio PA, book commissioning editor to freelance writer. This expert guide also lists relevant training schemes and courses, salary ranges and numerous case histories, providing inspiration, insider information and invaluable advice.

**Cosmopolitan Guide to Working in Retail**
Elaine Robertson

The retailing business is the country's biggest employer, providing jobs for one in ten of the UK workforce. What kind of career opportunities can retail offer you? From window dresser to buyer, personal shopper to department manager, this informative book will help you choose the right career.

*published or forthcoming:*

**Cosmopolitan Guide to Working in PR and Advertising**
Robert Gray and Julia Hobsbawm
**Cosmopolitan Guide to Student Life**
Louise Clark
**Cosmopolitan Guide to Getting Ahead in Your Career**
Suzanne King
**Cosmopolitan Guide to the Big Trip**
Elaine Robertson and Suzanne King